THE LEPER COMPOUND

THE LEPER COMPOUND

Paula Nangle

BELLEVUE LITERARY PRESS
New York

First published in the United States in 2008 by
Bellevue Literary Press
New York

FOR INFORMATION ADDRESS:
Bellevue Literary Press
NYU School of Medicine
550 First Avenue
OBV 640
New York, NY 10016

This book was published with the generous support of
Bellevue Literary Press's founding donor the Arnold Simon Family Trust
and the Bernard & Irene Schwartz Foundation.

this book is supported by
literaryventuresfund
investing in literature one book at a time
www.literaryventuresfund.org

Cataloging-in-Publication Data is available from the Library of Congress

Book design and type formatting by Bernard Schleifer
Manufactured in the United States of America
ISBN 1-934137-06-2
FIRST EDITION
1 3 5 7 9 8 6 4 2

CONTENTS

1 : SVIKIRO

PENNY SPOTTED THE ANOPHELES MOSQUITO ONE MID-MORNING break at Hatfield Girls' High School. Most of form 2A lined the upper balcony, sitting on the sun-warmed concrete with bags of potato crisps, vigilant of prefects, their pleated uniforms bunched at their thighs for prime tanning. They shaded their eyes as Penny pointed. Then everyone saw the mosquito on the white railing, its pointed bill aligned with its body. There was a pause before they charged the form room. They blinked in the sudden, cool dark, breathless, uttering various bits of Afrikaans slang.

The anopheles was rampant this year, Miss Dunn said in biology. "I hope you've all been taking your quinine, girls." Colleen's face felt hot with guilt. She wondered if protozoa spun up and down her body in the flow of blood, drinking iron, bursting their way through valves. They would divide into numbers too long for a calculator. She played with her pencil, making it wobbly and buoyant. She had seen Ministry of Health movies about teen pregnancy. A girl, an actress, rubbed her temples and shook her head with secret knowledge. "I'm pregnant," the girl finally said to her mother.

"I forgot to take my quinine," Colleen told the boarding mistress, and gave her the aluminum packet. It was moist and crinkled from the sweat of her palm. The woman held it before Colleen's face, its intact green pills in horizontal rows, something to read from left to right and understand completely.

★ ★ ★

Long after Colleen grew up, her father still talked about the malaria. "You weren't even there," he would say. "Mostly you were gone, you didn't even see me. I thought you were dead." He would repeat himself, marveling, she supposes, that she didn't die like her mother, one morning years ago, of an unknown fever. Colleen had thought she was asleep, curled up on her side with the tea tray steaming next to the bed. The parquet floor was cold through the rubber feet of her pajamas. Her mother had not been dead long, they said, because when Colleen had climbed in next to her, she was only limp, only sleeping, her hands cool, not hot like the night before, and Colleen rested her head against her mother's warm chest. After a while, she noticed how her head did not rise up and down the way it usually did—a kind of ride, since at seven she could no longer be rocked—and she wondered if her mother was teasing her, holding her breath, and Colleen held her breath too, and no one moved, nothing, not even their eyes.

Malaria must have seemed more definite to her father, an infection with a household name, perhaps a thing he could stop with his knowledge of its seriousness. He flew up to Salisbury in a single-engine Cessna. He stayed on the sixth floor of the Monomatapa Hotel, as if he were on holiday. Colleen remembers chills, and the infusion of chloroquine, lukewarm with the burn of ice. The hospital had been the dark gray of a back stage, an outer world. Her hand seemed used to flapping in the air. It had tried to catch mammals with peacock-feathered wings, reached to touch soft, wrinkled faces with sad eyes. Sometimes the faces would leer. "Go away," she would say, or "Fuck you," and her father's chair would scrape across the floor in a surprised way.

"Open your eyes, Colleen." Her father had tilted her distracted chin toward him. "You're in hospital." He spoke to her as if she had lost her hearing. His mouth stretched his face. His skin was dry and transparent from the sun and reminded her of Mapipi's phyllo pastry. "Do you know where you are? Rhodesia." The loud sounds pierced her head. "Colleen, what day is it today? Monday." She dreamed of surprise quizzes at school. She felt unprepared.

They came home to Nyadzi after the fever. Colleen stayed the whole rainy season, a convalescent in her father's houseful of menservants. The house echoed without her sister there—it was the first time they had left her alone at the hostel without Colleen nearby. For a while, she noticed the space that Sarah was not in, the absence of Sarah's harmonica, the way her sister quietly breathed into the metal reeds. There were people's feet in the hall, and loose parquet tiles sliding around. She startled at the rings of the phone, or her father's cursing into it, bullying the missionary neighbors off the party line. His conversations with the foreman vibrated through the transom windows. He mixed English with Shona, even though the foreman had studied agriculture at the University of Rhodesia, and usually interpreted for him. Her father only seemed to know Shona for "coffee" and "bean" and "plant," and emphasized the words with a certain zeal.

Colleen's father and Mapipi swathed her bed with mosquito netting. They tugged daily at the prolapsed mesh, tying the strings taut at the bedposts. Colleen would wait in the chair, wearing sunglasses, squinting out across the valley, where low clouds dispersed sheets of rain and columns of sunlight. She could see the corrugated iron roofs of Nyadzi Mission, and the Wiri River, high in flood, bright then dark then bright. Women knelt on the few remaining slabs of river rock, scrubbing and wringing. Newly washed clothes hung on flat-topped savanna trees along the ravine. Sometimes children squatted on rafts they'd made out of orange-and-red detergent bottles. They twirled over new rapids and disappeared under the bridge, and floated into sight again.

Or Colleen would just lie there, in bed, with the net dropping down, while Mapipi and her father argued above her. "Pull the bloody thing." "No, Master. I have too much on my side." She stared up, greasy haired, stifled by the humidity of her own sweat, breathing and rebreathing herself inside the gray space.

She'd acquired a habit, from the delirium, of gesturing. The forefinger twirled in clear cursive, place names, person names, Shona pronouns. She imagined she knew sign language. There were long silences when she pretended to be deaf. Two spiders hung from opposite corners of her ceiling. They drew up their legs, soft and pliable as pipe cleaners. Their movements were deliberate and steady. They did not require sudden painful turns of the eyeballs. Sometimes they noisily killed flies and dropped them, gray-coated balls for Mapipi to sweep into his hand. Or the balls landed in glasses of flat Coke, and after a while the surface of the drink wobbled back to a line that was never exactly straight, a constant molecular tremor Colleen could not quite see.

Julia Chonongera, the mission nurse, checked on her twice a week. Colleen would wait for her, for the first sound of her female voice in the kitchen, talking Shona with Mapipi. Colleen had listened to the nurse negotiating with her father over her pay. "I have never treated a European," Julia said. Along with her usual tasks, she was busy caring for one of the schoolteachers, Miss Maenga, at the mission. "Some days I may be late," she said. Colleen noticed that her father didn't argue with her. Everyone knew—even he must have known—that Miss Maenga had cancer.

At first, Julia came from Miss Maenga's house preoccupied and quiet. Once, while taking Colleen's temperature, she nodded to herself. "You are quite like your mother," she said. "The little girl, your sister—she also resembles. But you in other ways." Colleen nodded, waiting for Julia to take the thermometer from her mouth, relieved that someone had noticed. Colleen tried to impress her with her form-two knowledge of anatomy. Julia might talk broadly about disease. She was an expert on leprosy and sleeping sickness, and even diagnosed Colleen's mother: "It was probably encephalitis. Are you sure she had a terrible headache?" But they rarely spoke of Miss Maenga, and of the cancer, a Western word that Julia muttered unnaturally. She said that it did not belong at Nyadzi with all the other kinds of death.

Colleen tried to identify Miss Maenga's house from the cluster of mission buildings along the mountain. During noon storms, she would know that rain clattered on Miss Maenga's metal roof. There would be steam on that window. The teacher might lie there and wipe it with her finger, draw a face or write her name, Kudzai, which meant praise. She might blow over it and smudge it and look at the swirling imprints of her fingertips. But this was something Colleen would do, she knew, if she had a bed next to the window. A person who was going to die soon, a person who knew this, would be wiser than a god. Possibly, she thought, Miss Maenga was too distracted by the pain to do or think anything. Colleen would lie inside the netting, without moving, becoming uncomfortable and stiff, hoping this would lessen Miss Maenga's pain and wondering, was she awake? Why hadn't she told anyone? How could she let it spread to her lung? Then Colleen turned on herself. "Why did you forget the quinine?"

"There it was on the surface, on her breast," she blurted to Julia one afternoon.

"Every time she took a bath and rubbed herself with soap," Julia said after a pause.

"How did she find it?" Colleen asked. "How does a person know? How can they say 'This is a lump?'" She rubbed her fingers anxiously along the knobs of her ribcage.

Julia laughed. "For you, my girl, I would not worry yet. Mine are so often filled with milk that it's hard to tell, even when the baby drains them. It is best if a breast produces milk, a woman is safer."

Colleen brushed her hair at the edge of the bed. She did not want Julia to leave.

"I think Miss Maenga should never have worn a bra," Julia said. "Hoisting up her breasts and separating them like a white woman." Julia filled a syringe with a yellow substance. She flicked it. Colleen smelled yeast and vitamin. "In India, women wear saris. No one has breast cancer there. They do not imitate white women in their dress."

"The missionaries might never have let her teach without one," Colleen said. "They might have sent her home."

"You're right. It is not her fault." She looked closely at Colleen, tapping the syringe thoughtfully onto her left hand. Her eyes were the shape of fish, moving or poised to move.

"There are different poisons, Colleen. Many reasons why things go wrong."

"Like Juju?" she asked, breathing in.

"Well, maybe. Just another scary story for you. The curse on the Maenga family."

It was true that Miss Maenga's immediate family had all died tragic deaths: bus accidents, a brother, innocent, hanged for treason in Salisbury. After the trial, Miss Maenga's fiancé canceled their wedding. He'd already paid a renowned *lobola* of Barclay's Bank bonds and more than the usual amount of livestock, but still he moved away, out of the country, to Malawi.

"I've heard you can protect yourself with pork fat," Colleen said. "Hung in the doorway of a bedroom."

Julia was rummaging through her bag, pulling out cotton balls and a bottle of rubbing alcohol. When she looked up, something was missing on her face, as if she were focused in front of Colleen, or beyond her. "I need to start teaching people about lumps."

"What would it matter?" Colleen heard herself say, like a quote from a set book, how male characters might speak standing with cigars. She could see her literature teacher, who would probably write "futility" on the board and pace back and forth in her platforms. Colleen realized that she could not separate her feelings from ways of acting, or trying to act, and she wasn't sure if the emptiness was real or pretend.

"Time for your B12 shot," Julia said. "You can talk to me all you want, and distract me, but you're still getting it today."

Colleen pulled down the shorts of her baby doll pajamas and endured the long ache, imagining, as usual, Miss Maenga's pain. "My dog killed her chicken once," she confessed. She had been home from boarding school during Rhodes and Founders weekend. "The cancer was growing when I sat with her that day."

"It grew inside her for a long time," Julia said. "I am certain she knew. She would get up every day, and do each thing the same, but know all the time, deep inside."

"She was so nice about the chicken," Colleen said.

"That was the last of the *lobola* chickens," Julia said. "You probably did her a favor. Perhaps she was reminded less of Kenneth Mtetwa after that."

Two years before, Kimmy was a full grown puppy. He'd acquired the menacing look of European guard dogs at gates in the cities. Colleen's father made it a point not to care about security, and felt annoyed when Kimmy no longer resembled his retriever mother. Colleen was eleven then. On the day of the chicken, she and Never Dzunga had been riding on the back of a donkey wagon, a two-tire trailer constructed from the body of an abandoned Fiat truck. The tailgate was down. They sat between loose wood poles and steadied them, watching their feet bump along the rocks in the road. Kimmy sniffed into crevices, then scrambled to catch up. Never's father reined in the donkeys at the soccer field. Women were making bricks from clay mud for a new classroom. The bricks dried under the sun in different rows of brown. Never's father examined them. He stopped to talk to people at the well, shaking hands, eventually sitting down on a rusted kitchen chair. He gestured to Never and Colleen with a ceramic pail. They watered the four donkeys, nuzzling them, listening to the heat of the slow afternoon, cowbells, cicadas, the sound from metal roofs like wire snapping on a petrol-tin banjo.

They had followed Kimmy along a path to the teachers' houses. It was shady with fruit trees. Never picked a grapefruit and peeled it like an orange, offering segments. "*Unoenda,*" Never said suddenly, poking her on the shoulder. Colleen was It. They still played hide and seek. Colleen ran ahead and hid in the Maenga maize patch, pushing the stalks softly, careful not to trample. Never was close behind her, jumping down the steep part of the footpath. Pebbles scattered. She stopped at the fork and hesitated. Colleen stood very still. "Colleen," Never called. "*Onai!* Kimmy!" A trick, Colleen thought. She did not come out.

Miss Maenga's rooster crowed. Kimmy barked and growled savagely, the way he fought with baboons. Colleen heard clucking and one smothered squawk. She rushed between the rows and found him in the Maenga courtyard. Kimmy jerked his head from side to side, grunting into the carcass of a large hen. Her feet clicked together, helpless, twiglike. The rooster stalked the yard, glaring.

Miss Maenga leaned tall against her door frame, still dressed from the mission school, in a dark cotton blazer and java print skirt. Her hair was shiny with oil, tight in a chignon. Kimmy dropped the chicken and lifted his face to Colleen, panting, cheerful, his whiskers dark red spikes. Kimmy nudged the dead bird.

"*Asi canai*," Colleen apologized. "He's never done anything like this before." She pushed Kimmy away from the chicken with a turn of her knee. She could see the purple of Never's dress behind the aloe garden.

Miss Maenga had a permanent frown, as if she strained against a great load, pushing hard at something. Passing her in the business district, Colleen had noticed it before, her face sinewy, except for the flat bridge of her nose and curved regal nostrils.

She waved her hand, dismissively. "It is OK. His ancestors were wolves. A part of him wants to hunt."

"He will never do it again," Colleen promised.

"It does not matter with this hen. Her eggs were no good anymore." Miss Maenga's eyes, squeezed up, made small by wincing, were soft and analytical. They had a wizened look of a very old, perhaps Oriental man. Colleen looked back at her.

"*Uya*," Miss Maenga said. She led Colleen into the open coop and passed her several beige eggs, warm from recent brooding. "Drop them into the slop bucket," she said.

The eggs splattered, the yolks brown and red, smelling like the sulphur of hot springs. Colleen plugged her nose. "You see," Miss Maenga said. "Now don't worry. She'll make a good stewing chicken."

"I could pluck it for you," Colleen offered, though she had only before seen Mapipi scattering quills to the wind, brushing off his cutting board in readiness. She wanted to stay longer in the swept clay yard, with its poinsettias and lemon trees and the green wall of maize.

Miss Maenga picked up the chicken by its legs and carried it dripping to the step. "Let's both do it," she said.

They sat, tugging at feathers, the bird between them steadied by their hands. Sometimes Colleen did not pull hard enough at the feather's shaft and bits of down remained on her side of the chicken. She suggested a tweezers. Miss Maenga returned from the kitchen with a match. She held a flame to the tufts. There was a smell of burnt hair, the smell of curling tongs at boarding school on civies day. Kimmy and the rooster seemed foreign and separate in the courtyard.

The mission bell clanged, echoed, and they heard voices in the dining hall, the next level down the mountain, a clatter of ceramic dishes and the scraping of chairs.

"Dinnertime," Colleen said, knowing they did not eat at the farm until seven, after her father's sundowners, when he paced with a tinkling glass. She hoped Miss Maenga would not request help gutting the chicken. It slumped in a goose-fleshed mass, veinous, white, awaiting a knife.

"Goodbye, Colleen," Miss Maenga said. She lit another match. She dabbed and pulled away. Her face glowed an orange brown, relaxed in its absorption.

Kimmy trotted beside Colleen. She called him newly learned swear words. At the footbridge, she threw a stick. Kimmy splashed into the Wiri after it, clamping on, then turning in the current. He paddled, looking steadily at her, his neck extended. The blood was gone now from his mouth. Water lapped quietly around rocks. "Come on, boy," she said.

Getting over malaria, while her father waited to fly her back to school, felt like a developmental milestone, required, demanded, the way he taught her to cycle. Colleen's weakness confused her. She fancied that it was some kind of resistance. She believed it had to do with Miss Maenga, with being white, that she refused to flourish of her own volition. She was too sluggish to really consider it. Why should anyone thrive, she asked herself, turning over, closing her eyes, while Miss Maenga got sicker? Recovering or dying, they shared the suspended stale time of days, their progression to dusk when the generators roared on, the dominant present. They would both know, flat in bed, how time passed, how it moved the same way as growing, a stillness that did not seem to happen without measuring its progress.

Wryly, Colleen's father called her names. "Larva." "Prima donna." "Invalid." He and Mapipi raised their eyebrows when they talked about her. She wondered if maybe she was faking it. Lying down, she didn't feel much different than she did the time she and Penny had curled on the cots in sick bay, writing comic strips under the sheets. But walls spun when she walked, and she would stay close to them, palpating her way along, stopping, pressing her forehead against the cracked plaster.

One morning, after a loud thunderclap, she leaped half awake from bed, seeing only bright gray spots and the sudden floor. Julia was called. She came with her baby wrapped on her back in a plaid blanket. Julia sat down on the bed and pulled Colleen's lip up over her teeth. She lifted Colleen's hand, running a thumb over her fingernails. "You are whiter than any white I've seen, look." Then to Colleen's father, "Send Mapipi to the butcher. She needs liver. Her blood has not recovered. By now it should have."

Every Friday they drove to Mutambara clinic for blood tests. Mr. Haan gave them lifts in his Combie, after morning assembly and his first-hour math class. He'd pick Colleen and her father up by their own truck, stalled beneath the vined carport for almost a month, its tires gone flat. Mapipi continued to brush off jacaranda petals and bird droppings. Colleen's father declared that he would never buy a domestically made car. He'd wait for parts from South Africa. He argued over the phone with customs officials.

Mr. Haan considered chauffeuring part of his missionary work. He was known to pick up whole lines of Africans at the bus stop. People expected informal sermons above the roar of the diesel. Colleen's father would ignore him and smoke Chesterfields, tapping them into Haan's ashtray stuffed with American gum wrappers. Mr. Haan worried for people, about hell. His right eye twitched nervously behind his bifocals. Colleen always politely kept his gospel tracts, folding and refolding them gently in her pockets.

Julia flagged them down one Friday in front of Sekundiri grocery. Miss Maenga was with her, in the small square of shade from the store, resting against several burlap bags of mealie meal. They must have been waiting for Haan. "Are you taking Colleen to Mutambara?" Julia called to him. She helped Miss Maenga up, and they stumbled to the back of the Combie. Miss Maenga gripped Julia's waist.

"You should ride in front," Haan insisted.

"That's OK, *Baba*." Julia absently cupped and patted her hands, a thank-you gesture. Haan slammed the back door behind them. He peered for a moment through the grime of the door window. Colleen pushed aside Shona hymnals for them to sit. Miss Maenga panted, heaving. Something rattled in her chest. Her breaths made a wailing sound. "Help her, make it stop," Colleen wanted to say to Julia. She felt restless, even frantic, and swallowed hard. Miss Maenga crouched on the opposite bench soldered to the wheel well. *Is she afraid?* Colleen wondered, but she could not tell. There was only her open mouth and bulging, immobile eyes. Colleen wanted to barricade this blank struggle from the rest of them, and fidgeted with her pink sunglasses.

"Colleen," Julia said.

"What?"

"Show some respect."

She looked away from Miss Maenga and did not meet her eyes again.

"You will get oxygen at Mutambara, *sisi.*" Julia's Shona was rapid next to Miss Maenga's ear. Colleen had to think hard if she wanted to listen. Julia saw no reason to speak English to a dying woman. "The oxygen will make it very different, you'll see."

Colleen sat across from them. She watched the road through the back window, retreating, slipping away behind curves, behind outcroppings of rock. Sometimes Haan's Combie seemed to drag, as if it were being pulled backward into a gorge. She waited for Haan to gear down, for a change in the rattle of the engine.

It does not happen. They are sliding, all of them, over the edge, tumbling on top of one another, African, European, the American, sick, dying, vigorous. The Combie rolls in midair, grazes a boulder. Layers of earth fly past, orange and yellow and black. Miss Maenga's face falls toward her, unchanging, frozen in a labored pull of a breath. *She doesn't care*, Colleen thinks. There is the buckling of metal, the brush of acacia against the window as the truck settles, they are all dead. Colleen looks around. She is relieved for Miss Maenga, who moves quietly, the way a person gets up in the morning without disturbing the others. It is her own quizzical face again, and she measures Colleen briefly before she goes.

"*Unonyara*, Colleen," Julia said. Colleen blinked and wiped away drool. "You were dreaming. I watched your eyeballs turn so quickly behind those lids." Haan reversed into a parking space. They saw the red-tiled roofs of the Mutambara compound.

Julia found a wheelchair, kicking at its brakes. Haan asked to pray. They stopped under a palm at the entrance. He suggested they all hold hands, though it was only Miss Maenga's hand that allowed itself to be clasped, and he seemed to realize this, the two of them holding hands, and he dropped it into her lap, flustered. Julia scuffled impatiently in the gravel. She moved her foot back and forth leaving a foot-long clay path. Miss Maenga's eyes were closed. Her head lolled backward. Haan read quickly from his flipped-open Bible.

Inside European outpatient, her father lit cigarettes, but otherwise did not look up from his Wilbur Smith novel. Colleen studied the front cover, an active picture of a striding suntanned man, and in the background a woman, composed, buxom, and behind her various mine workers in hard hats, awaiting orders. Penny had been reading the same paperback, up at hostel. She'd shown her various explicit passages. Colleen sat ready for the blood test with her sleeve already rolled. She balled her fist.

People passed in the hall: intermittent footsteps, the occasional squeaking of unoiled trolleys. Colleen saw the red of Julia's canvas raincoat. She turned around and paused in the doorway. "It is so quiet here," Julia said. "The non-European side is packed."

"We're still waiting," Colleen pointed out, competitive.

"Well, I'm heading back now, on the Shushine bus."

Before Colleen could ask, Julia said, "They gave her morphine, for the pain. It stopped her respirations."

"She died," Colleen said. It was as though she had picked up one of her father's single-sentence business cables off the dining room table. Prices are down. Stop.

"Yes. It is good."

"Did they know morphine might do that?"

"It is a kindness. I regret that I did not bring her sooner."

Colleen felt an odd alertness. She remembered her Barbies after a catastrophe, conversing amid prone and supine figures and dismantled doll furniture, the overturned plastic miniature beds. "Maybe it wasn't her time to die yet," she said. She wondered if Julia had told her something that her father, smoking and pacing, shouldn't hear.

Julia shrugged. "Her spirit was already outside of her."

Miss Maenga's grave bordered the coffee farm and Nyadzi Mission on a small plateau of tribal trust land. The place was seldom used for burials. People preferred to bury their kin, especially the babies, in shallow holes behind kraals, protected from vultures and baboons by heaps of sandstone. Colleen's father resented the new grave. "I'm going to get my drinking water from the springs," he said. The mountain sharply rose up beyond the graveyard. It shadowed the markers into a gray haze. Clouds were often low enough to swirl there, in ethereal wisps, moving slowly off, to terraced maize patches and thatched roofs, where they hovered alongside the smoke of cooking fires. Colleen imagined sometimes at night that a mud slide would wash Miss Maenga down to them, rolling to a standstill before their kitchen door, hugging herself tightly.

Miss Maenga's cousins had placed a long stick down into her grave. Julia showed Colleen the stick on her first walk. "It will be hard for a tunnel to form in this mud," Julia said. "The stick will need to stay for a while." She took off a sandal and picked chunks of clay from its heel. "I don't know what her cousins were thinking. Who do they expect to remove it? They live on the other side of Rhodesia, near Plumtree. Who has time to come and watch the hole for a caterpillar?"

"How do you know which caterpillar is her spirit?" Colleen asked. "Supposing more than one comes out?"

Julia stood with her back to her, looking across the valley. Circles of water glinted: the full reservoirs of the irrigation system, and a baptismal tank outside the mission church, blue-green and still. "I hope you're not poking fun," she said. She pulled her beaded hair forward across her shoulder and held it, examining black frizz at the ends. "After the caterpillar is seen," Julia continued, glancing back at Colleen briefly, "people welcome the spirit above the ground. Then she finds a *svikiro*, a medium, among us."

Colleen felt a cold anxiety, as if she were meeting boys from Cranborne hostel. She knelt and fingered a plastic flowered cross at the head of the grave. It was wet and smelled of new dolls. "From the missionaries," she speculated. "Mr. Haan maybe."

"She taught at the mission school for fifteen years, right up until the month she died," Julia said. "To the Americans she is a saint. Her soul has gone to heaven."

"To us, she is a *mudzimu*," Colleen said, testing the word, "a wandering spirit."

"Us," Julia echoed, laughing in a polite way. She did not say more.

During her father's siesta, Colleen began to walk there by herself, comparing daily erosion from the noon downpours. The stick emerged, sometimes shorter, often longer, settling in the clay mud. She might gaze around, furtive. She was violating something, being there, a thief, continuing to steal what was African, parts of Africa, and make it hers. Understanding was only a new way to mark territory. Sometimes she felt ashamed. She lingered at the grave, stubborn not to go, and yearning vaguely. Lizards darted out from behind rocks. The mountainside dripped and trickled. There were soft dove sounds. She did not see a caterpillar.

"You're ready to go back to boarding school," her father said one afternoon. "Anemia or not." He sat on the veranda in his brown safari suit. Colleen caught her breath. She had been climbing the steps. He must have watched her, picking her way across the valley. He wiped the sweat off his forehead, back into his hair. "How often do you go over there? You were nothing to that woman."

"I know," she admitted. She tugged at the French doors, which were sticky from the humidity and beaded with rust.

"What for, Colleen?"

"I'm looking for a caterpillar," she said, sheepish, and felt her face flush and the tears come up, and she jerked her head to the side. Her father didn't say anything. She waited and took some breaths. "I want to be the one to see it."

"You have to be one of them," he said in a brisk, informative way. He was not taunting. "You have to be one of the family," he reminded her.

"Maybe not," she argued.

"Your mother's ashes are in the pantry," he said, as if he were offering her a choice on a menu. He traced the wrought-iron coils of the table. "She liked the pantry. I'd find her in there a lot. Standing between the shelves. Pushing spice tins around."

Colleen thought of the window in that room, small and square, its leaded glass imported from England before sanctions, and the cardboard box wadded with Saran wrap. The box was eye level behind baking canisters and about the same weight. It could be held on top of two palms, or in one, balanced, pulled by gravity. Nothing went further. The room was airless. Flecks of tea leaves and sugar granules crusted the shelf. She might hold the ashes and still try to make the weight words, send it to words like "there" or "somewhere." She'd think of Haan's tracts, the scary ones, sketches of repentant spirits in hell, or others, rising up from coffins, standing at bright thresholds, their speech printed inside neat white circles. Earthly survivors raised their arms and encouraged one another to rejoice.

"We should've found another lift that day, back from Mutambara," her father was saying. "Perhaps with someone in the six o'clock convoy. Children are quite impressionable. I didn't think."

"I'm not a child, in any case."

"Well, Haan surely acted like one. Going on about his bloody evangelism. Seizing the most morbid opportunity."

"He didn't hardly speak at all," Colleen said.

They had been wandering around the Mutambara parking lot. Haan had re-parked the Combie near a utility door, but seemed, at first, to have forgotten which one.

"Miss Maenga's gone to be with the Lord," Haan had said, with the exuberance of the tract people. He rubbed his temples and pulled at his twitching eye. He unlocked the truck. His keys were like small bells. The engine started up, clattering. Colleen unrolled the front window. Her father was tense and restless, squeezed next to Haan, who reached over his thigh for the gearbox. Miss Maenga's body lay in the back, in a tarpaulin wrapped loosely with duct tape. Colleen pretended she wasn't there. Her father smoked. Ash flew past her. She leaned outside for room, squinting down at the moving truck and

the new black-tar road, and her flying yellow hair, at speed so fast it
was still. She opened her mouth wide in the hot, fast, evening wind
and closed it, making hollow sounds, like the inside of a shell. Her
father nudged her.

Haan turned sharply at Wengesi junction, and the body shifted
and thumped. "Do you mind terribly if I close this?" her father asked
Haan, sliding shut the window between the cab and the back.

Behind them, Miss Maenga's arm had come loose from the tarpaulin. It lay outstretched, with her wrist turned inward and her two
longest fingers unbent, as if she'd been stopped in a gesture, something she was trying to say, mid-thought, pausing. Colleen watched
the hand, trembling on the corrugated truck bed, poised, it seemed,
to write a message. She strained her head sideways to decipher it.

2 : CRAWL SPACE

IN THE YEAR AFTER COLLEEN HAD MALARIA, SHE DREAMED EVERY night about larvae and reptiles. It seemed all she did was have nightmares more real than her own life. One dream involved rowing a boat over a sandbar inhabited by snakes. She would scuff across the sand in the reflecting light, and in an instant the snakes were in the boat, small and fast; the water at the stern rushed forward as she jumped away.

She also believed there were noises coming from the trapdoor underneath her bed. She told the boarding master about it. "'Chittering sounds,'" he repeated. "What is a chittering sound?" He was busy with the accounts at his desk. Colleen stared helplessly at the MAYBE TODAY sign above the door—maybe the Lord is coming today, it meant, or "as a thief in the night." The boarding master and boarding mistress were evangelicals from Wisconsin who'd come to Rhodesia after UDI. They admired Ian Smith's stand against the world. They'd become permanent residents and no longer needed work permits. Colleen did not like to think about the Rapture, or the tribulation period, but everyone had to walk under the sign to get to the dining hall. The junior school girls were crossing the courtyard now, her sister, Sarah, lingering behind them; breakfast was over. "You're hearing things," Mr. Fairbridge said. "You're nervous about exams."

"Not quite nervous enough," Mrs. Fairbridge said. "All yesterday afternoon in Penelope's pool?—I can tell by your sunburn—and then spot swatting back here." Mrs. Fairbridge glanced briefly at Colleen over her bifocals. "Up at four A.M.—in the loo. Hardly an example we want for our younger girls." Mrs. Fairbridge unlocked the medicine cabinet and began to set up her tray of asthma treatments. "Self-discipline," she said. "You don't know what it means."

Then Mr. Fairbridge was talking. Did he need to have another chat with her out on the netball field? Should he have Caephas bring out two chairs? Should he speak to Penny's parents? How was Colleen going to manage in form four or sixth form? Maybe she needed to spend more mandatory prep time in the prep room. Perhaps Beth should tutor her.

"Enough, Ronald," Mrs. Fairbridge said. "It's quite simple. No swatting before the bell."

Colleen retreated into the central corridor.

"No last minute swatting," Mr. Fairbridge called after her.

'A person might as well study as listen to that thing in the crawl space,' Colleen thought. She went out to the bike shed and strapped her homework onto the back of her bike. 'They are so weird,' she thought. 'Like I really enjoy it. Sitting on the bathroom floor with *19th-Century Europe*.' Colleen jerked hard at the bungie cord. This morning she'd been finishing up an essay on Louis-Philippe when Mrs. Fairbridge had walked in and sent her back to bed. "Don't turn on your lights, don't wake Bethy." Yet there was something pleasant about the bathroom that did linger in Colleen's mind every time she studied there, the echo of her pen dropping from her lap, how the tube lights blinked in reliable intervals and the cistern refilled. She liked the way the stall doors slammed and pipes resounded to all the tubs and toilets in the whole compound. After the first birds, everything would start up again. The night would be over. Her assignment might not be done, and she might get order marks against her house. Obed Magida and Caephas, his nephew, would come up the path from the *khayas*. Pans started in the kitchen. Milk arrived on a truck. The bell would begin, Mr. Fairbridge squeaking down the waxed hallways with the bell. Many nights, in her room with Beth, the Baby Ben ticking under Colleen's pillow, she would dream it—someone like her down the hall, inside this bathroom, someone thirteen as well, maybe even earlier in the morning. Only in the dream, the pink tiles were gone, the bathroom had become a kind of platform in the center of dense bush, and stairs led up to it from all sides.

When Colleen had returned to hostel earlier that year, she did not want to take a bath. She washed her hair in one of the three pink bathtubs, and she used a cloth to wash her face and under her arms and between her legs. For more than a week, she could not even look at her breasts under the beginner bra, a hand-me-down from Penny. She was certain the pain came from breast cancer. She felt sure that tumors were growing in various stages on her body. She could not bear the prospect of actually finding one. Then she started her period. Out at the desk, with Mrs. Fairbridge capitalizing Kotex across the ledger, she bought a second bag of the Rhodesian-made scratchy weave pads. She stained the sheets and her mattress. She blushed at the thought of Caephas and Obed seeing such sheets in the laundry. At school, a prefect reprimanded her for wearing a jersey tied around her waist, and Colleen showed her the uniform skirt underneath—the pleats caked and stiff against the back of her legs—and she and the prefect nodded together, knowingly. During supper Colleen raced through her shepherd's pie and stood as usual in Obed's line for seconds, but then she ran for the bathroom and vomited into a flushing toilet. The pain stopped and started again like heartbeats. Mrs. Fairbridge had come in behind her and placed a hand on her shoulder. Colleen was snorting chunks of acid into her nose. "Has a family member talked to you about menstrual periods or pregnancy?" Mrs. Fairbridge asked. Colleen swiped her mouth and clutched again at her stomach. She felt her face, her whole scalp flush along the parting of her hair. Colleen had not yet readjusted to the mattress springs on her bed. She dreamed that night of sand lizards trapped beneath her, rearing up around her, and Mrs. Fairbridge's face, which broke up into pieces, miniature light-bulbs, and tiny mechanized sprockets, like the broken watch Colleen took apart once in church, flying, scattering, in the noise of distant crickets.

★ ★ ★

Because of all her dreams, Colleen was not exactly sure that the sounds under the bed were real. Before exams the noise grew louder. There was a heat wave—"October, the suicide month," Mr. Fairbridge kept saying—and Colleen wondered if it was just the way the floor responded to such humidity. She noticed how the pages of the Ministry of Education notebooks curled and uncurled themselves at the corners—was this what she was hearing, not just one tiny rustling, but an accumulation of such movements under the floor? Rainy season would make it go away. It was a matter of time. Her roommate, Beth, said she didn't know what Colleen was going on about. Mr. Fairbridge told Colleen she was not getting enough sleep. She replied, in what she hoped was a biting tone: "Because the *sounds* keep me awake." Mr. Fairbridge said that maybe his wife was right. Maybe Colleen was unbalanced, or hallucinating. It might be the effects of malaria. It might not. Maybe she needed a sedative. Mr. Fairbridge pointed out that if she didn't like Hatfield, there was always Rest Haven, or the asylum at Nkachini. Colleen went to her room and slammed the door. She sat at her desk and stared out through the overgrown bougainvillea. Had Mrs. Fairbridge said that? Colleen could hear her, at tea in the dining room, with her acquired British accent. But it didn't matter. Hallucinations. She thought quickly of Sarah and Sarah's imaginary friends, Dank and Scott. That was nothing though, a way to cope with being a type of orphan. Colleen listened with renewed interest to the nightly squeaks, shudders—wings so tiny they would only be seen under a microscope. What insects were they? At times, she felt protective of them. Possibly they did feel like part of her mind. Yet she never heard the sounds at school, or at Penny's, or in the bathroom. Still, Colleen wondered how her roommate slept. At night, when the sounds were strongest, Beth would be there, across the room, in the light from the transom window—Beth's shoulders, Beth's framed 5 x 7 photo of her parents on the bedside table, and her white Bible with its ribbon bookmark tailing from the pages. There were the rhythmic snores, and the pauses between in breaths and out breaths, when the floor underneath them buzzed with sound and Colleen would think, "Beth is awake, she is finally hearing it." One night Colleen tried to pry the trapdoor open with a butter knife, cutting through layers of wax and dirt. When the door jogged a little, Colleen nudged it back and forth.

"Voetseg," Beth said through gritted teeth—the bedposts had been rattling—and Colleen dropped the knife, startled. She could not lift the door. "Please go to sleep," Beth said in her normal voice.

Colleen had been reading a book that took place in Wales. She dreamed she was visiting a woman in prison on the Irish Sea. A chaplain led her inside. Colleen followed the chaplain along a row of beds. "Here she is," the chaplain said. The woman tried to sit up and look at them. Colleen thought she knew the woman, but she had never really seen her before. Colleen sat on the edge of the bed. The lumps in the mattress began to take on forms. "They're nothing," the chaplain said, but his voice had become high. From behind the chaplain, Colleen observed the tumult inside the mattress—monsters, demons, trapped rodents, something about to be born. The woman herself seemed to be physically suffering, unable, unwilling, to leave the bed, wedged between the moving humps. Colleen began to hear chittering under the floor. She'd become so used to the chittering she hardly noticed it. For as long as she could, she clutched the mattress. "Stop," she commanded, but she was not going to be able to save the woman, she must save herself, and her voice was unsteady, and she folded her hands and put them to her lips to keep them steady and to pray.

Colleen tapped hard on Mr. and Mrs. Fairbridge's bedroom door. "I can't sleep in that bed anymore," she called out. It was two A.M. on the Baby Ben. She'd not even hesitated before knocking. She stood in the echoing hall. She must have pounded louder than she thought. She knocked again. The banging reminded her of the British South African Police, how they'd raided a Christmas gathering last year at Penny's house—a potluck Penny's mother had organized for the domestics in the neighborhood, the usual distribution of Christmas boxes. The police had checked identity documents of all the Africans. Colleen felt a same vulnerability, as if right now she herself was not the one thumping her knuckles on a solid metal door. The B.S.A.P. had taken some people onto the police truck while dogs barked behind hedges, and everyone blinked in the headlights. The other Africans were allowed to leave, lining up single file under the trellis while a torch was shone one last time on their faces. The officer read names off the identity documents: Abednigo, Lazarus, Elijah. Colleen had thought of prophets, participants in miracles. The grass under Colleen's feet had been a bright glowing green.

Mr. Fairbridge opened the door with an expression Colleen knew he'd have: his mouth ajar—"that gormless look," Penny called it. Mrs. Fairbridge was tightening a rain cap around her curlers. "What's wrong with your bed?" she said. "You like your bed." A pulse moved in Mrs. Fairbridge's neck. She usually wore a muslin scarf. Mrs. Fairbridge was probably right. Colleen didn't like to get up on Sundays, she napped a lot, read in the bed, sat there in it. She had become fond of her bed, pushed into its corner behind the shelf, and for the most part she liked how the mattress springs rose up around her in their malleable lumps.

"Go with her, Ronald," Mrs. Fairbridge said, and Mr. Fairbridge did follow Colleen into the room to listen for the sounds. There was a small breeze. Palm fronds scraped against the roof tiles. Beth's breathing had become softer, and Colleen felt tired and uncertain now, listening to the calmness of the breathing. Mr. Fairbridge stood there in the light from the hall. "You have to believe me," Colleen said. She'd heard this said before on TV, this kind of appeal. She felt the same sense about her, as if she were in the TV room watching RBC commercials, completely aware of a scene being acted. She was acting. Yes, she had truly created this problem in the crawl space, she'd made it up—why would she need Mr. and Mrs. Fairbridge like that? She immediately regarded herself with extreme suspicion. She felt dizzy with the treachery. How could one ever define oneself, announce with any sureness, "I am this," or "I'm that," if one knew so little? Beth was awake now, hugging her knees. "I'm so sorry," Colleen blurted out, and ran for her own bed.

★ ★ ★

The next day, though, when Colleen came back from school, she found the bed pushed aside and a crowbar next to the trapdoor. "Out of the way," Mr. Fairbridge told her. He and Caephas tramped into the room with a clinking metal bottle and a hose. "Do you understand what to do?" Mr. Fairbridge said to Caephas.

"Look here, Caephas," Mr. Fairbridge said, as he pried open the trapdoor—and the sound was there now in the room, and no one denied it.

"*Aiwa,*" Caephas said.

Colleen peered from behind Mr. Fairbridge, down into the hole, at the writhing of larvae and pupae and new insects, a buzzing of the tiny wings. Caephas was climbing down into the crawl space. For a while, Colleen saw the movement of his torch. "It won't take long," Mr. Fairbridge was saying. "You've only got the surface area of this room," he called down. "If you've had enough, I'll do the one on the west side."

Caephas didn't answer. But Colleen heard his boot stamping, and the sound itself, pausing now, starting up again. Sometimes it was higher, almost volumeless, like the far-right keys on the piano-room piano, which usually made no sound but sometimes might be heard like the aftermath of RDF sirens. In the beam of Mr. Fairbridge's torch, the worms moved like navy beans on low-boiled water. Colleen hoped they were dying. She felt mean spirited and confused. She thought of the plagues of Egypt, part of a verse, a God voice, "all forms of pestilence." She thought of the movie *Frogs* she had seen with Penny. What was it about Mr. Fairbridge, kneeling there in his safari suit?—his back to her, this sense of being consumed, overtaken—not Caephas down there in the actual place with the canister, but Mr. Fairbridge and her, as if together in a dream. What were they punished for? What did they both know? Because of this feeling, and though she was right about the worms (she'd been right all along), there was no triumph.

An odor of hard sweet insecticide filled the room. Mr. Fairbridge leaned now over the hole. He finally turned around and looked at her. His face was red, and his bone-rimmed glasses defiantly reflected sunlight from the window. "Okay, Colleen," he said.

"Okay," she said and went to the window, and rolled it open, and pressed her face against the cool of the burglar bars.

3: THE EARTHQUAKE

THE MAGNITUDE OF THE EARTHQUAKE WAS POSSIBLY A FOUR, THEIR father told them, after ringing his friend, the geologist at Shabani mine. There had been nothing on the radio. They'd felt earthquakes at Nyadzi before, small unsettling pullaways under one's feet, as if stepping onto the gangplank of an ocean liner, their father would say. Yet no one else they talked to had noticed it—not even the missionaries across the highway, with their wind socks and Fahrenheit thermometers and cheerful fascination with storms. "Feel blessed if it was a quake, and not one of the new bombs," Gordon Beck, the station head, told Colleen. These bombs were going to be used, he said. The *Herald* had issued a warning: terrorists were being armed by Russians and perhaps the Chinese.

Colleen said that no one noticed the earthquake because it occurred almost simultaneously with the singing of the *Madzimai*, which happened every year on Easter morning. The *Madzimai* wore red dresses with matching bandanas and performed biblical reenactments and musicals. They came from tribal trust lands as far away as Ndima, and met in groups down by the river. Easter was their largest gathering of the year. They would rise early like Mary Magdalene and march before dawn to nearby farms and kraals. The women carried lanterns and chanted. They sang hymns with a rousing force that did shake windows and set buildings to tremble; corrugated iron roofs would vibrate throughout the district.

That morning, Colleen had put her head under her pillow when she heard the gate grinding on its hinge. Kimmy charged the front door and whined. Her father turned up the shortwave in his room —the BBC *World News*. It was six o'clock. Colleen could feel the weight of the women, swaying and dancing up the drive, their rhythmic stamping, the force of numbers. Even though she knew some of them—Julia Chonongera, Vaida Moyo—all were *Madzimai*—the Easter march made her feel anxious and vulnerable, and at the mercy of something collective that would never involve her. Sarah loved the march and would stand at the window waiting for them—"Here they come," "They're coming," "They're here."

It was their first Sunday of April school holidays, another Easter— it might even have been last year. She and Sarah had been on the train all of Saturday and had arrived home late and drunk hot Milo, and then they played with the dog. Sarah pulled Colleen's quilt off, and told her again, "They've knocked."   Colleen could hear the women gathering along the retaining wall, ululating. She searched through her suitcase for her robe; she had not unpacked. When she opened the door, the *Madzimai* were already heading down the hill, on their way over to the mission. They were singing *Kudenga*. She and Sarah kept humming part of its chorus as they heated up their oats, a low drone, *endai iyo*: it meant going, go.

While they were eating breakfast, the sideboard began to rattle, as if a convoy of lorries had gone past, and then another, and again, another. Decorative teaspoons clinked together, swinging from their notches. Sarah took her serviette holder and held it firm in her hand. The window seemed to drop lower and let in more light. Colleen was so used to the shimmying of the train that for a moment she accepted the earthquake; she had been reaching for the marmalade on Sarah's side. Her instinct was to proceed as usual. The jar slid away from her. Two plates on the sideboard pitched forward; one, the copper, reverberated on the floor; the Paragon landed, cracked, and spun before it shattered. Kimmy walked through the glass before Colleen could stop him.

Their father had been in the pantry. He called the dog, who limped toward him, bleeding. They chased Kimmy through the house. The goal seemed to be to catch him and remove the shard from his foot. The parquet tiles clattered together like pucks on a shuffleboard. The quake had subsided. Colleen and Sarah and their father and the dog circled around inside the house. "Chreikie," her father was saying, slapping his hand on his forehead. "No, girls, the hall. The hall. Away from windows, down, like this, down," and he dropped to the floor with the dog between his knees. Everyone was breathless and panting. "This is stupid," he finally said. "It's over."

"Probably not a good place to be anyway, in an earthquake," Colleen said.

Her father began to laugh with relief. "Chreikie," he said again.

Sarah was laughing too, with her sense of permission to do so, a high-pitched giggling that led almost immediately to hiccups.

"Right, love," their father said to her. "Deep breaths."

The dog wandered off, his feet clicking, and paused to gnaw at his wound.

"Let's get that glass out of Kimmy's foot," their father said in a hearty way—it reminded Colleen that he was not really used to them yet. He was still in that cheerful mode, always lasting a day or two—the effort at welcome, as if resolved to be happy to see them, or happy, maybe, as best he could—when Colleen knew he would avoid arguing with her, and she could do more or less whatever she wanted. She and Sarah had been gone since New Year's, when he had given them, and even a few students from the mission school, rides after midnight on his new Honda 90.

They heard Kimmy lapping water off the floor in Sarah's room. Her fishbowl had fallen and lay cracked and empty; gravel seeped from scattered mounds. The goldfish flipped languidly. It was easy for Sarah to scoop him up and shelter him in the palm of her hand. His fins flared. She followed her father to the bathroom, where he was running water into the sink.

"The water's too cold," Sarah said as the fish floated to the surface, belly up.

"I think he's had it," their father said. "In any case."

Colleen picked moist gravel from between her toes. The fish darted sideways and then rolled over and shot back down again. He could not seem to hold himself upright in his usual position.

"I wish he'd make up his mind," their father said.

"I'm not watching this anymore," Colleen said.

Colleen returned to the bathroom after bandaging the dog. Her father had held him while she'd prodded between the claws with her eyebrow tweezers. She'd shown her father the piece of china, but he had gone searching for a needle and suggested she dig around some more with it. "I won't," she had told him. It would be on her then, her father said, if Kim got an embolus in his bloodstream from a loose fragment. Had she heard of that? Emboli could kill, immediately.

In the bathroom, the goldfish hovered near the drain plug, resting.

"He'll be fine," their father called. Colleen heard him sweeping glass into the dustpan. It was Mapipi's day off. "He's a sturdy fish. Used to jostling on train rides back and forth to Salisbury in a Pick-n-Pay bag."

Sarah stood tense and immobile above the sink. "No," she was saying. Her fists were clenched. She winced. She opened and closed her mouth.

"Don't worry," Colleen told her. "He looks OK to me. After he's rested for a while, we could put him in this casserole dish."

"He's really strong," Colleen said. "He was out of the water for a long time, don't you think?"

"Do you want to try another dish?" Colleen asked. She disliked having to make such an effort. It was too much like the kind of talk she'd make with her roommate at the hostel, and she felt a similar nervousness. "Is it deep enough? I've heard fish can sometimes jump out. The edges don't curve over, you know, like the fish bowl did."

Sarah was ignoring her, or did not hear her at all, which seemed much worse, especially since it seemed to be happening now at school. Sarah's teacher had mentioned certain lapses to Mr. Fairbridge last term. Colleen had heard him on the phone in the hostel's foyer, through the transoms: the only place free of his voice was usually the prep room. *Not Sarah. She's a brick. Plays by the rules. We never see her in a dwall around here. Absentminded? Her sister is. Could be the apple doesn't fall far from the tree.*

"Sarah," Colleen said.

Sarah blinked and blinked again. Her eyes moved slowly and furtively behind Colleen. Colleen glanced back: the scale was there, a towel rack with the threadbare, iron-stained towels Mapipi had put out for them. "Not so," Sarah declared. From behind her teeth, she muttered something else, which sounded to Colleen like Afrikaans, the way the sound *ge* was formed at the back of the throat. Colleen looked around for their father. If he were there, Sarah might stop it, this trance. But he was on the phone now, and Colleen did not call out to him—something a subprefect would do, she thought. If these were the friends again, she did not want to displease them. Could it be, was it them? The earthquake had likely done it, brought them back. Colleen always found herself deferring to these friends as if they were real. When Sarah was seven, she'd called them Dank and Scott. Another one, a bad one, was Deju Daju. "Deju Daju is here," Sarah would say, cringing. Colleen would get goosebumps. "That's creepy," Colleen would tell her father. "Well, you had fears," her father would point out. "No," Colleen remembered telling him, "not like these."

It had been at least a year—Colleen had stopped keeping track. It was best not to think about this, Sarah outgrowing the voices. Colleen refused to say it to herself, as if any kind of dismissal in her own mind would invite them back. When Sarah used to talk about them, it was at home, and only in rare confiding moods, as if having come to a decision. It seemed she could not, must not, keep it in. There would be a rush of fervent telling. She would hardly pause between breaths, the meandering stories, Dank and Scott doing this or that, usually something mundane in Colleen's opinion, or predictable—jumps, dares, pranks—things Sarah may have seen someone do at school. Sarah would describe it all with zeal. She savored each word. She beamed. She would wait with feverish eyes for Colleen's reaction, as if an important announcement had just been made. Colleen always felt she should clap her hands. Even when Colleen was younger, she seemed to know not to dispute the stories. She remembered thinking, 'that's a lie,' but she'd understood it lacked the deception of lies. Back then, Colleen wanted to think of Dank and Scott as true, in the way that she believed in the characters of chapter books. Out of an emerging new politeness, she'd felt she must do this.

Now, with the goldfish in the sink, there was a small wave. The fish rose up in the swell and swam back down again. "Did you feel that?" their father called from his study. "An aftershock, I suppose."

Sarah peered closely at the goldfish. Colleen busied herself with putting gauze back in the medicine cabinet. She would not show interest in these friends again, she decided—if that was what had been going on these last few minutes. And it might not even have been Dank and Scott. The fish was in peril. Sarah had only been fearing the worst—she was only ten, who wouldn't?—promising something to the fish, praying, willing him to live maybe. She must root for her fish. Stay there or else. It required her complete attention. A kind of game or superstition. Colleen could not remember being so serious at that age, so steadfast. She wondered if this was what might be lacking in herself. Her sister spoke again. "No, I won't," she said and averted her face—she wedged her head, her ear into her shoulder. Her eyes had the calm detachment of someone on a telephone.

"Dad thinks we were at the epicenter," Colleen said, hoping the word might in some way seem interesting enough. She would have to explain it. Then they'd look up various details in the Britannica.

Sarah turned to her as if enlightened by some idea, but then past Colleen, with a tilt of her chin directed elsewhere. She smiled, her fairly new teeth still far apart. She had not heard Colleen, or she'd heard Colleen, and it didn't matter, and the fish didn't really matter, only euphoria, that private euphoria that seemed beyond her years, wise, serene, as if she were older than Colleen, older than anyone.

"Who were you talking to?" Colleen asked.

"My fishie," Sarah said in a high-pitched baby voice, the way Colleen, but not Sarah, sometimes talked to the pets.

"You're weird," Colleen said. "And guess what, you little *skollie*? I don't believe you."

Sarah shrugged. "The center of the earthquake?" she asked. "Why were we at the center of the earthquake?"

"Because we were. Because someplace usually is."

Sarah didn't answer.

"We can look it up, but it's the plates moving under the ground, or something like that, but it has nothing to do with us."

"Really?" Sarah said, in a way that reminded Colleen of Mr. Fairbridge. "Are you sure?"

"Yes, I am," Colleen said.

"Why did you say it has nothing to do with us?"

"It doesn't!" Colleen said.

When Colleen returned that afternoon from the mission school—she'd been invited to their end-of-term debate—her father and Sarah had gone to Melsetter for tea. She'd hurried up the drive after hearing what she thought was the station head at target practice. She ran and stumbled over an unfamiliar groove. There had been stories of his stray bullets ricocheting off rocks. In the dimness of the house, she caught her breath. It still seemed odd to be home. What she missed was her bike in Salisbury, there, not here—it had never been here—safe from earthquakes, locked inside the chain link shed until she came back to it.

Her sister's goldfish had been transferred to a ceramic washtub. He darted around freely in the new space. The house smelled of furniture polish. Sarah had decorated the rooms with doilies; she must have found them in the pantry. Colleen sneezed from the dust. Their mother used to buy doilies from roadside vendors as an excuse to chat. Sarah would not have known that. Colleen's stuffed animals had been rearranged in interacting poses on her bed. She closed her window through the burglar bars. Smoke wafted up from a fire at the compost heap near Mapipi's *khaya*. He was burning something plastic. In Sarah's room, the stuffed animals wore tea cosies pulled down over their ears. Sarah had covered them all carefully with beaded nets that Mapipi used for the sugar bowl. They reminded Colleen of brides, or characters in costume at a dress rehearsal. They seemed paused, with a look of self-consciousness that was almost animated.

Mapipi had come up to the kitchen to remove his meat from the freezer. They exchanged the usual Shona greetings. Colleen asked him about the earthquake, but he said he had been with his wife in Muusha.

"It knocked over the Paragon plate," Colleen told him.

"*Idii*?" he said politely. "That is why there are pieces down in the fire."

He turned to leave and then reached for something he must have placed just outside the door. "Colleen, what is this?" he asked, handing her a warped and ashy can of Pledge. "I brought it to show you." It was still hot, the metal peeled back raggedly from a hole where the cap had been.

"You must never put these bottles in the fire. They explode. Did you hear it explode just now? That popping like a gun? See this sign. It is telling you right here—contents under pressure. Should you be teaching your sister to play with fire?"

"I wasn't here," Colleen said.

"You girls were at the compost heap when I arrived from Muusha this afternoon. I heard Sarah talking to someone! It must have been you."

"Maybe the dog. Or my dad?"

"*Kunyepa*."

"It is not a lie," Colleen declared. "I was at the debate. I'll tell her though, not to throw canisters in a fire like that."

He shook his head. "Good night," he said.

"She likes to clean sometimes," Colleen called out to him from the door.

"There are children who could have used these toys," Mapipi retorted.

Colleen followed him down to the fire. It had been kindled with bits of dry grass, which were still scattered around. Colleen could see along the hill where a scythe had been used. Potato peelings steamed; the heap itself had been too damp, or densely packed, to set alight. Colleen found a stick and poked at a deflated ball that over the last year, had already become an occasional chew toy of Kimmy's. It was now even more concave, gummy, and oozing. Its vapor rose in the air. Colleen did not see any other toys, no dolls or stuffed animals, no disturbing rejects from the display in their rooms—that had been her fear. She saw the blackened fish bowl, broken Paragon pieces with their Tree of Kashmir design, a toothbrush.

"She likes to clean," Colleen said again. "At least she's not a hoarder."

But then she noticed, smoldering, popping in the coals, fragments of colored glass—the glass eyes, antlers—one of Sarah's miniatures. Perhaps it had been found broken after the earthquake. It could have fallen that morning with the plates.

"We do not want Sarah to get hurt," Mapipi said. "We must ask her, 'Why not use the garbage can?' But here is another thing. The station head at Nyadzi is RDF now. Would you believe it? Mr. Beck! A volunteer! I do not want to draw his attention this way. We do not need that man in our business over here."

Bats were circling indecisively above them, as they always did at dusk. A dropping sizzled on a fringe of embers, which flickered and then collapsed and disintegrated.

"Look at this," Colleen said.

"That too must go," Mapipi said and nudged a bottle of her father's shaving cream out of the fire with his boot. "I had not seen that one."

The bottle hissed, and there was a sweet soapy smell, exactly like the warm bathroom in the morning after her father had finished his shave.

"She should go see a doctor," Mapipi said. "I will speak to your father about this matter."

"What? No!" Colleen said. She turned to face his tinted glasses that looked, in most light, like sunglasses, and then enviously, behind him, at his *khaya*. She heard a radio—a xylophone—from its small high window. How could she compare? she asked herself. Sometimes she wondered if she wanted everything, every experience that wasn't her own. But she kept on going, tallying his advantages. He lived alone, the *khaya* off limits, behind poinsettia bushes. There was his clothesline of drying skins and pelts for the drums, the intermittent buzz of flies, the compost heap which was really his domain, he used it for his garden, his house in Muusha, his family they rarely saw—that he rarely saw. Colleen hated that he knew so much about her, yet another person weighted with this banal awareness of her—who she came from, what they were. She drew him down into the shame she felt for herself, his knowledge of their flaws, all flaws odd and intimate and ordinary.

"Don't do it," Colleen said. "Or not yet anyway."

"No then, Madam."

He had never before called her that.

"Madam?" she asked, blushing.

"You are right. We will wait."

The phone was ringing.

"That is probably Beck, asking about the explosion. I promise you. It will be him."

The phone had stopped ringing when Colleen got back up to the house. While there was still some light, she sat down at the kitchen table and tried to start the lantern. The generator had not come on. Colleen wondered if the earthquake had shaken a wire loose. The phone rang again.

"Gwen and I were worried," Gordon Beck said. "Especially with you girls home right now from the capital."

"We accidentally threw a bottle of Pledge onto the fire."

"Don't you think you've had enough excitement for one day?" Gordon Beck teased her merrily.

Colleen realized that the mantle in the lantern had frayed. She searched in the junk drawer for another one, then fitted it and struck a match. She listened to the high blowing sound of the gas and turned the lantern up to a flaring white, and then back down, until it was steady and even.

Her father and Sarah arrived with Chinese takeaways. They had gone on the motorbike to Melsetter. Sarah unpacked the boxes and started to open the fortune cookies with her helmet still on.

4: HENDALL PLUERE

WHEN SARAH RAN AWAY FROM HOSTEL, IT WAS SURPRISING TO Colleen that no one searched her exercise books. In Sarah's room, past the carefully made beds of the three other form ones, the sheaf of paper was right there, folded in front of Sarah's map handouts—capitalized, "I won't go." Colleen expected such words. It came almost as a relief. They would find her. That her sister had had some kind of motivation, some unwillingness, Colleen felt assured; even, in a vague way, complicit. She paused for a full, complete breath. Next to several magnificently spiraling circles, the ink hard and blotched, her sister had written, "ask Hendall Pluere." In the other notebooks, the careful science diagrams, or her Afrikaans translations, there was nothing.

Her father had flown in that evening, and sat now with BSAP officers and RDF soldiers and the Fairbridges—every chair in the dining room had been used and tables pushed aside. A Form One prefect, Joy Ring, was recounting Sarah's last statements. Most of them were inane echoes of what the girl, Joy, had said. They'd talked about an upcoming gala the girl was swimming in. Sarah had been doing that lately, a habit of pleasant repeating. The adults, especially Mrs. Fairbridge, took it as a kind of politeness. The servants even asked her to say the Shona over again—she rolled her *r*'s perfectly. It reminded Colleen of the way Sarah had trilled as a baby. Most of the younger girls considered Sarah malicious. "Your sister is mocking me," they would tell Colleen.

Colleen, still in her games jumper, could not bring herself to walk across the room and give the paper to her father. She passed it to Mrs. Fairbridge, who read the words out loud with a tremulous voice. But who was Hendall Pluere? Mrs. Fairbridge asked the room.

"No one," the prefect said. "He's not real."

The girl was told she could sit down, and Colleen moved aside for her. "They're absolutely sending me!" the girl hissed to Colleen from behind her hand. "'Who's Hendall Pluere?' Can you bear it? They don't know her at all."

Two Queen Elizabeth girls said they saw Sarah the next day at a Cranborne rugby game. She had been under the bleachers collecting spilled popcorn. There was some question about the validity of their story. One said that Sarah (a Hatfield girl in a wrinkled uniform and muddy anklets) stood in line at the tuck shop to buy crisps. The other said she'd stayed under the stands and run back and forth, and someone had thought it was a baboon. Cranborne had trouble with baboons because the rugby field backed an open stretch of bush. But later that night, Sarah was found in the bush, next to her own small campfire, not far from RDF's training base. The girls received house points and special pins for their vigilance.

Colleen never saw her. She'd been taken to casualty at Central, and then on to Rest Haven. Although their father was still in town for another week, the hostel continued as usual. Colleen kept going to school. She wrote tests and discussed them with her friends. She was at the beginning of her final *A* level year. That first week, she felt irritated with Sarah for causing such a disruption, nothing else. In her mind, Rest Haven felt temporary, and necessary, "and not a moment too soon," she told her friends. This was Sarah's cure, she believed, and beyond that, Sarah would resume her life. She would grow up to be perhaps slightly odd. Colleen didn't mind.

On a Salisbury map, the bush across from hostel extended the width of the suburb of Hatfield. It bounded the Cranborne playing fields, and stretched north to the industrial outskirts. Along Queensway, it was used by RDF for training maneuvers. Peripheral paths had been made by domestics, Cranborne boys, animals, and occasionally in the news someone was struck there by lightning, seeking shelter under the acacias.

It began to bother Colleen how little anyone noticed that Sarah was gone. Even Colleen needed to remind herself. This seemed her duty. Colleen recalled the times at hostel with her sister, making a conscious effort at nostalgia, but they had rarely seen each other. Their assigned tables went up in different lines for meals. Prep time and bedtime were staggered from Standard One to Sixth Form. At tea, they'd sometimes met at the same table, with Mrs. Fairbridge at the head. Sarah was always the best groomed. She had dark blonde hair, which she wore in two ponytails with beaded hair ties. Her parting was always severe. Mrs. Fairbridge prompted Sarah and completed her sentences. And Sarah sat right next to Mrs. Fairbridge, passing out peach tart or scones. Sarah would strain the tea, concentrating, the tip of her tongue between her teeth—always with such intent obedience. Colleen sometimes felt she and Sarah might as well not have been related. There was no need. Sarah had Mrs. Fairbridge, of all people.

Once or twice a week, Colleen and Sarah did push each other on a swing in the front garden. The tree faced Albert Road. One of them would curl the rope around and pull the swing back so the other could twirl, first rapidly, spinning down to a complete stop. Colleen remembered what they'd said: "Your turn," "My turn," "Can I have one more turn?" "Get off," "Don't go in yet." Across the road, in the bush where RDF practiced military moves, they would hear megaphones and helicopters, all out of their sight.

Colleen wondered what her sister had observed, out there those nights and days. She must have watched the schoolboys on their bikes—their shortcut to Cranborne, their smoking hideouts—and at the other end, the drafted boys, slightly older, in drills. The helicopters would have been flying over. How had they not spotted her? Would Sarah ever talk about it—what these things meant, what she saw in them? Colleen did not know how to ask. Colleen understood that Sarah was instructed to run away. She had set up camp and lived in this military field. She had followed her own order to flee and hide. Colleen asked herself, if she had been a little more bossy—a type of leader, "a role model," Mr. Fairbridge would say—would this have happened? Had her sister retreated to these authorities because she herself, Colleen, was not one? She refused to linger on it.

"Who is this Hendall Pluere?" their father said to Sarah one day, shortly after her admission to Rest Haven.

Colleen nudged him, furious. 'What a blunderer,' she thought. No wonder Sarah was sick.

"I don't know what you're talking about," Sarah said, as if indignant, with a stagey whisper. The name must have still been important enough to deny. But her eyes were clear, and it seemed possible now to Colleen that she didn't know.

The psychologist pulled them aside. "She feels it, not quite as a voice, but a force—a pressure if you will."

"That helps," her father said ruefully, to Colleen, sideways, under his breath. She felt embarrassed in front of the woman, who had heard him. Colleen believed they were scrutinized and compared, and perhaps blamed.

"That's in your head," her father said as they walked to the parking lot. He would be leaving in the morning and would not have to come back for awhile. Nyadzi was four hundred kilometers away. "She's really rather nice," her father said about the psychologist. "Sincere."

"I hate her," Colleen said.

"I suppose you'll be in here next," her father said.

On some Saturdays, Colleen would take the bus downtown and then transfer out to Mabelreign, and walk a kilometer from the bus stop to Rest Haven. Out here north of town, the elevation was even higher, one of the highest points of the plateau, and the clouds seemed to hang low, as accessible as flapping laundry. Sarah lived in a long, thatched rondavel called Emmaus. All the buildings had biblical names. Rest Haven had been started by a missionary. Coming toward the rondavels from the road, in the moving cloud shadows, Colleen was reminded of dreams, and her fear of heaven.

5: THE LEPER COMPOUND

COLLEEN CLUTCHED HER HEAD TO STOP IT BUMPING THE LOW CEILING of the back of Mr. Haan's truck. Ruts and potholes worsened as they turned at a *v* in the road and they reached the steepest part, with the clinking of rock against metal rising above the roar of the diesel in first gear, and she and Heresekwe lost their grips. They fell from their places on the low wood benches lining the sides. They slid and bounced. The truck lurched and they flew together against the tailgate, which opened sharply; they were tossed out. They stood and stretched, face-to-face with the almost vertical road, laughing, watching the missionary truck ascending the mountain. Mr. Haan was oblivious to their exit.

Colleen pushed aside scrub and shuddered at the straight drop to an unoccupied valley, mostly odd rock formations, boulders balanced on top of each other, and savanna: no timber forest here, no kraals, no mealie patches. It was borderland, although nothing marked what was officially Mozambique's, and Colleen realized she had never been this close to it—a forbidden country now; the borders were closed. She ignored the urge to step off. She selected a jagged rock from the road and dropped it down the cliff, hearing it scud and click. "My father punctured his petrol tank on a rock like that," she said. "I always wondered why Julia rides around in that donkey cart delivering her medicines. It seems so slow and, I don't know, pastoral for a Westernized woman. Yet more sensible than a car."

Heresekwe winced. "Perhaps she does not want to be Western or European. You whites think we all do." His voice rose and fell in his favorite expository fashion, as if he were leading a form-four debate. He had been the debate captain at Nyadzi until March, when the security forces had detained him. "He is lucky to return as a student," they had said.

Colleen shrugged, used to Heresekwe's rebuffs about her white Rhodesian mindset, and tried to ignore the influence of her government boarding school and life in the southern suburbs of the capital. It took a day by train to reach the highlands, and each school holiday, in a lurching compartment, she and her sister changed out of their uniforms into dresses that weren't pale green. They would roll their blazers into rumpled balls while the train shunted onto a different track and sunlight flashed in the door mirror. Colleen would think about transforming herself: she wondered if she could be more than one person. At her father's coffee farm, the students from the Nyadzi mission school would try to change her, make her a reformed white girl. She believed herself to be pliable—she was not her father, she told them.

Colleen saw a horned goat skittering through the bush. Heresekwe brushed her fingers with his and looked ahead at the American trying to remove a pump organ from the front seat of his truck. "Mr. Haan, I will help you," he called. He maintained his gait. "Besides Haan, and Julia and her husband, and me, no people come here. We are superstitious. Fearful."

"Julia says you can't be infected if they are already on the antibiotics," Colleen pointed out.

"Ah, Colleen, when you are nonchalant, I feel very worried."

"Well, I guess I'm supposed to feel impressed that you come here every Sunday."

"No." Heresekwe's voice became hushed and speculative. "I don't know why I want to show you." He squatted to help Haan with the organ. Colleen walked beside them, clasping the bench.

"I see that you two must have rolled out the back door," Haan said with his occasional tic-like squinting. "Got to fix that door next time I get to Umtali. Glad I decided to put the organ in front." He gasped a little. "Not that I mean—I—"

They lifted the organ over six chipped steps to some kind of veranda or platform.

"We had a good rainy season this year," Heresekwe said. "It made the roads very difficult. But at least there is no drought." He nodded pensively, polite, traditionally revering his elders, fake yet sincere. Colleen stared sideways at him, rolled her eyes.

The lepers were assembling. Heresekwe jumped down below the platform and chatted to them. They did not look too different from where she was sitting, behind the organ, surreptitiously applying lipstick. She clamped down on a tissue and studied the red shape on the white square, blotted lines and pores. She remembered tracing jacaranda blossoms with her mother—Sarah a baby then, wavering upright, trying to put the pencils in her mouth. She had pulled a face, drooling—how the paper had acquired a likeness of the pressed petals. "We've made new flowers," Colleen remembered saying.

Haan rippled through the thin pages of his Bible. He pulled his reading glasses off and on. He called "Hi, Hi there," to the lepers. He climbed down and shook their hands. Colleen watched him. She thought, 'What's he trying to prove?'

She pushed her shoes on the pump of the organ. She made a timid sound with her fingertip, middle *c*. They waited, huddled in the orange clay courtyard. Some were smiling, weird grimaces, dissected noses, wild white eyes of blindness. The sky was thick blue, it was hanging low, it could be touched. She searched through Haan's dead wife's chorus book, seeking something without sharps or flats, and found "Higher Hands Are Leading Me." Colleen had never heard it, and she played it poorly. She could feel Haan's loss of his wife. She recalled her playing at the Nyadzi Mission church— chords, Dorian scales, ancient music. His wife had mostly stopped and watched people sing. She would add huge sounds to the ends of percussion, hearing in awe the African harmonies. Colleen remembered the woman's mouth ajar and her eyes half closed. Colleen listened, her feet barely touching the pedals, to *Kudenga* in phrases of united repetition. A leper played a drum. Music was everywhere. Her fingers tapped plastic, the silent keys. She felt the longness and shortness of them, saw black and white rectangles converging blurrily, made joining sounds, pressed her foot down over and over, lifted up, down, waited. Dissonance did not seem to exist.

But suddenly Colleen made a loud mistake, *b* flat and c, enough to cause silence. She could have rung a bell, a microphone might have squealed. Heresekwe looked cold. He stood with his arms tightly crossed around his hand-me-down sport coat. He gazed beyond her, with the distant formal look of Africans in photographs. For a second Colleen felt lost and desperate, as if he had left her here to stay. He took the chance to open. "*Mangwanani,*" he said. "I will interpret for Baba Haan."

Haan began, blinking his eyes as if to clear his mind. Heresekwe had told Colleen that Haan taught math better than he preached. He seemed to take Haan's halting words and multiply them in Shona.

Haan talked of miracles. Colleen had been told this was a weekly routine, a popular one. Haan tottered above the courtyard, very tall, almost dizzily. He tried an occasional Shona word that his interpreter colloquialized. Heresekwe immediately translated the missionary's verse, "'Rather fear that which is able to kill both the body and the soul.'" Then he gave his own input, pieces of *Paradise Lost*, his set book, half-quotes and paraphrases, "'Spirits . . . not tied with joint or limb . . . choose their own shapes.'"

Both males were excited now, speaking loudly. Colleen envied the oral privilege of men. The audience hummed in low monotonous oneness. Heresekwe spoke alone now, about ZANU, freedom, Zimbabwe. Haan nodded. People were waving arms. They waved whitish stumps, white-gray parts of fingers. But their eyeballs were turned up inward or crossed, and their scars made stiff masks of distraction.

Heresekwe removed the sport coat and rolled up the sleeves of his winter school uniform. Clouds moved past the next mountain and sun shone dimly through them. Colleen refused to look closely at the audience, squinted at the encroaching blur of an even lower sky. Mist had become heavy. She touched the dampness on her blue wool jersey. After a while she felt cold and sleepy and rocked faintly to the lulling, unfamiliar sounds of someone else's language, words she recognized leering emptily out of the mist, unconnectible, like the bandanas and coats of lepers in front of her, bright purple and orange, splotches rising up from the mass.

Guinea fowl screeched at a woman striding along the east wall. She carried a large box. It was Julia Chonongera. She beckoned to Colleen. Colleen turned around to see if there was someone else behind her, and she left her place to find Julia at a small mud outbuilding. Julia waved Colleen to a straw mat on a hard dung floor.

"I thought I'd save you from another hour of those two," Julia said, laughing. She untied the blanket around her back and pulled Tonhorai, her youngest daughter, from it. The baby wimpered, her fat legs still flexed, indented with creases from the blanket. She blinked at Colleen and gazed purposefully back at her mother's blouse, pulling java print aside and opening her mouth onto a breast. Julia supported the baby with one arm and unpacked vials and syringes, large jars of rattling pills. "How are you, *musikana*? How is boarding school? Soon you will matriculate? And then university." She paused. "Heresekwe told me you are thinking about Cape Town."

"I don't know where to go, really," Colleen said. "It's good to be home."

"Your father is well?"

"Quite well," she said. "He and Mapipi are busy with the new irrigation. They want to start some grapefruit." Colleen pulled at her single blonde plait, held it in front of herself as if it required measuring. She hardly saw her father. He did not want her to learn about coffee and chicory. She spent her days in the valley, at the mission. At night he would drink whiskey, and rant about selling the farm. But since the ambush at Nyadzi junction, eastern border property had devalued. "I'll have to keep it," he would say, standing before his reflection in the dark window. "I'm staying." He would pace the floor.

Her father took curves at great speed. Once, while driving Colleen and Sarah to the train station, he forgot to straighten the wheel and Colleen reached across to pull it back. His grip had been fixed and strong. Sarah was muttering to her imaginary friends in the back seat and had kept going steadily—the same tone, so familiar, secretive—even while the car swerved into the road and stalled in high gear. Colleen and her father had stared at each other. He seemed briefly to acknowledge her. When Colleen had turned to Sarah, she was looking calmly out the window down the cliffside.

"How is your family?" Colleen asked Julia.

"Very well, thank you." But Julia persisted. "And the little *mwana?*" she asked.

"Sarah's at Rest Haven," Colleen said.

"Ah, no," Julia said.

Tonhorai burped and played with Colleen's shoelaces. "Some dapsone arrived today," Julia said. She dropped pills into cups one by one. "This is it, see? The best way to kill the evil *Mycobacterium leprae.* Least toxic, least expensive." She smeared ointment onto gauze squares as if she were buttering bread. "I am surprised the Ministry of Health supplies us with anything sometimes. I've never personally seen a white leper." Julia's beaded hair ticked and jingled as she worked. She syringed sterile water into vials. Colleen watched white powder float and dissolve.

"These lepers all look like lions," Colleen said. She remembered staring at a lioness through a Combie window, through binoculars at the game park, memorizing her face as she stretched and yawned and sniffed. "Like how Ian Smith reminds me of a rodent. But maybe they all have similar lineage, a same gene or something."

"That is quaint, Colleen. I like that," Julia said. Her gold front tooth glittered. She was considered a great beauty in these parts. "They are indeed leonine, but it is because they have no eyelashes or eyebrows. Still it is uncanny, what you say. The cause, though, is a germ, a hand-to-hand spread. People just don't know they have it and infect others. There is one man here who did not get treatment until very late. He probably infected half of these people when he was out in the community. That is him, over there." She pointed with a half-filled syringe toward a wall past the courtyard. A seated figure languidly poked a cooking fire with a long stick. Colleen held Julia's baby and peered down at him. He was not at church with the others.

"And then," Julia said, briskly making sucking sounds with her plungers, drawing from her vials, "he turns out to be dapsone resistant. I could not believe it. I'd only heard of this sort of thing happening. I did some puncture biopsies and carried them to the lab at Mutambara. M. leprae remained all over him." She clucked her tongue. "I felt frightened. He was a vector that could not be saved. Plus he seemed so, I can't think of the word I want, *anofara*, smug, victorious."

"Anyway, it was rather unsettling." She spoke in a lower, whispery way. "Now he gets rifampicin. I continue to wear those yellow garden gloves up there when I treat him. And use his fire to boil them in a pot when I'm done."

Colleen watched the man. "He looks pretty ostracized," she said.

"He should be," Julia retorted. Colleen was propped on her elbows. She played peek-a-boo with an intent Tonhorai, absorbed the odor of the straw mat, of shrouded fires inside huts in winter, smoke knotted and twisted into the fibers during weaving. Julia sprinkled rubbing alcohol on cotton balls. Dogs barked. Colleen waited, then heard the shrieks of baboons and dogs fighting. The roars and lulls of the meeting had stopped. She did not hear the low background sound of Heresekwe.

The lepers waited in line outside the hut. Someone jerked water from a pump, and they swallowed their medicine. Julia taped dressings onto wounds. The baby crawled toward Colleen in her knitted suit. It was mealtime—cast iron and tin and ceramic clinked throughout the compound. Colleen stepped outside the hut with Tonhorai against her hip and smelled the newest cooking fires and some Sunday meat.

"Are you hungry, my *shamwari*?" Heresekwe was lighting a Berkeley in the mist. He struggled with his match.

"Yes," Colleen said. She felt ravenous, consumed the odor. "What is that?"

"*Mbudzi*," Heresekwe told her—a goat—"and yams and beet root. They cooked extra for us." Heresekwe gave a metal spoon to the baby, who clamored to get down and began to pierce the clay ground. Colleen looked back at Heresekwe. She viewed his long body, his cheekbones, a faint scar along one, the brown eyeballs that gazed above the lower lids, a line of white beneath them, the pupils continually darkening with her, through her.

The medication line had diminished. Colleen took his cigarette from his mouth and placed it in hers. "Haan is coming," Julia called, and they moved behind the hut.

They watched the one lone leper against the distant wall. Colleen dropped the cigarette butt and pressed it out with her loafer. Heresekwe grabbed her fisted hand and held it before him, disentangling the fingers and thumb and intently, absently touching them.

"Does your skin feel different?" he asked. "Like there is a force around you? I look at my skin when I am here, and it always has the goose bumps."

"I feel cold, that's all. I keep thinking about lighting the donkey boiler when I get home and having a bath."

He nodded. "You might still feel that way, even in summer. It is always cold here. The skin forever crawls as if it is hearing a sacred tale." He opened wide his gray, oversized sport coat and pulled her next to him. She stared at the torn maroon lining, pressed against the heat from his body, found the hot skin of his side beneath a loose shirttail.

Haan yelled that it was time for lunch. They moved apart. She pushed her hair behind her ears. Heresekwe looked at her, and then down at *kikuya* grass sodden with mist. Colleen pulled her skirt hem even with her knees. They were knobby and pale beneath blue tights.

"The food is pretty good here," Haan called heartily.

Fires sizzled and bounced along the south side of the clinic wall. Two or three already pulsated with gray-and-orange coals. Colleen glanced inside a large open door and saw in the dimness a long row of cots along a cement floor. Shapes tossed. They curled and recurled restlessly under army blankets. Shapes were lying still. The room was mute. People tried to nap.

The lunchtime fire was mostly embers. A woman dug down into them with a stick and nudged hotter ones around a black pot. She expelled blackened mealies from the bottom of the fire. They rolled out along the ground, steaming. She picked one up in her hand and offered it to Haan, the oldest. He winced and dropped it, waving his hand in the moist air.

"*Asi canai*," she apologized repeatedly. "I forgot that hot things burn."

"Just because you feel no pain does not mean you have special powers," Julia teased her gently. "I suspect that you also burned your hand and you just don't feel it." She reached toward her. "May I look?"

A pink streak crossed the woman's outstretched palm. There was a space where her ring finger belonged. Colleen noticed white, scaly scabs along her forearm. Julia found some aloe leaves in her skirt pocket and squeezed them onto the burn. Haan shook his head that he was fine. His face moved along the mealie as he bit and chewed. Colleen peeled hers, removing the silky hair and the husk and throwing them in the fire.

"You are all numb to some degree," Heresekwe said, quizzical. "I didn't realize. I knew it moved along the nerves." He tried to change the subject, probably sensing his affrontive directness. He commented on the flavor of the corn, and offered to help the woman as she dished root vegetables and goat bones onto a large tin platter. He passed the *sadza*, heaped high in bowls. They all crouched and ate, dipping fingerfuls of *sadza* into the main dish.

"We thank God, my son, that we are blessed with a painless disease. And that Mai Chonongera can halt it with her medicine." The woman spoke dreamily. Colleen thought the woman was quite brave, even saintly, but Heresekwe frowned. They washed their hands in a metal tub, and he passed Colleen the soap beneath the water.

Julia had left Tonhorai sleeping on a blanket, her face coated with orange yam. The leper woman sat near her. She moved her hand above and along the length of the curled baby, as if to caress her. The woman's face sagged. There was a stretch of hard ground between them.

It was time to visit the infectious leper. They crossed the courtyard and began to climb down along the eroded terrace. A gust of smoke blew slowly at them and changed direction. Colleen wiped at her eyes, sniffed, and hoped her mascara had not smeared.

"I sometimes tire of coming here, Mr. Haan," Heresekwe said, batting irritably at the smoke. "I detest this happiness. The grisly optimism. They are like a new tribe. Perhaps their minds are corrupted with numbness. I am not surprised at their political apathy."

Haan squinted hard, thinking of something to say. Julia stepped from the doorway of the mud hut. She was wearing her yellow gloves to her elbows. "They are isolated. How can they know what is happening? And if you bring a Rhodesia Herald? What then? Everything is censored," she declared. "Many are immobilized throughout our country, and it is not because of leprosy."

"Anyway, they're not happy," Colleen said. "Aren't their faces all pulled that way from the scars?"

"When I was little, I used to think zebra skeletons were smiling," Heresekwe said.

Haan asked how close they were to Mozambique. Heresekwe raised his eyebrows. Haan said he figured about one or two kilometers. The nearest border post was outside Umtali.

"You still think they could help somehow with the cause, Baba. Because they're right on the border." Heresekwe looked briefly at Julia. He shook his head. "I sense that they would be sellouts."

They descended upon the man at the bottom of the slope, along the north wall. The man could not see them; he was blind. Colleen wondered where his irises were. His muscles were wasted.

Julia muttered tersely and gave him a capsule. She examined a small wound near his elbow and threw her gloves onto the ashes of his fire. They smoldered and fumed. She climbed the hill. Haan prayed over the man while Heresekwe interpreted. Colleen watched Julia holding a basin high above her head and hurtling its water through the air. She carefully toweled her arms, waved down at her, and blew a kiss.

The man wore a plaid blanket. His thighs protruded from the blanket, ending at the knees—dusky stumps, scales caked with ashes and dust from his fire. Colleen regarded him.

Heresekwe said in English how she would enjoy freakshows at the circus. He was sarcastic, restless. "Shut up," she told him. Haan suggested they get the organ in the truck. They said goodbye to the man.

"*Musikana?*" The man pivoted his head and gazed out behind her. He asked her name.

Colleen told Heresekwe she would join them in a minute. She wanted to practice her Shona.

"He speaks some kind of dialect. Good luck."

She heard them panting up the hill, especially the missionary. "Don't touch him," Heresekwe added, turning and looking back.

For a while, Colleen and the man exchanged long textbook Shona pleasantries. He said he was from Mfumvufu, near Nyadzi. It was where a narrow river moved through a rocky gorge, where a sign on the road told people to change gears. He spoke Shona oddly, like her, as if it were his second language. He asked where she lived, inquired about her family. Yes, he said, he knew that farm. There were two or three farms before the junction, and then the wattle plantations. She told him that her sister was *penga*—she wanted immediately to say it—never before, *crazy*, Sarah—how scornful it made her feel, and vindicated somehow, calling her that. Their mother was dead, she told him. "*Runyarara,*" she said, a word which meant the same as sleep. She was only asleep. She thought of it, not wistfully, as usual, but in the way she might shrug her shoulders. She felt gruff somehow, and defiant. Around this man, she seemed to dismiss them both, as if she might not even know them, nor her father, no one. She thought vaguely that she might understand Sarah if she could stay thinking this way—people she knew seemed to veer away from her in her mind, and disappear, like essential figures in a recurring dream.

He wanted to tell her a story. The scaly stumps that were his legs looked like used kindling. They were the color of ash. Colleen stomped and kicked some powdery white coals. She knelt next to the gray white circle and wondered where he urinated, palpating the ground for dampness.

"There was once a time when the world knew only animals," he began. "Then the first ancestors emerged from the ground. They rose up from holes and caves and peered out from behind rocks. The first ancestors learned a secret language that gave them the knowledge to become immortal." He ran lumpy fingers along the smooth wood of his crutches. "I hear you breathing," he said. "You are close to me."

"Across the fire."

"They could become immortal by changing into snakes that shed their skins or chameleons changing colors. But this metamorphosis could never be observed by another person. We changed our forms alone, a very hallowed time, and exalting beyond anything I can describe." His voice seemed to change; there was less rasping. Colleen asked herself how she understood some of the more complicated words he used—it was not possible, even after all the Shona lessons with her mother's friend, Vaida Moyo. But she decided she was finally bilingual. Maybe it just happened like that—one day, one moment.

"We could change back into human forms. We impregnated and became pregnant, which created the mortal ancestors. But one immortal stumbled upon two others procreating. On the same day, he came to behold another shedding skin. One can never behold acts of immortality.

"The penalty: a curse permeated only the bodies of every immortal spirit. Mortals could die. We continued to transform physically, but the process altered, and we started to decay alive. We have lived among mortal lepers since ancient times. We can never heal. We rejuvenate enough to rot again, over and over."

"Why do you infect mortals?" Colleen asked, as if he told her the truth, remembering how Julia held him responsible for many new infections.

He ignored her, turned his head. She unbent her knees and scrambled up. His blanket had fallen away. "You are perhaps a trapped spirit," he said. "You could somehow undo this curse." His penis perched upright from his crippled body, engorged, flawless, the foreskin rolled back against him. She felt a familiar pang across her pelvis, then nausea. She shook her head to clear it. She must think objectively about the surprising contrast.

"You have beheld me." He covered himself. "Now touch my face."

Automatically, Colleen brushed his forehead with the ends of her fingertips. She was a priest. She blessed him in some way. He continued to murmur softly. She was now a freed spirit, he said. The sky will lift. She will lose her body. These eyes and fingers will disappear first.

"Feel the skin that is yours," he told her. "It is teeming with sensation. The spirits of the first ancestors are stroking you. Lepers touch you to be healed, and you fade with each touch. You are alive forever, invisible like wind. You stir this putrid air, disperse it."

Her fists had been pressed against her eyes. She saw black and gray. She was dizzy, as though she'd whirled around and around in a circle.

"Come on, Colleen," she heard Heresekwe. "Can you understand him? I can only make out a few words. He talks gibberish. *Anopenga?* Do you think he's mad?"

Colors returned to her vision. She nodded slowly up and down.

On the ride home, Colleen and Heresekwe sat together on the floor in the back of Haan's truck. Their backs pressed against the cab as the truck tumbled down the mountain. The pull of gravity steadied and soothed her, and she saw Haan's bald patch through the window when she turned around. They dozed back and forth on each other's shoulders. Deep ruts jolted her awake. Her spirit flew out, startled, and after a while came back. A sudden afternoon sun glowed through the flesh of her closed lids.

6 : HOT SPRINGS

COLLEEN WAS ALONE IN HER SIX–BUNK COMPARTMENT—NO ONE
wanted to take the night train anymore—wrapped inside her bedroll.
She leaned against a steaming window, its Rhodesia Railways insignia
impressed onto both sides of the glass, and beyond that, the dark blowing bush. This train made fewer stops. It blasted through villages. It was
a night of wind and rain, cold even for August. The clouds rushed past,
orange tinged; bush fires raged. *Guti,* she'd heard this weather called.

Her father had phoned before she left school for the August holidays telling her she could pick up her ticket at the Salisbury station.
He told her there had just been "an occurrence" at Nyadzi mission.
Over a period of days, thirty-four students had absconded, crossing
the border to guerilla training camps in Mozambique. The mission
school had been closed by RDF. Some teachers and students were
arrested. Her friend had been detained again, her father said—the
interpreter the missionaries used, the boy from Sabi.

The train passed through another fire, the glowing savanna, a sudden
heat. The engine was grinding uphill, and the cars rattled now through
corrugated-iron back buildings of Rusape and Inyazura, servants' quarters, warehouses. Colleen took Heresekwe's envelopes from her purse
for the second time that night and reread his rushed notes from last
school term. One was postmarked in mid-July, his fountain pen splattered across pulpy lines of exercise book paper. Heresekwe believed that
the post was tampered with "by Smith's agents," and wrote like the

opinion pages in censored foreign news magazines. Or he would allude vaguely to their own past conversations. "The *Herald* is all lies, Colleen," he had told her. "There is no need for the protected villages," he'd said. "Those people are only prisoners of war." In the letters he asked her, "Do you remember what we talked about?" Or, "This is what Rose and I explained down by the dip tank." She knew that mostly he told her nothing. She searched his last letter for any kind of tension. It would have been written during the week of the absconding, right before the arrests. He talked in a newsy way about the protected villages. People from Ndima tribal trust land had already been moved by RDF; their huts had been burned behind them. They lived now in a guarded camp at Skyline junction, behind a security fence. They could not come and go as they pleased. Nyadzi would likely be next. "So many people are behind the gate now," he wrote. "You will have to see it to believe it."

But for his poem—he sometimes copied verses from his Sixth-Form anthology for her—he had chosen parts of Matthew Arnold's "To Marguerite." It made her flush with anxiety.

> Who order'd that their longing's fire
> Should be, as soon as kindled, cool'd?
> Who renders vain their deep desire?—
> A God, a God their severance ruled;
> And bade betwixt their shores to be
> The unplumb'd, salt, estranging sea.

These words, vain, severance, sea. It was not that she didn't think it had pertained to the two of them generally. It was how much more he must have felt it pertained to them than she did. He was the one who had copied it down. And now.

Colleen was to spend the first week of August at Hot Springs with her father. They had been invited by the new district commissioner and his wife, who picked Colleen up at the train station. "We're just Clive and Nanette to you," the commissioner's wife said. "Do call us by our Christian names." They adored her father, they told her. He had been "super" company for them while they were "out in the bundu." They asked after Sarah, and nodded with concern, as if they had been longtime family friends.

Umtali was overrun by new military trucks, and exuberant soldiers making catcalls. The previous month, a missile had been shot across the border from Mozambique. After breakfast at Meikles tearoom, Clive made an excursion into the suburb to show Colleen and Nanette where the bomb had landed. There was a hole on the regularly mown grass inside a busy roundabout. It had tunneled into the ground without exploding. Clive said that this was providential, a sign that God was on the side of the Rhodesian Front.

They met up with the convoy south of town, and joined another one at Wengesi junction. A9 was empty. The only oncoming traffic had been army lorries overloaded with Africans—women, babies on jostled backs, older men, children. The bush smoldered; smoke blended with low clouds to form a wispy fog. Clive and Nanette's car was second in line from the armored truck, and Colleen could see two soldiers on the top, vigilantly rotating their guns.

"They need to bloody well speed this thing up," Nanette said. She turned back to Colleen. "No wonder your father refuses to ride in convoy!"

"Quite right, we're sitting ducks," Clive said.

"I suppose it's the fog," Nanette said. "Poor blokes up there, waiting to get picked off. But smell the springs! Bloody horrid really. I can smell the springs already."

"Me too," Colleen said.

"We're still about twelve k out," Clive said.

"Sulphur," Colleen said. "I think it comes from the earth's crust."

"Not just a pretty face, hey," Clive said. He had a pleasantly smooth voice which reminded Colleen of the disc jockeys on Radio 5. He braked and geared down behind the car in front of them. They passed through a business district. "Craft market, police camp, bottle store," Clive said, pointing. "The metropolis of Odzi."

"That's where they're holding the Nyadzi detainees," Nanette said.

"In there?" Colleen asked in a conversational way. There were two Quonset huts with aluminum awnings over a row of front windows. "Will they be released?"

"I hope not," Clive said, laughing. "No, actually, Colleen, we've sent them to their deaths."

"Ach, shame," Nanette said.

"No, sorry, sorry," he said. "I couldn't resist. Most of them have already gone to their homes. Or rather to their assigned P.V., if they're lucky enough to have one. The school is closed, you know. I believe they've kept a few yet, the headmaster, and one or two of the boys."

"I shouldn't have brought it up," Nanette said to Colleen. "Now that's all we'll hear about till teatime."

"Such a setback," Clive said. "Did their absconding distract us from the relocations? Most definitely! But they're only hurting themselves."

"Darling, darling, we're on holiday."

At the springs, Colleen swam in the pool while Nanette and Clive sat at the open bar drinking cane and Coke. Africans in chef hats grilled lamb on the *braaivleis*. Everyone wore down jackets and talked about how cold it was. The temperature had dropped ten degrees from that morning. Breath steamed. The pool steamed. Colleen loved the hot water, with its reek of sulphur. She floated in her snagged and faded Speedo, and the drains lapped and gurgled. She gasped for air and dived back down again into the hot rolling silence. For what seemed to be minutes at a time, she did not think about her sister or Heresekwe in their locked compounds. The only other people in the pool were a retired couple from Gwelo, who told her about ancient bacteria that still thrived at these springs, much like billions of years ago, before animate life.

When her father arrived from Nyadzi, they had dinner and went back to the bar, where Colleen was allowed Cinzano and lemonade, and the men took turns lighting Nanette's cigarettes.

"What are we doing here with a D.C.?" Colleen asked her father as soon as they were back in their own rondavel. "Why are we with these people?"

"Are you speaking to me like that?" her father said. "A little self-righteous are we?" The waiter had provided a tray for him, with a bottle of J&B, a souvenir glass, and a bucket of ice. "Well, the poor bloke can't help it, Colleen. He's actually quite a free thinker. These are difficult times. Complicated times! Sometimes one has to follow orders."

"You just like his wife," Colleen said to him.

Her father smiled viciously, wiped his hand over his face, and shook his head. He reached into his glass for a piece of ice and popped it into his mouth, crunching.

"No," he said. "No, I won't say anything. I will keep my mouth shut."

"Good!"

"Bloody hell—there's you and your liaisons," her father said. "Surely I have the wrong daughter locked away?"

Colleen thought it best to stay quiet. She had been hanging her tops in a musty central wardrobe with a full-length mirror on one of its doors, and she pushed the door back away from her impatiently.

"Well, at least we're here," her father said in a conciliatory way. "A proper holiday for you."

Her father had met Clive and Nanette at a security meeting that June in Melsetter. He'd been the only farmer who refused to install a security fence. Nanette had invited him to dinner. During Colleen's winter school term, they had spent much time drinking together. Colleen's father seemed impressed with how Nanette could hold her alcohol. They sat now at the bar until late, under the high beams of garden light. Colleen could hear them after she had gone to bed. There were other commissioners at the springs, and a group of civil engineers who talked endlessly about land mines. Unlike the other wives, Nanette argued politics with the men, calling herself the devil's advocate. Conversation was now all about race, the recognition of an enemy. The bar waiters stood nearby in maroon caps and, in the day, gardeners trimmed rhododendrons. Debates raged, shot glasses clinked, the resort staff proceeded, and even Colleen began to wonder if they really heard this talk.

Nanette was tall and athletic with short black hair that she combed behind her ears after she'd been swimming. She would wear her jacket over her swimming costume until the sun was high in the sky, her hands in the pockets, and walk back and forth between the pool and the bar. In the morning, she drank screwdrivers. Often she swam with Colleen; she said she had been on the Western Province swim team, "a hundred years ago." Her dark tan—her husband called her his "little kaffir"—

blended on her legs with two long purple scars, which she told Colleen were from surgery after a car accident. "They're so ugly, I shouldn't even wear a cozzie," she said. When Nanette gestured, or beckoned a waiter, Colleen could see another scar, meandering and white, without pigment of any kind, on the ball of her hand as it joined the wrist. It folded and opened into the lines of her palm. Colleen thought that she must have held out her hand at one time to break a fall.

"She's quite lovely really," her father said to Colleen on the second day, as if he had always thought otherwise. They were sitting in bleach-smelling chaise lounges, with Nanette doing laps, skillful backstrokes, the pool a warm, choppy mist.

"What do you make of her?" he asked Colleen.

"She seems fun," Colleen said. "Livens things up a bit."

"Yes, that's it," he said. "Spot on."

After awhile, her father picked up a towel and stood over at the edge of the pool. "Come out from that soup," he said in a gruff way to Nanette. Colleen felt embarrassed for him. She looked back down at her magazine. Nanette treaded for awhile in the deep end.

"Give me a hand then," she said.

When the waiter arrived the next morning with the tea tray, asking in a low voice, "Coffee or tea," Nanette answered. Colleen at first thought she was dreaming. From Colleen's father's room, Nanette rushed to the bathroom with her fist pressed over her mouth. The toilet flushed; she was retching. Colleen unlocked the burglar bars and opened the door. She picked up the tray and brought it to the table.

"It's tea," Colleen said to Nanette when she came out. Colleen stirred in her own sugar and passed Nanette a cup.

"Thank you, Colleen," she said. Between sips, she reached out to hold the table for support.

Colleen could hear her father snoring in the next room. Nanette's cup rattled. She set it back down on the tray. "I must get back. Don't say anything to Clive, he may not have noticed." She stood at the door behind the burglar bars and watched the other rondavels. There were other trays on the *stoeps*, and no one had come out yet. "My dear, we were all so pissed out of our minds. Use discretion, hey. Promise me, hey."

"I will, I promise," Colleen said.

That week, Colleen made friends with a group of South African hikers, who had just arrived from Chimanimani National Park. They were camping in the empty caravan park behind the resort's thatched enclosure. Because no one else had claimed the campsites, they'd arranged their tents in scenic locations along the bluff. Out here, even more than at the pool where the springs flowed, Colleen could smell the sulphur and other salts, perhaps iodine. She found herself thinking of potatoes, craving them—the thick air seemed to infuse her with a vaguely primitive appetite that she couldn't describe. The South Africans taught Colleen about the mineral content of the spring water, how geothermally heated water could hold more dissolved solids—lithium, calcium, even radium. The women and one of the men were Michaelis Art School students or graduates; they had all at some time attended the school, and talked knowingly and confidently about their projects. One of the women, Robin, had brought along a sculpting wheel so that she could use different types of mud and clay from places on their trip. She would paint the pots later. Colleen liked how they demanded nothing of her except her willingness to let them demonstrate their lifestyle. She sensed that the lifestyle was probably more enhanced, more defined, if they had an observer. She admired what seemed to be their fearlessness, here in a war zone, which appeared truer and more real than her own. She felt it had to do with the way they gave only a select attention to their surroundings. They encouraged her to do the same—she must free up her energies, focus. She must look—*see*, they emphasized—with the eye of an artist. Several of them had been involved in a movement in Cape Town called "I Live," which enabled them to make decisions without regret. All choices were possible and right. There was no wrong choice except doing what one did not want.

One afternoon, during one of their excursions down to the Odzi River to collect mud, they started a bonfire to fend off Mopani bees and smoked dagga. Len, the man who had gone to Michaelis, stripped off his shorts and stretched out under the sun. The women followed, and then the other man, Graham. They were used to nude beaches in Cape Town, they said—Sandy Bay, parts of Llandudno, if the tide was low. Colleen did not feel ashamed of her body. She was thin and tall, though pale; she burned rather than tanned—but she left her jeans and shirt on and sat holding her knees. She watched the river and the fire. Len lectured her about inhibitions. The five of them seemed almost pagan to Colleen, stretched as they were around the fire in languid poses. A hawk glided. Robin went down to the river to dig for clay. She moved back and forth with a shovel and a bucket. The men watched. One of the women, Carole, appeared to be sleeping. The skin around her groin was peeling from sunburn. Len stood up and added more kindling to the fire. Colleen tried not to stare. The dagga had not relaxed her, had made her, if anything, more vigilant, more acutely aware. She should not have smoked it. Len returned to his spot next to her and rested on his back with his eyes closed. Colleen watched a group of ants at a nearby anthill. Their movement seemed frenetic and cooperative. She felt, she was determined to feel, that Len and Carole and the others made a mockery of such movement. That was their intention, their choice, they would tell her. She immediately chided herself—not even out of sixth form and she had become a kind of prude. Yet strongly, with this fear, came an exact, fleeting desire for all of them, their exquisite indolence, especially the oldest one, Len.

There was no trail leading away from the small beach except back uphill to the resort. Len wanted to search for more branches, and had already set out in another direction—toward a reed-filled area which seemed a likely place for snakes. "Would you be happier if I put my shorts on?" he asked Colleen, bounding back for them. His body was stocky and capable seeming. He checked the pocket for his pipe and matches. Getting back into the pants—tight cutoffs —he tugged, tried to pull taut his stomach, and struggled slightly with the zip. "You're afraid of us now," he said to Colleen.

"I'm not as green as you think," she declared.

Len swished for awhile through the reeds. They could see the back of his head, and then could only hear him, remotely, singing.

"Mind the crocs," Carole called to him.

Robin had come up from the river with the collected mud. She set the buckets down and leaned on the shovel. Graham began to get dressed. Carole walked over to the reeds and peered inside.

"Len!" Robin called.

"Hey boetie," Graham called.

"Vok," they heard Len say, as if from a distance, but the clattering of metal and ceramic might have been next to them.

"Are you all right?"

"Someone's picnic," he called back. "I tripped over someone's bloody *kos* in the middle of a river. You must come see this, come here."

He stood on a small peninsula surrounded by a variety of trampled ferns. Rapids surged around a fallen tree. The current of the river seemed to flow in two directions. Inside a green tarpaulin, Len showed them rows of cast-iron and ceramic pots, a pile of plastic plates. Flies buzzed.

"Odd," Len said. "The odd River Odzi." He laughed.

"Amazing," Carole said.

From a chicken, Len pulled off a complete leg, a drumstick attached to the thigh, and took an exaggerated bite. "Chreikie, I'm hungry," he said, chewing, swallowing. "Lovely." He gestured to the pots. "Enjoy," he said. Carole and Graham were vegetarian and sampled the greens. One pot seemed to be cucumber soup. There was mealie bread wrapped in foil, sweet potatoes, a cantaloupe, several ripe avocados. "Mealie meal?" Len opened the *sadza* pot and looked at Colleen.

"Don't be afraid," Carole urged Colleen, offering her a boiled egg, already peeled. "It's all still fresh. It won't hurt you. I promise."

Colleen took the egg and ate, wishing she had salt and pepper.

"I'm not quite getting it," Robin said. "What is this doing here?"

"A ritual of theirs, most probably," Len said in his knowing way. "An offering to the gods?"

"Colleen, what do you know about this tribe's culture?" Robin asked.

"I don't think it's an offering to gods," Colleen said.

"Who knows?" Len said. "You'd be surprised what they don't tell you."

Graham stood with his arm lolling over Carole's shoulder. Colleen had become used to the nakedness, especially since the men were now partially dressed. Robin knelt down and carefully replaced the lids on the pots. "You shouldn't have eaten anything," she said. "None of you."

"'Should' isn't really a word," Graham reminded her.

Beyond the reeds rose an embankment with a path occluded by short, thick trees. Four women passed them carrying baskets on their heads. Robin and Carole waved to them.

Colleen went twice to the Odzi business district. Both times, she'd found a lift with Robin, who wanted to buy soapstone at the crafts market. Colleen told Robin she had a friend who worked at the police camp. The Quonset building smelled of wax and metal, like an old elevator. An African behind the desk explained to Colleen that only chaplains could see inmates. Colleen gave the man a letter for Heresekwe, which she had rewritten several times. In the letter, she stated that she wished him well. She'd not been sure what else to write down; she feared implicating him further in some unknown way. Mostly, she had difficulty believing he could even be in the building with her. At the springs, it was the same. Her wavering loss of belief in this fact—him here, locked up—convinced her that she lacked any real steadfastness. She wondered why they even called it a camp. The floors were a polished red tile. The walls were white. She had heard before—Heresekwe himself had told her—that inmates got tortured here, at Odzi. It had always sounded so ominous when people talked of it. But the place seemed clean and civilized. Nothing would happen. Nothing had happened. He would not be hurt. She refused to think in those ways. It was helpful to be inside the Quonset hut. She liked the signs on the wall —red print on a white background covered in Plexiglas—office, infirmary, kitchen. The clerk seemed cheerful. Colleen forced herself to imagine Heresekwe as a kind of obligation. Doing this seemed easier than she would have otherwise thought. From somewhere in the building she heard voices that did not sound tormented.

On the second trip to the Odzi district, a convoy was assembling in the parking lot outside the police camp, but even after that, Colleen stayed in the crafts market and wandered from one stall to another. She told herself to just start walking, to just go over to the police camp—

Robin had barely noticed the last time—but instead she purchased an assortment of beads. What would the point be anyway? she thought. She could not visit. People from one of the safari busses had crowded the market and were tapping in tentative ways on the marimbas. Children chased each other with calabashes. There were rows of wooden baboons, with clumps of real gray fur, and better carvings of the game animals. Colleen examined a fragile-looking reedbuck.

Robin spent all of her time in the soapstone section. Earlier that week she had purchased a lizard, because she'd been told by another vendor that lizards were bad luck. The soapstone vendors did not heckle. They polished their pieces with corn oil. Some sculpted. The ground was littered with chisels and oily rags. "Colleen, come here," Robin said, beckoning. One of the artists sat chiseling the bust of an African woman and seemed nearly finished, the stone a different gray than the others, the color of cemetery monuments and downtown statues. "Do you like it, hey?"

"Yes," Colleen said. "Is it granite?"

Neither the artist nor Robin answered her. Robin was shaking her head slightly in a type of awe. The gray made the stone's expression easier to immediately see, as if facing some kind of strong light, the chin tilted slightly upward. Colleen had never really looked at one of these sculpted faces so closely—the way Robin's rapt interest seemed to insist—and the face contradicted itself, or changed itself, the more she watched it. At times, the face appeared wistful and long-suffering, which Colleen liked the most. When this seemed to slip away from her, she started searching again for it, the way she might look for a necessary name on a long, posted list.

The artist chiseled quietly, her knees drawn up under her. The bust was in her lap. Robin knelt down and held the stone chin in both of her hands. The artist examined something above the ear and redid a fine groove; her elbows pressed into the bust to steady it. She was finishing up the braids, which had been etched to a point at the top of the scalp. She pulled back the chisel and brushed loose particles of stone away. Colleen thought of Mrs. Fairbridge at hostel, doing nit checks with a lice comb. The artist peered at the head with a same absorption, with a particular task to complete.

Robin caressed the chin in a kindly way, tossing her hair back over her shoulders, her fingers moving across the eyes. The bust seemed now to perch in the artist's lap as if released to its own life. The face had changed again, or possibly it had always been this one set thing, resolute and poised.

"So beautiful," Robin said, breathing. She let go and sat back on her knees.

"You must buy it," Colleen said.

"I might," Robin said, standing and brushing off her jeans. "I like the detail at the brow and cheekbone. I'm going to look around first."

Another vendor waved to Robin, and she went off to look at copper silhouettes. Colleen was tired of the market and wished they would leave. Beggars rattled ceramic tins. She saw Haan, the missionary, in a new sombrero made from breadbags, passing out Bibles from the tailgate of his Combie. People walked past her with Gideon New Testaments. Some set them down on folding tables while shopping and left them. The safari tourists jostled past her. Africans called out. Robin bartered cheerfully. Colleen half-admired her style. She wondered why it wasn't, or couldn't be, something to cultivate in her own self—a certain regard for the Africans without actually thinking of them at all, and if so, mildly, pleasantly. Everyone seemed to be outside of Robin. It wasn't only the Africans. All things, including Robin's Michaelis projects, seemed secondary to the single combined, almost palpable thing: the goals and plans and ideologies of the group, Robin's group. To think of it, Colleen felt lonely and unsure of herself. She did not know what she wanted. She felt a dull fullness, like the yearning after a heavy meal for something vague that was not even known. She bought a set of bottle-cap coasters for Sarah. Sarah would place them around as decorations in her room at Rest Haven. Colleen worried that Sarah would ruminate about some hidden significance in the bottle-cap labels. After a while, she waited in Haan's line for a New Testament.

"They let me see Heresekwe the other day," Haan told her in an unusually gossipy way. It was something of a boast. "Even though I'm not really a chaplain."

"A missionary is sort of like a chaplain," Colleen said. "What did he say?"

"He asked me to pray for him," Haan said, distracted now by the people behind her. He was passing out books as well, with titles like *Nothing but the Blood* and *Saved by Grace*, and she stepped to the side of the tailgate. People stood around reading.

Colleen could suddenly hear it, Heresekwe speaking to Haan—she had seen them enough together—*pray for me, could you pray for me.* She imagined Heresekwe sitting on a floor, or in a chair. He would look up when he spoke. She could hear him. This was something he would have said to Haan. He would likely have meant it. When did Heresekwe ask for prayer? Her mind reeled with her sense of him, and what she believed to be his despair, or conflicting remorse, that she could not really name or understand.

"And what an answer to prayer!" Haan said to her, with a rare smile that reminded her of an animal baring its teeth; one of his incisors was a fang. "He's home safe now with his mom and dad. When I got there today, he'd been released to Sabi!" They'd see him soon, Haan told her—the mission school would be reopening during the August holidays, to make up for lost time. In his happiness, he'd taken on the tone of his sermons, the climax before the invitation. "Weeping may endure for a day, but joy cometh in the morning," he said.

On their way back to the springs, Robin talked to Colleen about Carole's recent miscarriage. This had happened before they came up to Rhodesia. She said that a successful pregnancy had much to do with aspects of the moon, especially moon to Pluto. Colleen said she had also heard something about the moon. Robin said that Carole had been pregnant long enough to purchase a few baby clothes. She'd even bought a used bassinette and moved it into their co-op in Observatory. Len had wanted Carole to have his baby. He tried to stop Carole's bleeding with an herb called feverfew and some wild yam. Carole had nearly died from blood loss, the nurses at Groote Schuur had told Robin. She was given several pints of blood in a transfusion. Len had been angry with Robin for bringing Carole to the hospital because he felt they should have given the herbs more time to take effect. Robin said Len had spent a long time looking at the fetus. He'd told them later how he'd removed it from the toilet after they left for casualty. It had been a difficult time for him. Robin never felt the same about him after that. She used to be fiercely jealous of Len and his other women, but after that she didn't really care. She said that she still couldn't stand it when Len referred to her and Carole as his wives.

It was the first time that week that Colleen had been given any sense of the South Africans' own history, aside from hiking anecdotes and their art. That moment, she could see it more clearly than her own life, Len pulling a fetus out of a toilet, or more likely—brazenly—the clots of blood and tissue, scrutinizing them, trying to see himself in them, gazing awhile at this thing. What had he then done with it, once he was finished? She knew not to ask. The lighthearted Carole nearly bleeding to death. Maybe the herbs would have worked if Len had known what he was doing. Colleen was certain he hadn't. She wondered why Robin had told her. Maybe to discourage her—Colleen—from Len, a warning, an urge to make known the dissent in their group. To remind her that this was not her group; she could not be bound the way they were bound. All week, her involvement with the South Africans had dominated her thoughts. She had allowed it, as long as she could believe them not to have facts behind them, facts and realities as set, as established, as anyone else's life—as her own. This life seemed to fly back at her, into her face, as Robin drove, Sarah, Heresekwe, her father and Nanette, O levels, A levels, Rhodesia itself. As Robin talked, Colleen heard herself commenting, even exclaiming, without the empathy she felt a person should have.

Their last night at Hot Springs, Colleen's father asked her if she would like to go for a walk. He wanted to watch the sun go down. Nanette had told him that sunsets were best seen from the campground. He said the hedge and tall cycads depressed him because of the way they blocked eastern and western light.

There was no actual sun—it had been occluded by the smoke, which had been in the air all week, and low, dull clouds. The bluff above the Odzi River was vast and bare. The South Africans had gone with the afternoon convoy to Beitbridge. Clive and Nanette had also left and were on the way back to their post. Clive had pressure on him to "facilitate" the next relocations north of Nyadzi junction.

The bluff seemed unfamiliar with the pup tents gone. Colleen paced from one mashed square to the other. "This one was the storage tent," she said to her father. "They slept along there in those two." It seemed important to explain how the camp was set up. She stood in a patch of flattened kikuya grass, and looked out over the wide shallows of the river.

"People come and go," her father said. "Maybe you'll see them someday in Cape Town."

Colleen thought it kindly of her father to make the effort to reassure her. He did not do it often. She understood that he believed she missed them, Carole and Len and Robin and Graham. To her it seemed more that she marveled at the profoundness of their absence. Around them, she'd taken for granted that the bluff could only be there in one certain way. It was only there that once. She had accepted this assumption. Her father sat down on the picnic table and smoked. The fire in the cement pit had been doused with water, and when her father tossed his cigarette into it, the dampness gave way to a brief gritty plume. In a nearby wire dumpster, Colleen could see the spray cans of Doom, which they had used for the mosquitoes.

Colleen brushed aside what looked to be baking powder, and probably turmeric—Carole had recently made soybean bobotie—and sat on the other side next to her father. She felt relieved to be with him.

"It's nice out here," her father said. "The real Africa." There were electrical hookups for the caravans and signs on the cinderblock bathrooms which said WHITES ONLY. The sun itself, behind the smoke and the sulphuric vapors, could have been the sun of any time. Colleen wanted to believe that she knew what he meant.

WHEN COLLEEN RETURNED TO NYADZI FROM HOT SPRINGS, HER mother's friend Vaida Moyo had dropped off some new Shona translations. Vaida had also been gone, in Sekubva with her husband, but the security forces were reopening the mission school; teachers were expected back early. Colleen started working on the translations immediately. She felt more anxious than usual to impress her, as if by not doing so her mother might fade entirely from Vaida's memory. She was not sure why it still mattered. In the afternoons, she studied physics—she had barely passed the winter exam.

Mapipi seemed preoccupied with his drum business, and was often down at the khaya. The goats shot by RDF after curfew had not been claimed. This gave him a surplus of skins, which flapped heavily on the clothesline. There was always a faint smell of decay. Lately, he went every weekend to Umtali, sliding his instruments onto the back of Haan's truck. Colleen had seen him there by his display, on a lot near the BP station, drinking purple Fanta.

It seemed to Colleen that Mapipi now played his drums all the time. He had even moved one up onto the veranda, and would tap on it between various tasks. He sometimes did not let up, an endless pounding that echoed off the ridge. Colleen's head would thud. One day she had thrown her textbook down in a rage. "I wish he'd shut up," she said. She rolled the windows closed around the house, furiously. "He's not any good anyway."

"It's a code," her father said.

"You're joking," she said, although she had heard about the *mujibas*. For some time, she had assumed Mapipi was one. No one would say for definite.

"True as."

"He told you that?"

"Seems obvious to me," her father said. "Listen sometimes when the army is around. He's warning the chappies up in the hills."

The afternoon before Nyadzi started, Colleen reviewed her translations with Vaida in the school's library. She was hoping to see Heresekwe. But Vaida speculated that he might not be coming back; perhaps his parents wouldn't allow it. Vaida said she wondered whether he'd actually been released. She reminded Colleen that the news had only been hearsay. "Or the police camp may have told lies to Mr. Haan—why should we believe them?"

In the distance, they heard RDF soldiers calling out announcements on megaphones, rudimentary Shona and bits of Chilapalapa. Colleen noticed that soldiers had been hiking up the steep road to the mission school every day. They would leave their Land Rovers on the highway, mounted on the embankment. With the school reopening, they were searching Shushine busses and randomly checking the bags of returning students. Colleen could see the soldiers now, running and jostling with the megaphones, turning them playfully in different directions. "Bioscope!" they were announcing, almost incidentally. "It's bioscope time." Several pretended they were a band onstage with microphones; Colleen knew the song from the hit parade. The soldiers seemed collectively to be in a festive mood. They beckoned at the window. "Hi baby," someone said. "What are you doing here?" Another had a bottle of Castle in his hand and pretended to be a ringmaster. "Step right up and come to the show," he called, grinning, laughing, embarrassed. Colleen saw primary school children running after them, clapping hands in thank-you gestures. A soldier with brightly colored epaulettes stood on the path and passed out Crunchie bars. "Bioscope," the children were all saying.

"I guess they never see any movies," Colleen said.

"Movies!" Vaida said. "You mean 'Films by the Internal Affairs.'" But when the soldiers entered the library, Vaida stood up and obeyed them. "They are only bringing us messages from their puppets," she told Colleen, as they followed the others down the road to the primary school.

A teacher pulled the shades. It was two hours before curfew, the sun already behind mountains. People whispered. The children giggled in high pitches and chased each other around desks. Soldiers escorted more sixth formers into the classroom. Vaida removed her steaming glasses and wiped them on her cardigan. Her eyes shot around in the dimness. An African operated the projector. "Black outside and white inside," Vaida muttered to Colleen, but the man did not seem to hear her. Colleen never knew what to say to comments such as these, considering her own race.

At first, there was only the projector light on the cracked wall, outlines of faces, shadows. Alongside the small desks, Colleen could read poster boards labeled with *koki* pen—shapes, numbers, words, construction-paper triangles, rectangles, magazine cutouts, one horse, two cows, three goats. Another board labeled items of clothes in Shona and English. A coiled strand of multicolored tinsel dangled from the ceiling, although it was August. The film tape made a snapping sound; something was wrong with the reel. The man took it off and examined it. He placed it back on the spool. The projector fan whirred. Soldiers closed the doors.

The first film took place in Durban, a comedy dubbed from Afrikaans into English. It was about a family's seaside holiday. There were various pranks and calamities. The dubbing resonated oddly over the constant boom of the surf. In the classroom, small children shook each other's shoulders, exclaiming *maiwe*, frightened by it, excited. They sat poised on their benches. Most of them had not seen the ocean. "*Onai!*" the children were saying.

"See what?" Vaida said glumly, her chin in her open palm.

In the film, a speedboat thumped across waves and spun expertly to a stop. The water-skier had been left behind. The boat turned around. There was much banter between the skier and the people in the boat. Sun flashed in different angles on the water. When Colleen turned away from the screen, she saw Heresekwe. At first she had not been sure: she told herself it was just that she'd wanted to see him. She wanted a person—any one of the Sixth Formers up there by the door—to be him. She had gone to the film hoping he would be there. He looked younger than he had in April, or maybe older. Something about the way she had not been able to immediately recognize him made her feel slightly agitated. She watched for a movement in his face—nothing. She must have lost the exact memory of it. He stared at the movie. But his arms were at least crossed; this seemed normal. Light flickered steadily. She felt an awareness of present time, as if it had its own energy and demanded something from her that was more rigorous and precise. Heresekwe turned. The room went dark again. The scene in the movie had changed, and changed again to the glare of the coast. Colleen could not concentrate now on the propaganda Vaida had warned her to look for. The movie seemed innocuous and stupid. He must have arrived earlier, on one of the Shushine busses—had he looked for her? She wondered what would matter now to him after three weeks in detention. Freedom of movement, absence of pain. Disbelief in this life outside. The more she tried to imagine his suffering, the more she felt envy of his imprisonment, for altering him, taking away his feelings for her as she believed it must have.

She remembered being with him in April, high upriver, above the Wiri waterfalls, how he took away her breath. There had been prisms in the mist like frantic tropical fish. They'd shared a flask of warm *maheo*; it had barely had time to ferment. She had felt heat inside her like a light. They were motions along themselves. She felt she was nothing but processes. She blinked to glitter, to particles of water in air. He murmured Shona, and his face became quiet.

Heresekwe lifted his head and looked out over the valley. "The beats of your heart are unsteady," he said. "There is not a set rhythm there. It feels like a code, Colleen, a special message."

"A heart defect," she said, as if she were fond of it, but she felt for the first time a certain shame. "It's supposed to go away. Sometimes it reminds me of Mapipi's drums."

Heresekwe gazed sharply at her. He buttoned his shirt. "Perhaps you are in sync with him," he said. "In any case, I cannot believe I never noticed it before."

"I would like to be a *mujiba*," she said. But it seemed immediately a coy thing to say; she regretted it.

"You don't tell lies well enough," Heresekwe said, laughing. "And you don't play drums." He avoided her eyes.

Colleen reached for her sandals. She thought about the way Mapipi warned and summoned the guerillas who'd been taught to understand him. Or the women, who were said to deliver their daily meals. Colleen had heard that these women would hide land mines in slings under maternity dresses. She tried to imagine such purpose, such clear intent. Even the land mine itself passed, as she imagined it, low over the ground to grateful hands. It would be interred under a hard dirt road, the earth trembling. It would vibrate, explode.

They stepped along the boulders, made leaps down, down again. They ran and slid along the gorge. Trees dripped. The river began to meander and flatten and gather mud. It was when they heard cowbells up ahead at a footbridge that they saw two Africans perched next to cattle like herdsmen. They leaned on their rods, or guns, or fishing poles. Colleen stopped on the path, but Heresekwe seemed not to notice; he kept going calmly toward them. She supposed it had been all her thoughts about Mapipi, or the *maheo* wearing off—she felt nervous, jittery. But the men did seem to be fishing. Neither were in camouflage. Colleen caught up with Heresekwe. They lost sight of the men as they rounded a bend. Colleen still wanted to lag behind. She could not think of what would happen when the river straightened. Maybe they had not been fishing. She felt consumed by an icy suspicion and waited for it to go away. When the men came into sight again, their guns (rods, poles) were gone. Or what had they been leaning on? Colleen was alone. She may as well have been alone. As she came steadily forward, she had a vague notion that she was being delivered to the men. But she did not believe herself to be betrayed. It had to do with her uncertainty about the men. She didn't know what they were—herdsmen, guerillas—if guerillas, whether they meant her any harm. She could not know. It went around in her head, this confusion, and alertness. The younger man had a wound on his forehead which he had tied with a floral scarf. The pastels were the most beautiful thing she had ever seen. Another thought seemed to be that she would deliver herself. Heresekwe, her love, her feeling for him, seemed as nothing. Her ears closed and rang as if she had dived to the bottom of a pool and stayed there willfully. She was here. Her life was nothing.

The older one held out his hand to Colleen, and then the boy her age, from Nyadzi; she had seen him before at debates—this calmed her, until she remembered that he had absconded several months before, had crossed to Mozambique in the first wave. Or so she'd heard. But people had come back. Some had never actually gone. He was likely one of those. She felt her wrist moving coglike in the tribal handshake. She shook their hands numbly. They started the greetings.

"*Maswere se?*"

"*Ndaswere*," she said. *I am fine if you are fine.*

Colleen realized that Heresekwe had still been beside her. She had stopped noticing him. It was his turn to shake hands. Then the greeting needed to be repeated over again. Then she and Heresekwe crossed the footbridge, which required concentration—one of the planks was missing. Possibly the men were fixing it. She proceeded from one action to the next. She struggled now with the urge to run.

"You are very quiet," Heresekwe commented, once they were on the other side, and further downriver. "*Unofara?* Are you feeling happy? We must go to that place again."

Had he already forgotten about the men—were the poles not guns? Or did she just wish they were? Now that the danger—if there was danger—had passed. And the student who had absconded— what was he doing there? Colleen could not resist dwelling on it. Yet she felt certain she could never speculate about these things to Heresekwe. She could not ask him. Maybe he didn't himself know.

They walked along the riverbed for awhile. There was no one around. Heresekwe took her hand.

After an expert switch of reels, they watched the next film—the new government minister, an African, the Honorable Chief Chirau. He wore a gold chain around his neck and a yoke with the Rhodesian Front insignia. He was gentle and reassuring. Colleen tried immediately not to like him. He had an easy smile. She felt herself wanting to like him, his casualness, or cheerful conceit, that seemed almost American. She thought she had heard that he'd gone to college in Pennsylvania. "The government is here to help you," he said.

Vaida practically snarled into Colleen's ear.

Chief Chirau looked back down at a sheet of typed paper. "We are richer than the Africans in Zambia and Mozambique," he said. He listed examples. He gave statistics. He wished to remind them of the Ministry of Education, the Ministry of Health. Now it was time for them to accept the protected villages. Relocations would begin very soon. They must all want safety from the *magandanga,* the terrorists. He promised cash rewards for information. Colleen felt dazed and vapid. Vaida had begun to wheeze. Colleen heard "liar" whispered, even spoken around the room, but it was dark and the generator roared.

"The film is broken," she heard the operator tell a white soldier. They examined a third reel.

"Ach, no, man." The soldier laughed. "It's quite fine, Simeon. You simply don't want to show it."

"It is getting close to curfew, sir. People might be shot."

"We all know where they've been tonight. Now let's get on with it, hey."

The last movie showed three ZANLA soldiers entering a village, laughing, talking. Everyone seemed familiar. They ate *sadza* at a fire. Someone brought them beer in a cement bucket. Children touched the guns. The soldiers put on the safety catches and let the children aim them at the bush. Colleen had seen the guns before on TV up at hostel, the frequent special messages on RBC ("an assault Kalashnikov, a terrorist weapon"), especially during Mission Impossible. But it was not the usual government portrayal of terrorists. It seemed to have actually happened. Someone must have been watching them, filming them. Then there was a campfire, and what could have been the morning of the next day. The ZANLA soldiers got up and stretched. One smoked a cigarette. There was the whole thank-you ritual, even soft percussive sounds of cupped hands.

The next scene showed security forces and military police in tight shorts and combat boots. One sat on the grass, contemplative. Colleen observed his suntanned inner thighs. The men commented about three sets of boot prints. The camera zoomed in on the ground. These soles were made in the same factory, the men said. They had not been made in Rhodesia or South Africa. All of them agreed.

The three ZANLA soldiers were now setting up camp in a clearing. They were not actors. Colleen knew it. After muted shots from an unseen automatic, the men fell. The picture moved in. The picture shimmered and refocused. One death was slow, the man cried out for his mother. Colleen saw the haze in the room, the flying dust in the tube of light. People tried to leave the schoolroom, but the soldiers blocked the door.

Colleen listened to the primary schoolchildren chattering softly. The movie showed a hyena on a leash. "*Kunoipa,*" people were saying around her—the hyena, the lowest thing, the bearer of evil. Even the youngest children knew this, even Colleen.

The hyena was taken to the dead soldiers. It was a scavenger. It rolled itself on the bodies. Someone outside the camera held the tugging leash. The hyena ate. The camera paused on a man's entrails, bloated coils. The movie ended in grayness. There were words: "Produced for the Branch of Internal Services."

Despite the smell of someone's vomit in the hot room, people did not rush for the open door. Parents rocked crying children. Others stood blankly and milled around. An older woman started to wail and ululate, but people rushed to stop her. A hand was slapped over her mouth. Vaida sat still. Colleen stayed next to her. Night had come and the curfew was forgotten. The security forces gave a warning gunshot. Desks and benches scraped. People were asked to form two orderly lines at each door. Heresekwe made his way back across the lines toward them.

"*Mufundisi*," Heresekwe said to Vaida. Colleen saw relief on her face. She had not yet seen him in the room. He shook Colleen's hand—dry, hot palms. His look was brief acknowledgment.

Outside, children darted past them, breathless, intent. Colleen heard tripping over rocks. One of the soldiers shot again into the air, dispersing a group crossing the soccer field. There was gradual light from the moon; it had just risen. Colleen kept swallowing. It seemed as if she could have been there at the campsite—she took the pictures, she held the camera, but sometimes not steadily. She'd watched the scene that way, with almost a greed, a determination, searching for ways to understand the cameraman. Was it a man, a white man? Where had he come from? And then the sniper. And the leash holder. It had all helped to distract her—this effort. But in a room surrounded by Africans, she'd still identified with whomever had worked to make the movie, the avengers. Or she believed she had; she feared that she had.

"Such manipulation," Vaida finally spoke. "They studied our folklore. They used this hyena to control us."

"We need to know what they are saying to the people," Heresekwe said tiredly. "The last film will be impossible to counteract."

"I have heard about this flick," Vaida declared. "They have showed it on the northeast border. One good thing. Perhaps they are desperate."

"Ah, no," Heresekwe said.

"Just don't go on about how guilty you feel, Colleen," Vaida said impatiently. "I think I can sometimes read your mind."

"I didn't say anything."

"You don't have to," Vaida said. "And don't be cheeky."

"That they showed Colleen, one of their own," Heresekwe said. "That is reckless. That is desperate."

"Perhaps not," the teacher said.

Colleen breathed deeply the night air that had begun to smell like cooking fires. They passed candlelit doorways of metal shacks.

"I suppose everyone is asking you about your imprisonment," Vaida said.

"Yes."

"It's true what is said about the nails?"

"Yes, it is true." He appeared used to interrogation. He meant nothing in this tone. He could be lying or telling the truth.

"Well, it is good, *mukomana*, that they did not touch your brain. I wondered. You are not yourself. Not speaking your mind. Saying what you please." She watched him. "Normally you would have been incensed by this shocking thing tonight." The moon had become bright and they walked fast, Vaida gasping for air.

"I am," Heresekwe said. "I am incensed by this," he added, in a way that reminded Colleen of Sarah.

When Vaida had gone up the diverging path to the teachers' quarters, Colleen asked Heresekwe, "Did you get my letter at the police camp?"

"No," he said. "I was not permitted letters."

"I left one there for you," she said. "I was there at Hot Springs."

This did not seem to interest or surprise him. Neither did he go into his usual diatribe about the springs, how it was "a microcosm of the Rhodesian universe."

"I am glad to see you," he said.

"I'm glad you are safe," Colleen heard herself say.

Inside the veranda, he paused and then gripped her shoulder with an outstretched hand. They stood there clumsily. Colleen felt the distance of the length of his arm. It seemed almost as if he were pushing her away. She thought of the way her teachers awarded pins for house points, reaching for the upper lapel of each student's blazer. The awkwardness made her certain she wanted to step forward. She ran her fingers along the line of his jaw, a roughness of whiskers. She felt a pulse in the hollow of his temple, and the scar just under his eye. After a while, he pulled her next to him and began to kiss her; their heels scraped on the flagstone. She could see the kerosene lamp in the kitchen and listened to her father's shortwave some-

where. He was tuning it, the frequencies overlapping, the squeals—
Voice of Zimbabwe over Radio Mozambique, an acquired energy in
the announcer's voice, almost a deliriousness. She heard her father's
footsteps.

"Your friend is with ZANLA, the teacher as well." Her father
stood with his bottle of J&B. He refilled his glass. His eyes gleamed.
"The boy coordinated all the absconding. I am certain of it." He
spoke in a rush of words. This odd new involvement—she had liked
her father better when he seemed disengaged. She supposed it was
the influence of the commissioner. Surely Clive had set him to thinking this way; he had known all about the arrests. "But the boy must
not have talked," her father said. "They couldn't prove anything."

Colleen wondered why her father had not yet been shot. His
farm, the land issue. He seemed like a good target to her, leaning
against the front window on the glass. "I'm surprised the security
forces didn't just shoot him," her father said. "Probably something to
do with that bumbling idiot Haan, publicity, what with Kissinger
just here."

"I don't want to talk about this," Colleen said.

"Dangerous, yes." He absently offered her a Chesterfield. He lit
the cigarettes. "Well, my girl, we don't care if we live or die."

Colleen inhaled all the smoke she could. The cigarette became a
rapid ash. She reached to close the yellowing drapes.

8: THE LAST DAY AT NYADZI

VAIDA MOYO'S SON WAITED AT THE KITCHEN DOOR WITH A PAIL OF mangoes. "Vaida wants you to come for tea," he said in recited English, and Colleen recalled the demanding nature of her requests. The boy's teeth dominated his growing face, and he breathed through his mouth. He had his mother's gap, though Vaida's had long ago been filled with gold, her one act of vanity. Colleen had seldom admired it because Vaida never smiled outright.

"I can make mango chutney with all these." Colleen patted her cupped hands together in a thank-you gesture, without thinking, and then said "*Mazvita*," as if she had not been gone five years, two thousand kilometers away at university in the Cape. These highlands, *Chimanimani, Vumba, Nyanga*, were better known back then, before she left, as the operational area.

Sometimes Colleen felt as though she'd fled, joined the exodus. *Rhodies*, the South Africans called them. Her father stayed, maintaining his coffee farm with Mapipi and John. He liked to brag that he never drove in convoy. He left his curtains open at night. He didn't own a security system, or even the fashionable nine-millimeter hand carbine.

Sarah had been sent to a special school in Bulawayo, on the other side of Rhodesia. It was the safest city during the war, the school's director had pointed out. Sarah spent each day in social-skills group. She learned beadwork and other crafts. She attempted to imitate African designs. The students were taken on field trips downtown and purchased artwork from vendors by the city hall. Colleen always wondered how the bartering worked out, if it was stressful, whether a therapist stood nearby and acted as an intermediary. Sarah had been given a diagnosis, or Colleen had finally heard its name (Sarah had blandly told her, not her father)—Childhood Onset Schizophrenia. This was something rare, the doctors had told Colleen's father, who still claimed, at times, that Sarah had a new form of autism. There were years to go yet, Colleen's father said, before her autism would be rightly understood.

Colleen and her father met Sarah once a year at Christmas break. They were given a fourteen-day supply of Sarah's pills, and a release was signed. Colleen's father arranged to house-sit for friends, who vacationed every December on the Wild Coast. Colleen did not see how the friends could otherwise have stood it. The house was in the suburb of Montrose, cut off from the townships by Mafeking Road, wide and paved and two-laned, and a field of savanna that burned almost daily during droughts. There seemed to be no other event, no activity except the passing of courier bikes, the occasional ringing of an ice cream bell. Colleen and her father had been told not to overstimulate Sarah. They watched TV when it came on at night. Her father switched it off at any hint of violence, glancing quickly at Sarah, and Colleen would argue with him about turning it back on. During the afternoons Colleen read newly purchased paperbacks from Kingston's. Occasionally she would call out to the dairy board man, and she and her sister would go through the gate and buy Fudgesicles. Sarah would stare with some interest into the box on the man's bike; steam rose up from the hot ice. On New Year's Eve they would walk tentatively through Centennial Park and look at the lights. The days were endless, and Colleen napped so much with Sarah that her father wondered if she had sleeping sickness.

"Why can't we just go home to Nyadzi?" Colleen would ask her father during these holidays. She would make detailed plans, suggestions for next time—Colleen could fly up as usual, and they could all drive home along A9. Sarah liked riding in a car. They could travel at different times from the convoy. They could cross the Sabi at Birchenough Bridge. Sarah might or might not be interested. It would feel like their trip through the Karroo before Sarah's first admission to Rest Haven. Sarah needed to get out of this dull town, Colleen would insist.

"I won't spend all that money to bring you home, only to have you blown to smithereens," her father would say. "The mines are bad, I'm telling you."

Colleen scoffed at him until the year he rung her, weeping. She had not heard him cry since her mother died. The dog had accidentally leaped upon an antipersonnel mine. He'd been fighting with a baboon on the dry Wiri riverbed. There was little left of either animal. "I do have his collar," Colleen's father said. Kimmy had managed to stay alive through years of curfew, when security forces shot at anything that moved after dark, especially the Africans' goats and cows. The valley would stink of rotting carcasses, the skins, the meat salvaged every daybreak by enraged herdsmen. Vultures would swoop down from the orange escarpments and make their way up again.

Colleen followed Vaida's son along the footpath. "You have grown tall," she said. She had never before seen him stand. He had always been on his mother's back, or a sister's, regarding Colleen sideways. They walked, single file across the valley, past the mission schools and clinic, the rows of boxlike grocery stores, purple and pink against red-clay ground. They passed Mhapisa's bottle store, dark beyond its screen door, the corrugated iron roof dazzling in the sun. Marimbas and xylophones competed with static on a shortwave radio. A group of children played marbles in the dirt. It was a quiet afternoon. 'Heresekwe will not be here,' she reminded herself.

She had forgotten about all the loose rocks, their perpetual chipping, the rubble, and slid down as the path narrowed. The boy handed her a branch. Colleen removed her sandals and smacked them against a slab of limestone. She could see Vaida's house above her, a Nyadzi mission building. Vaida stood in the courtyard plaiting a daughter's hair. Perhaps it was Rindai, the one they sometimes called Choice. The girl's head tilted backwards over a rusted kitchen chair. Vaida was still large, from years of *sadza* and meat and childbearing. Her ankles were swollen. She wore a pair of men's shoes without laces. They exchanged Shona greetings. Vaida put down the metal comb and clasped Colleen's hand. Rindai dashed away, her unplaited hair, heavily oiled with Canola, tapering to a thin pointy tip. She reminded Colleen of a unicorn.

"You're still too thin, and wearing pants, too. All dressed like a Hillbrau girl."

"I am not," Colleen said, laughing, and tugged absently at her beaded earrings.

"What would your mother have thought?" Vaida led her into the house. Colleen listened closely for her wryness. Sometimes Vaida teased. Her face—what Colleen could see of it in the sudden dimness—was heavy and guarded.

Vaida had admired Colleen's mother's ascetic ways. Nyadzi had been shocked when her mother married the coffee farmer across the valley, a worldly man, already divorced. Colleen had been born five months later. Her mother lost her foreign support money. "You are no longer a missionary," the field director told her. But they needed another midwife at the clinic and she returned, timid, never bossing the Africans around.

She had survived Vaida's scrutiny. "Why did you like my mother?" Colleen would ask Vaida. "'Why?' Because when you are in the middle of a breech birth, you have a baby coming out of you backwards, and she is there, you not only begin to like her, that person is the only one in the world." Colleen had often seen the two of them on the back steps of the maternity clinic. They stared ahead beyond the clotheslines, the flapping diapers, the rinsed out sanitary pads. It was difficult to interrupt them. "We are talking, Colleen. Go play."

Vaida lit a gas burner and adjusted a kettle onto the single plate. "What do you think of independence?" she asked casually. They used to speak of independence in hushed voices. "And now, here it is— 1983, a few years already passing. I do not like one of the ministers, but for the most part I am very pleased."

"I'm sorry to have missed Bob Marley at the ceremonies," Colleen replied. Anything she said would be subject to attack.

Vaida removed her cat-eye glasses to clean them.

"'Zimbabwe' doesn't exactly roll off my tongue yet," Colleen admitted. "I keep thinking about the Zimbabwe ruins. Stone corridors. It's strange, it's like the name of somebody's new baby. I want to just say 'Rhodesia.'"

"Then you want to pay tribute to Cecil John Rhodes. Remember we have knocked down his statue."

"That isn't what I meant," Colleen said. "Anyway, I'm moving back. I have two interviews in Harare next week. The hospital and an outpatient clinic."

"Don't expect them to be impressed by your extensive study of Afrikaans."

"My project," Colleen said pointedly, "was about the positive influence the Cape Colored have had on the language, all the innovations."

"Colleen," Vaida said. "Afrikaans is Afrikaans."

"I hate how defensive you make me feel," she snapped, but dropped her eyes.

Vaida measured the Tanganda tea into a sieve and poured water. Her glasses steamed. She steadied the teapot with its brightly colored tea cozy. "Have some Marie biscuits," she said, shaking the tin.

"It is good," Vaida said. "Yes, it is good to see you again. All the years you were growing up, we became used to seeing you every April and August and December. I would think to myself, 'The rainy season has begun. It's time for Colleen to be home from boarding school.'" Vaida sipped from her teacup and put it back in the saucer. "Now your sister we would never see."

"She didn't like to leave the house. It was the same in Salisbury. The same in Bulawayo. Unless she's in a car."

"Harare," Vaida corrected her. Not Salisbury anymore. But it was too much for Sarah really, losing her mother when she had barely been weaned. And then the nanny. The two of you at different schools half the time. I should have done more. And your father as well. But he's a difficult man, you know that. We never saw eye to eye."

"I tell myself that too—I should have done more."

"What could you do? It was beyond your control."

"Anyway, I haven't missed your drills in Shona tenses."

"Surely someone had to teach you the grammar. And they didn't do it in your white school. I couldn't have you talking that pidjin of your mother's. *Chilapalapa* kept her a colonialist. If one didn't know her, they felt patronized. I told her once, 'I am not your kitchen help. I am a schoolteacher.'"

They munched on the biscuits, and Colleen drank her tea, and felt warm, and almost secure. She supposed it was the sort of moment she'd come home for. In Cape Town, it was no longer her mother she missed, but Vaida, bartering over a sack of mealie meal, picking her up for weddings in her 1966 Ford Cortina. Colleen's mother, around Vaida, remained a presence. Colleen would long for this, for the way Vaida could speak about anyone who was not there—dead, in the city, at the mines—as if they mattered, as if they were still around unseen.

"They believe in spirits," her mother once told her, inside Vaida's house, the same two-room standard teacher's house, although all the mattresses had been pushed up sideways against the wall. They were at Vaida's first husband's funeral, or some kind of viewing; the coffin had been surrounded by mourners. Occasionally a woman had wailed. "To them, he is not really dead," Colleen's mother said, hoisting Sarah up on her hip. Colleen was seven at the time.

Vaida and her children, the ones older than Colleen, had been gaunt and thin from TB prevention medicine. Their eyes were a dull yellow. Colleen could not see the man's body. There was a smell of rot, like the rodents her cat sometimes lined up on the veranda. No one seemed to notice. It appeared to be just another odor, part of what the summer dampness brought out, a vapor, in the air with other vapors—old paint and Dettol and kerosene. Colleen had wanted to cover her face and stayed by the open door. She'd concentrated on the courtyard, on mist swirling past Vaida's banana tree, and beyond that on the segments of tribal trust land adjacent to the mission and the farm. Low clouds moved between mud huts and small terraced patches of maize.

There was a sudden flash, and people stepped away, startled, from the coffin. Gordon Beck, the station head, elbowed through the group, pulling glistening paper from a Polaroid camera. Colleen was used to seeing him with a camera, selecting exotic photographs for his supporters in America. He was often poised in the rock gardens, looking for flowering cacti, or unusual species of snakes. She had never seen the Polaroid.

"We don't take pictures of the dead," Vaida had told him, as he lay the picture on the kitchen table. Yet she picked it up and watched it. Colleen came over to the table.

"Careful, it's wet," Beck said. He held a sunburned arm out in front of Colleen, but she peered over it. First the poinsettias developed, freshly cut from bushes along the footpaths. A face emerged, like the carvings on Mapipi's drums. The necktie turned grayer, blacker, stripe by stripe. Colleen wondered when it would stop. Her mother pushed her head away. Colleen felt her mother's skirt against her cheek.

"This isn't a spectacle, Colleen," she said. But she examined the picture with Vaida. "It's the wrong angle, don't you think?"

"The best angle is at the head of the coffin," Vaida said.

People moved aside for Vaida, and Colleen and her mother and Sarah followed her. Looking down at Vaida's husband, lengthwise, they could not see the rigidity in his face. It seemed easier this way, where the smell was strongest, to consider him alive. He'd built his own coffin, Colleen's mother told her.

"It's too small for him," Colleen whispered. He was twisted sideways at the shoulder. "I don't think he measured it right."

"He wasn't himself the last few weeks."

Colleen turned her face back into the gray weave of her mother's skirt, feeling, against her hip, an assurance that this would never happen to her mother, to herself, a strange, early racial security: they were exempt. Vaida stood beside Colleen's mother. Colleen stared at their legs in nylons. Their heels scraped the cement, changed positions, mashed little clumps of tracked-in clay. They whispered above her.

Vaida was always a zealot about Shona. After Colleen's mother died, Vaida said she was determined to formally teach it to her. Vaida's interest in this project was sporadic. Sometimes there were school holidays when Colleen never saw her. Vaida remarried and had more children. Her new husband worked outside Umtali, and one year she lived there, translating the Old Testament with Canadian missionaries. She had given Colleen a Shona coursebook in standard five, and whether there at Nyadzi or not, Colleen studied the conjugations like rules of an elaborate game. She loved the sound of Shona, the long words with their repeating vowels.

One year—Colleen was fourteen—Vaida decided that local weddings might improve her tone. They would drive up the mountains in her crowded car, beyond the wattle plantations, where tribal trust lands bordered Mozambique. The air was always cold there. The brides wore long sleeves. Even on clear days, water dripped in orange lines down the whitewash of the clay brick schoolrooms. Colleen would begin to feel anxious when the singing started up, and the ceremonies were over, and Vaida disappeared into the crowd. Colleen would wander around with a Shona dictionary, searching for the color of her bandana among the others, and people would coax her—"Say it this way." They would laugh when she used slang and clap her hand.

Sometimes Vaida took Colleen to evangelistic services at the mission church. There were long monologues of rapid dialect in the afternoon heat. Colleen complained to Vaida that the African evangelists hardly paused to breathe. But she never refused to go. The church would be full to capacity—men on one side, crouched forward on benches, a dark blur of sport coats, and women on the right, knitting. Children crossed the aisle from one parent to another. People would dance during Shona hymns—Colleen tentatively stomped her feet. Much time was spent shaking hands. She walked in and out with other children. They occasionally passed crossword puzzles and comic books.

When the African church leaders first included ZANU in the services, the only sounds in the audience were the echoes of coughs. By this time, Colleen had turned sixteen. She'd begun to understand parts of the speeches, especially the liturgical-sounding chants.

> The people of Zimbabwe are many
> The settlers are few.

She started to wish she was not white, or at least not a farmer's daughter. The other whites at the meetings, American missionaries—scattered around the church with blonde hair or conspicuously bald heads—supported independence. But Gordon Beck was still the station head. Gordon Beck volunteered for Rhodesian Defense Force reserves and sometimes wore his uniform around the mission. He was gone on weekends, touring the country with white teenage singers from Umtali Baptist Church. The singers were to accompany him on his next furlough to South Carolina. He had organized scholarships for them at Bob Jones University. Beck's group sang inspirational songs on a Sunday radio program for the security forces. While Beck was away, Rhodesia was called Zimbabwe. Terrorists were freedom fighters. They were guerillas, *vakomana*, the boys.

"How is Heresekwe?" Colleen asked Vaida, carefully peering outside at the children over by the maize patch. They were collecting red peppers in their shirts.

Vaida answered slowly, watching her. "He's an ambassador now, or an assistant of some kind. Overseas. Someplace in Europe, I'm not sure." She scooped crumbs off the table into her hand. "You know he joined the boys. You were with him the night he disappeared."

"I didn't know," Colleen said blankly.

Vaida's foot moved sharply across the cement and began to tap.

"I mean, he didn't tell me his plans. Tambudzai told me afterwards."

"How? You were already on the train the next day."

"She *wrote* to me."

Vaida did not answer.

"He did talk about it that night," Colleen said. "I didn't think he was serious. It was exam time."

"Some teachers believed that Heresekwe wanted to avoid *A* levels," Vaida said. "That it was a convenient time to go. We were all divided about him. And the missionaries were there, in the conference room. We could not talk openly."

"It's true that he would have failed a few exams," Colleen said. "He was always leading those political meetings. Always talking to people."

"Yes. And up many nights. Guiding people across the border to training camps. Every third night."

"What?"

"You didn't know," Vaida seemed pleased.

"There was a rumor," Colleen said. "How he actively recruited for ZANLA. The security forces were paranoid. They even thought I was involved."

"He never told you then?"

"He never spoke of it directly." She sipped her tea, embarrassed, even ashamed that Heresekwe, her first lover, could have concealed so much from her. She floundered, readjusting all her memories.

She thought of him, shouting in the assembly hall, benches lined with Nyadzi students and adults and small children. Stray dogs trotted down clay aisles sniffing Heresekwe's feet. He would be frenetic and sweaty, shifting between Shona and English, suddenly leading everyone into an a cappella song like "We Shall Overcome," a dense sound, bouncing oddly off the mountain, low notes punctuated by shrieking ululatings.

"You're so much hot air," she had said once to him. "Why don't you do something about it instead of *gaaning on* all the time?"

Heresekwe had evaded the question. Colleen could see that now, in retrospect. He had taken her wrist and examined the inner part. "This is where you are truly white," he'd said and run his fingers along the veins.

The tea kettle whistled. Vaida spooned white sugar into her second cup. Colleen looked at the place where the first husband's coffin had been, a single mattress there now, with a faded Bugs Bunny sheet. "I guess I only knew what I wanted to know," Colleen said. "I liked the idea of people just sitting around here talking rhetoric. I must have."

"We kept many secrets back then, Colleen. I sometimes think it may have been best to have told you more. Though it is not our way."

"Oh, right, the *tsumo*." Colleen rolled her eyes. "*What belongs to a white man, eat it while you are on your haunches.*"

"And do you remember what that idiom means?" She might have been at the front of her class, expecting a memorized response.

"If you want to be friends with a white, you must be very careful in what you say, because these words can be used against you."

"Spoken as though you are one of us," Vaida said, and Colleen saw a brief glinting of gold.

"You could have trusted me," Colleen said.

Vaida lifted a cast-iron pot from her styrofoam cooler and relit the gas burner. She shook the match. "Do you remember the ride home from the *Ngani* wedding?"

"The time we got followed by an RDF helicopter?"

"Yes, Colleen. Think about that ride. It was getting dangerous for everyone. I hope you never told your father about it."

"I never told him anything."

There had been several people in the Cortina's front seat, men in suits. Vaida had been driving. "You were furious about the helicopter," Colleen said. "You were outraged."

"'Maybe it's just following the road, patrolling the road.' Remember you said that, Colleen?"

"I couldn't believe it."

She had been in back with the women, holding Vaida's baby. He bounced on her knees as the car lurched. Air had blasted through the open windows—dust, orange, they were coughing. Another baby pulled her mouth from her mother's breast and cried, and the mother pressed her hands over the baby's ears. The baby wailed, although no one could hear her over the helicopter; it hovered above them, and veered sideways as the road curved into the mountain. The man in the passenger seat drew his head back in and looked at Vaida.

"They *were* following us," Vaida said now to her.

"So were those men in the front seat guerillas?"

"No," Vaida said. "But there was quite a ZANLA presence at the wedding. Many of the boys were there. That day in my car, you were riding with *mujibas* and *chimbwidos*, all of us. We were very frightened that RDF would take us in for questioning."

Colleen knew more now, especially after the war, about reconnaissance. Men, the *mujibas,* had kept the guerillas informed about RDF activities, and *chimbwidos* carried supplies on their heads, weapons underneath their dresses. The RDF would respond by bull-dozing villages: they began to move people into the patrolled compounds with barbed-wire fences.

"You weren't here at the very end," Vaida was saying. "Everything closed down. The stores in the business district. Everything got boarded up. It was so quiet most of the time." She stared outside. The door had been left open by Rindai. A goat stood on the step, and his horns tapped occasionally on the face brick. Flies buzzed. The lenses of Vaida's glasses shone pale blue. She talked, casually, about war strategies, targets—district commissioners, or the white farmers who walked with machine guns in their fields.

"You could see them all at the Leopard Rock that last month. Civilians. They would shoot at anyone black outside, while the waiters served rounds of Castle lager."

Colleen thought about the Leopard Rock Hotel, especially in winter, with its fireplaces, and white tablecloths, and serviettes crisp and triangular, Nyanga just the other side of the glass and Mozambique beyond.

"Would you like a drink? You are old enough now." Vaida removed an old milk carton from the cupboard. She filled two jars with *maheo*. It was frothy and smelled of yeast. Colleen swallowed hers hard.

"Quite strong," she commented, and blew her nose.

"Colleen," Vaida said, refilling her glass. "What do you remember about your last day at Nyadzi?" There was a friendliness about her. But the question seemed rehearsed.

"I wish I had known it was my last day."

She had been home from Salisbury for a fortnight to prepare for end-of-school exams. Classes were over, except for the public exams right before Christmas. But after a week at home, her father had dropped her back at the train station. "You're not getting any studying done here," he said irritably. He was preoccupied and furtive. Colleen had spent the next week alone at the hostel with the boarding mistress. The senior wing was empty. She could still hear the echoes in the halls, the solitary bang of her toilet stall, the pounding of water in a bathtub.

Colleen's friend Tambudzai wrote her. *Heresekwe is gone*, she had said. Colleen wondered, 'What does that mean?' She obsessed about it. She paced in the empty courtyard. She had stared blankly at her textbooks.

"The air conditioner does not keep up. It could be broken," Micah says. They are alone in Mhapisa's, except for Micah. Colleen hears him cutting boxes in the back, and Thelma Houston, close, then distant, on the short wave, "Don't Leave Me This Way." They compare biology syllabi. They joke about sexual reproduction, as if this is not a sensitive subject, a cause of many sleepless nights. They practice words—gamete, zygote. They write the same Cambridge exams. No one can judge by color in England, though they must be able to differentiate among names.

Tambudzai has stopped using Ambi Cream. Her face is quite brown. It lacks a masklike chalkiness. They discuss boys. For Colleen, this school term, it is a prefect at Cranborne, a terrible rugby player, B team, with academic stripes on his blazer. He dates Colleen, but also a girl from Queen Elizabeth. Tambudzai is being two-timed as well. This expression, "two-timed," is hardly used in Salisbury, but at Nyadzi all of the students say it. They admire English slang; they love euphemisms. Colleen falls right back into it. She forgets about Salisbury when she is here. The smells are so different—no mown grass or chlorine. She thinks of the Cranborne boy, whether Tambudzai really believes she cares about the other girl—up there she seems to, but now those feelings are without intensity. She has no loyalties to her own concerns. She drinks the beer. She tries to recall last week, when she'd been with the boy in a Portuguese café high up in the SANLAM building. They saw, beyond the city, a maze of blue pools and red-tiled roofs blended into dry beige savanna, rolling, bluer and grayer and darker, the plateau under low, creeping shadows of clouds. She thinks about his face, his low voice, the way he wants to explain laws of physics with useful analogies, his need for her to understand. But the thing that seems clear is the view from the window, how they'd turn their heads from their coffee to stare out, watchful.

She never talks about Heresekwe. She has no words, she thinks, but besides this, she wonders somewhere, is it the covertness that she loves? He is using her, is she using him?

"I think Joe will reject me for the other one," Tambudzai says. "He put inside with *her*. She was getting fat, but now I am certain of it. She is pregnant."

"At least it's not you," Colleen says, then sees her face, tries to reassure her, disprove it somehow. "Didn't Joe cross the border months ago?" she asks. "How could it be him?"

Tambudzai shrugs, looks at the floor. Colleen assumes that all his relationships are over because he's at a camp, he's a freedom fighter. Tambudzai orders another beer.

"No, he is near Cashel," Tambudzai says quietly.

Colleen thinks, "He is probably a fruit picker."

She is supposed to meet Heresekwe at the dip tank. It's almost five. But they drink some more and decide to leave a message for Joe with somebody in Cashel Valley. They go outside. They are trying to figure out how to call long distance from the ticky box. Micah comes to help them. "Joe isn't worth it," Colleen thinks—a huge flamboyant chap who kisses everyone's hand. Micah smacks the box again and she's connected to Cashel exchange.

"Hello," Colleen says, to a voice, to static. "I can't believe this is just the other side of the mountain range," she complains to Tambudzai. "Here," Colleen passes the receiver to her.

The sun bores into Colleen's head. She shields her eyes. Tambudzai has put down the receiver. Three security force guys stand on Mhapisa's concrete steps. They wear khaki and guns. Colleen sees a jeep down the road at Cheriwa's grocery. The Portuguese soldier is gorgeous. They have eye contact. She figures he was conscripted. The other two are older, around twenty-five. The big blond one speaks, with an Afrikaans accent.

He wants to know why she and Tambudzai are wearing the same skirts. He speaks without levity or flirtation. Tambudzai explains. They bought several meters of fabric on sale in Umtali.

"When?" he asks.

"April," she replies.

The soldiers look to Colleen for validation. She turns away. The big chap grabs her chin and jerks her next to his face. "Stupid girl!" He pushes her backward in disgust. Tambudzai steadies her. He scans the bottle store where Micah is trying to retreat. "How is your mind?" he asks. She and Tambudzai are connected with terrorists, he tells her. Colleen is quite righteously convinced that this is not true. He asks why Tambudzai hung up the telephone, who were they calling?

Colleen feels quite cheeky. She has been studying *A Tale of Two Cities* as a set book. "'It is a far better thing that I do than I have ever done,'" she wants to say to him, heroically. Maybe this is how it feels to be brave. Her skin tingles. But she knows she's not afraid because he won't hurt her, she is white. She doesn't answer him.

"I thought you were an albino the first time I watched you. I could not believe it. Do they give you *dagga*? Do they drug you? Do you realize this is the operational area? Has your father disowned you? Ach, I can tell you think you are quite clever. A *kaffir suster*." The blond soldier grins now at her, a baring of teeth. He accepts a bottle of Castle from one of the others, drinks it down. The beer bubbles churn, orange in their brown-filtered sunlight. Micah has turned the music off. The business district is empty.

"Where did you call? Who did you call, you *bliksen se hoer*?" His voice rises to the pitch of an evangelical minister, chastising, enraged, without a pulpit to slam, and Colleen cringes. She tries to breathe. All this over phoning Joe. Ludicrous, even if he did cross the border. They don't know that. A romantic call to Joe Mutema. Tambudzai could do a lot better.

"We just called Cashel Valley," Colleen says. Who cares? They can run their asses off on some empty lead. Cashel, fruit farms. She provides a fake male African name.

The blond is calm now. He runs his fingers through his hair, beneath the beret. "The terrs sodomize their own people's children. They are going to kill you. And fuck you. They will all fuck you over and over after you are dead. And before you are dead too. But you will like that, hey?" He pushes his beer bottle hard into her abdomen. She clasps the bottle against herself, mindlessly, as he strides down to the Jeep. The other ones follow. Tambudzai is stoical next to her.

Music is back, crackling on the veranda speakers. Voice of Zimbabwe, shortwave from Maputo. People appear from hiding places throughout the business district. Micah serves a crowd in the bottle store. Women waddle purposefully, with babies tied to them, and on their heads parcels, pots, kindling. Nyadzi students cross the road. Low exclamations, *aiwa*, filter out of tightly packed groups as they walk past. Tambudzai and Colleen walk slowly, silent.

Heresekwe is leaning against the shed by the dip tank. He meanders toward them and steps over the cattle grid. "I see that you were delayed," he says to Colleen. "You two have been drinking again." He laughs. "What about exams?" But he squints at the jeep, grinding distantly up the pass. He opens a pack of Berkeley 30s and strikes a wooden match on a rock.

He listens to them, suddenly talking over each other.

"How did you evade them?"Tambudzai asks him. "That time last winter when they kept you in jail?"

He says he never answered. Or answered indirectly. Or perhaps he would tell harmless things.

"I did that," Colleen says, with a relieved feeling of having completed a checklist.

"You need to know what is harmless though, and what is not, *shamwari*." Heresekwe seems troubled. They hobble over the footbridge. The Wiri's water is muddy, rushing around great orange stones.

They talk for awhile in the courtyard behind Tambudzai's dorm. The dinner bell rings, and Tambudzai leaves for supper. Heresekwe and Colleen forget about curfew. After the warning shot, he runs down to the business district to call her father. *He can pick you up in his Combie.* It is too late to walk home.

Colleen waits in the dorm with Tambudzai, who moves aside on her bed and passes her one of their Action Comics. A girl washes her uniform in a corner basin. She wrings a blouse in her hands. Water drips. It is dark outside. The mission generator roars on. Glaring white light permeates the room, and they blow out the candles.

Loud voices and footsteps start in the distance, then subside and cease. Tambudzai's roommate perches at the curtain with her head cocked, eyes bulging. Colleen watches her. Outside a pebble scatters. A pebble drops down the retaining wall. Tambudzai squints up from her comic and pulls the lightbulb's string. They hear nothing. Then a cowbell tinkles, and a cow groans and stumbles over the rocks. There are several of them, cattle wandering around as usual. Colleen doesn't bother to decipher their shapes. She wishes Tambudzai would turn the light back on. There is a new sound now, a type of whispering near the window. It begins like rasping respirations. The cows must be sick. They are never healthy.

"Get under the bed, Colleen,"Tambudzai's voice is a tiny shriek.

She obeys. Her face is pressed into the bottom of the mattress. She recalls something she'd read in the *Herald*, that the guerillas move with the cows before attack. Whispers become shouts in Shona. An argument of some kind. Then Heresekwe's barrage of pressured Chindau, his cryptic dialect. Finally she makes out "*Endai! Endai!*" and the noise of people and animals dispersing.

Tambudzai shivers. Her teeth chatter. "It's OK," she says to Colleen.

Colleen stands bewildered in the middle of the dark room. "Did you get what they were saying?" she asks, curious.

"It's OK," she utters again, in a monotone.

Colleen hears the rattle of her father's diesel engine struggling up the hill.

Vaida ladled gravy into bowls and asked Colleen to dish up the *sadza*. Colleen tapped the spoon hard onto the rusted brims. There were several children besides Rindai and the boy—her nieces, Vaida said, and school friends. Vaida sent them into the courtyard. Rindai, the oldest, scuffled out slowly, balancing the smaller ones' bowls in the crook of her arm. "Eat something, Colleen," Vaida said.

Vaida watched her tear the *sadza* into pieces and dip it into the gravy. Colleen took her plate to the sink and washed it in a ceramic dishpan half filled with water. She dried her hands. There was one window in the room, pushed outwards with a stick, and high—one could only look out standing. Through the window, from this side of the house, were the long roofs of the mission school, the classrooms, as if she were in a tree directly above them, birds' nests in the gutters, and flat-topped savanna trees filtering voices. People were calling to each other in the courtyards. Someone practiced with a squealing microphone in the assembly hall. There was the occasional pounding of feet. Christmas beetles drummed erratically.

They sat on the retaining wall behind Tambudzai's dorm. Heresekwe was hunched forward over his bare knees. Colleen wanted to touch the coarse black hair along his calves. His white shirt was damp and plastered to his skin in places, the school-uniform shorts threadbare, his pockets weighted down with his calculator, cigarettes, the bird whistle he carried. They sat close. He smelled of Sunlight soap and sweat.

"Nothing will come of their interrogation, Colleen," he said. "Cashel is a big place, a lot of land."

"I can't imagine Joe even interested in being a freedom fighter. He was always such a yes boy." *Standiwe*, she and Heresekwe had called Joe, the giant baby, back in the days when they used to mock and joke, before Heresekwe's detention.

"All that time you spend in Salisbury, you only see the domestic help, those polishing the floors, spraying and mowing your netball fields. You forget to know us. How we pretend to agree. But deep down, even Standiwe is boiling."

It was true. The students who had absconded, the ones Colleen had known beforehand, never seemed very interesting. But then, they never talked to her, beyond polite greetings. They did not care whether they understood each other.

"Do you ever see any of them now?" Colleen asked. "You know. Julius, Kudzai, Ezekiel Dhube?" She wondered what they talked about: AK47s, methods of ambush?

"*Kwete*," Heresekwe denied in Shona, bowing his head and reaching for her single braid. He brushed the end of it against his open palm, back and forth, as if sweeping with a straw-colored broom.

"You do," she said. "You must."

He let go of her hair and turned to her incredulously, speechless.

"You say to me, 'You need to know what is harmful and what isn't,' but you don't tell me," she declared.

"This is a guerilla war." His pupils were huge in the dusky light, they blackened his dark brown eyes entirely. "We are trying to take over a country. What do you expect from us?"

"Always us."

The sun was down. The foothills had begun to silhouette. It was almost time for curfew. Colleen scrambled up off the concrete. He stood too, and reached for her roughly. He kissed her, but they did not open their mouths. Their mouths were grim lines, stubborn and sealed. "I don't know how to talk to you anymore," he said. His breath was warm on her neck, and his lips moved across her throat. "When I write to you, I sit for long times pausing. I hold the pen, I lie in bed and write my letters in my mind." He faced her. She could see herself inside his eyes, distorted. "But what I send is already censored, even by me. My letters sound like the *Sunday Herald*. We learn to speak, we learn to write in this country in the very tone of propaganda."

"I like the poems you copy."

"Written by Europeans."

They stood against the back wall. A toilet flushed in the lavatory. Colleen heard water in a pipe. His pelvis pressed against her. Her hands ached to unzip him. "You could go with me," he said, against her ribcage, a suggestion.

"To join ZANLA?" she gasped, midbreath, desire reversing itself backward, as if someone had suddenly shone a bright torch onto their bodies. "Heresekwe might begin to trust me," she thought. Her mind flew with new possibilities, another life, exchanging everything.

He half laughed, standing back. He was sly, he was teasing. They stared at each other. His face was shiny with sweat in the dim light. They both smelled of him. Colleen would go home and study, sit on her bed with the set books, and practice review questions. She'd rub her fingers along her neck and up to her nose, inhaling his scent of musk, corn, salted meat, fire. Her stuffed dogs would be there, and a dressing table strewn with makeup.

"Girls go to ZANLA, they get raped and abused," she said, for argument's sake. She had seen this on RBC. They interviewed girls who had escaped the guerilla training camps. Their faces were dark on the black-and-white screen, and averted. Someone instructed them to look at the camera. One had a swollen eye. Another breathed roughly through a crooked nose. Dark black scabs encrusted her nostrils. "Did the terrorists beat you?" "Yes," the girls replied together. Colleen had wondered, "Who really gave them these wounds?" Perhaps they had been threatened by the Ministry of Information. She did not know.

"There are many female combatants," Heresekwe said coldly. "But this is what I mean, Colleen. You don't know whose side you're on. You think I would do that. Take you to Mozambique and then act as a kind of pimp."

"We're talking nonsense," she heard herself say.

Heresekwe was silent.

"I guess I'd think about doing anything to avoid exams," she said brightly. "Crossing the border, that's the best. Right up there with driving off Skyline junction."

A bell rang. They heard the warning gunshot of the curfew. Heresekwe always ignored curfew. He had never been spotted by security forces while out after dark on foot.

"I'll call your father from the ticky box," he said. "He can pick you up in his Combie." Two people had been shot in the last week. Colleen had heard funerals in the valley, screams, wails, roaring unified songs. "You'll wait inside with Tambudzai?"

She nodded. She did not want to listen to herself saying another trite thing. But Heresekwe paused. He was still bristling. He stood with his arms crossed and rocked on his feet. Pebbles crunched under him. "I read in *Time* about rape," he said. "It is a traditional war act. A way to control the enemy's women and spread one's genes to the other side."

Colleen started to make her way around the building. It had become quite dark. She could feel her face, hot, flushing. She had listened to him speak enough to know when he was prefacing something. "Don't even say it," she ordered, in the clipped, forceful tone of her headmistress.

"Is that what it is with us, not rape, but a war act?"

"Get out of here with your stupid speeches," she said in a high, deranged way.

Vaida was busy removing a splinter from her niece's foot. The child gripped the sides of her chair while her aunt poked at the tough whitish heel. "Go pour water over it," Vaida said. She dipped the needle in Dettol and put it back in a tomato-shaped pincushion. Colleen could hear the girl outside at the pump.

"I should probably go," Colleen said.

"No," Vaida said. She bent to peer into a shelf, and the material of her housedress swung like drapery. The pincushion was placed on the shelf among other decorations. Colleen recognized a gift her mother had given Vaida, a Delft vase, which had belonged to her great-grandparents. She studied the blue-and-white pattern of the Delft for some presence of her own family.

"I have something yet to tell you," Vaida said. She came over to the table. "About that day. Ninth December." Her face was set. It seemed as if parts of it were dead. Colleen thought she had seen this look before, and the long breaths also, the way she paused before telling her African myths. Colleen used to sit on her mother's lap, staring at Vaida's face as if it might be something else separate from her, discarded by her, and then her voice would come from her mouth, a monotone. She would feel hypnotized. She'd blink and begin to nod.

When she was older, Heresekwe would talk about Vaida's lively class dialogues, how students distracted her from her lectures: "Otherwise she will make the people sleep." Colleen would say, "I know what you mean."

Colleen was not blinking now. Vaida's sighs were different, labored, maybe because of her weight—she'd been at least forty pounds lighter when Colleen was a child—or the heat, or her certain restrained agitation.

"The connection cannot be definite," Vaida said. "But there was a village near the fruit farms, Mhekwe, the other side of this range. It supported our cause and provided the boys with food and shelter between attacks. Tambudzai's boyfriend stayed there when he wasn't at the camps. An idiot. He'd call girls from the chief's telephone. He spoke on party lines.

"Security forces rampaged Mhekwe that afternoon. They killed children, raped and killed my sister and others. They even strung up the chief. Chiefs were their lifeline, you know. Big informers as long as the money was right. Every chief was made rich by the Rhodesian government.

"I fed my group of freedom fighters that night, here in my kitchen. We had just heard the curfew shot. A messenger child arrived. 'There has been a massacre, *vanobaya*,' he said. "I was told about my sister, Angelina. Security forces, RDF, had been in our business district that day. Everyone had seen them, or by then heard of it. You had not done anything intentional. You tried so hard. Such an earnest child. 'She is dangerous,' I told the boys. 'She is a loose cannon.'

"'She can no longer be exempt,' the leader said.

"So they found you. They moved with the cows. They were not going to harm you there. They would have taken you away from Nyadzi where no one would hear. 'Do not torture her,' I had called out after them. My mind was in an odd form of shock. It seemed as though I were refereeing them in a game.

"Heresekwe intervened. Actually, he saved your life. 'Why did the security forces pick Mhekwe?' he asked them. 'She never told the soldiers about Mhekwe. They must have known something else.' He became quite angry. There was not a boy who crossed the border who would not listen to Heresekwe. 'She knows nothing,' he had said. 'You destroy an advocate of unity and freedom. Is that not what we are trying to obtain?'

"So you left us. You went to the exams early. You left for Salisbury the next morning. Choice saw you at Sekundiri grocery buying Fantas for the drive to the station. You were giving cheek to your father. He at least realized you were no longer safe. You could not live between two worlds.

"Mapipi perhaps told him something: your life had been threatened, you were at risk. Mapipi was a good drummer. The RDF would think nothing of it, an African playing his drum. They would not suspect. Many times Mapipi saved the boys with his warning messages. This is why he survived. But we were certain on some points he was a sellout. We knew that Mapipi was loyal to his white boss.

"Heresekwe is still an enigma. Everyone has a story about him. He did go to Mozambique. No one would kill him just because he sabotaged a European's execution. He had a promising political future. But we never saw him back around these parts. He was one of those who went to China for special training. That is what I've heard.

"I believe he shocked himself that night. He realized he did not have the priorities right. He needed a new role. He needed to be free from such distractions of civilian life."

"How do you know?" Colleen said, swiping at tears. "Who do you think you are?" She couldn't speak further. She stood and clutched the table hard. There were gray swirls in the formica, and she concentrated on them. There were marks from a cutting knife, and one of the children had drawn a smiley face in blue ink.

Vaida remained aloof. Her glasses sparkled orange in the western sky. "I must tell you how it was. You have to understand the psychology of war. Friends, family, even one's own survival become secondary to the cause." She sat there rubbing the back of her ear with a forefinger.

"Your sister, the one who sold doilies outside the Leopard Rock?" Vaida nodded slowly.

"I didn't do it," Colleen said.

"It cannot be proved, one way or the other, who was responsible. The village may have been a planned target for quite some time. Or perhaps it was random. And the press ignored it, one tiny column in the *Herald*. What does that tell you? Of course they blamed ZANLA."

"Say I didn't do this, please."

Vaida was silent. She seemed to be searching for words.

Colleen was trapped, she closed her eyes. "I must get away," she thought. This village, Mhekwe. To be trapped, to not escape. Children ran, they hid, they were found. Adults, alive longer, there may have been hope, with that the fear, shock, limpness, a limp arm was tugged, a lifeless face nudged.

Vaida sat next to her on the floor. A kerosene lamp now burned shrilly on the table. Children chattered in the bedroom. 'I must stand up on my feet and go,' Colleen told herself, but she could not move. She could never think about being alive.

Vaida clutched her glasses and rubbed red, swollen eyes. "I go back and forth about this," she said. "Asking how I could have arranged for you to die. I argue to myself about the circumstances. I remember how our minds were in a separate mode. I have blamed you. Then I blame those of us who kept you ignorant, our traditional secrecy."

Colleen murmured something about going home.

"Here's a torch," Vaida said, flipping the switch. "I'll pick it up tomorrow, or sometime next week. I'll be down that way."

Colleen opened the door to smell cooking fires throughout the valley, gold flickers behind thick evening mist.

9: COMA GIRL

COLLEEN TRANSFERRED ZOLISWA TO IONIA INSTITUTE ON A Saturday morning. She had been indoors for a month, where windows were shaded to prevent dust and daylight glimmered like a shutter slowly closing across the lens of a camera. Zoliswa had probably never noticed this, or maybe preferred it, since light is said to be painful during meningitis. Her eyes would stare open. They did not seem to blink. When she was most alert, she would gag, or move her face as if she were sucking a cough drop, and lie, heavy, malleable as dough, her mouth sometimes pulled down wet into the mattress. The other children would stand far back from her bed, in their government-issue hospital gowns, and mutter in a type of unison. Someone would say "*isidumbu*," the dead body, and they'd scatter off, giggling nervously.

She and Zoliswa waited on the oval for the ambulance to reverse, a grayish Combie of the Cape Provincial Administration. It was the same make as police trucks, except those had steel mesh welded into side windows and were painted the flat yellow of chronic jaundice. The day was bright and lurid, and Colleen cowered from it, shifting the child. She glanced back inside the lobby, back at twelve hours of hospital time at night, penlights on children's sleeping faces, and the iridescence of the ward kitchen before breakfast, when she and Fiona might push open a window to draw on cigarettes. They tapped them into damp air, embers in darkness, while an orange line emerged along the east horizon, beyond the Cape Flats.

She covered Zoliswa with a nursery blanket. There was a breeze from down the mountain. She could smell fish frying in Portuguese cafés on Lower Main Road. The driver twisted his head backward out the window, and his chin doubled. "Going to Ionia?" he asked, as if it were a place with possibility.

"Ya," Colleen called back, and she heaved Zoliswa up against her shoulder, holding on tight to the back of her head. They walked past the fruit vendors. Zoliswa did not startle at the noise, their bartering, the pieces of languages, Xhosa, Afrikaans, English. Her legs dangled randomly in front of Colleen's. The driver opened the door for them and stood cheerfully beside the step. He held his arm out. "Careful, hey, nursie." His English, singsong, flirtatious, was Afrikaans-intoned. He had a pink face with small purple veins crisscrossing his cheeks, the result, possibly, of drink.

"She looks heavy, man," he said. "You can put her on the stretcher if you want."

"Thanks," Colleen said, and she watched him strap her. At five years old, Zoliswa had the muscle tone of a newborn baby.

"Ionia," he said, tugging at the extra leather. "Too bad, hey."

The ambulance moved slowly downhill, stopping and starting behind a bus. Colleen sat and listened to brakes, shifts of low gears. "It's OK, Zoliswa," she said, in case she could hear. Colleen held her hand. It was clenched, as if she were hiding a small trinket, something she had found, and she might open her palm wide to show her. "Look at this," she might say.

In the last month, Colleen had created a second child, an aware one, in her mind. It was a personality based mostly on speculation. The character seemed like her own self at five, sixteen years before. She was in Sub A at Melsetter day school—her mother alive, edging their car around the switchbacks between Nyadzi and the Junction; they would stop every day at the spring, a tap in a road cut, and fill thermoses with drinking water. Her anklets would always get splashed, and stained orange, and her feet would smell. The memory was so clear, and so connected now with Zoliswa that Colleen could not imagine her anywhere else beyond the hospital except Nyadzi—the Nyadzi she herself knew. Colleen despised this habit of hers, personifying Zoliswa like a thing, giving her some sort of white consciousness. But on E1, the real Zoliswa, the person before the coma, was known only to her mother. All Colleen knew was the aloofness of the mother's grief.

Colleen concentrated on times and dates: world events that happened during the spring of that year, when Zoliswa had lived a regular life. She kept reversing back to those dates, as if thinking about them might stall the Kei River epidemic, make its subsequent occurrence go away, move it, maybe, to a different month and another town.

At first people had thought it was encephalitis. Public health workers drew blood from captured birds, hoping to find a vector. The fever had spread. Sister DeKock ordered twenty spinal tap trays from CSD. She prepared an isolation ward. They talked about it at shift change.

"The nonwhite side is full," Colleen reported. "Muriel is the only patient on the white side."

"She'll probably be expired by the end of the week." Sister DeKock rubbed her temples underneath the bows of her glasses, which pushed the frames up to her eyebrows. Her brows became magnified and reminded Colleen of unshaven legs. "Well, Colleen, one has to be frank," she declared.

Colleen agreed, nodding.

"We'll move Muriel out, and put the Kei River kids in there," Sister DeKock said. "Her mother is with her, nay? They can use the side ward."

"Anyway, she's so prone to infection from the chemo," Colleen said. "She doesn't need to be around meningitis."

"Ya, that's it then." Sister DeKock squirted Jergens on her hands.

Ten victims arrived in Cape Town, and all of them except Zoliswa screamed through their lumbar punctures. Colleen had bruises from the struggles. The children were suspicious afterwards, even in the delirium of their fevers, when they would gaze at invisible things rolling between their fingers and thumbs, then fling out their hands and watch the plain air, as if something were fluttering softly to the floor. Colleen imagined dust and snow. But mostly it seemed like the bacteria itself, circulating around them, persistent and unseen, a fragmented spirit that twitched about in various shapes before lodging in the mucus membranes of noses, and penetrating spinal cords and the linings of brains.

Colleen and the other nurses swallowed large doses of rifampin each tea time, but after the lumbar punctures, no one used the protective face masks; the children were terrified of them. Still, they remembered Fiona and Colleen. Each child would shrink from them as they knelt down by the cribs with spoonfuls of green Panado. They all cringed during sponge baths, curled into themselves with eyes vigilant, alert, as if listening for a distant shout.

"I hate my peds rotation," Fiona had said. "I will refuse to assist with another lumbar puncture." Her teacup rattled. "I will." She nodded her head at Colleen in case she didn't believe her and slurped milky tea from a saucer.

"I don't know why people didn't get them done on day shift," Colleen said.

"Colleen, the clinic room is nothing but a torture chamber." Fiona lit a cigarette and glowered behind the smoke from it.

"It's like the doctor is the bad chap, and we're the so-called good ones, who talk nicely to them and then hold them down."

Fiona shook her head the way she listened to a Walkman. "It feels so political," she said.

"White kids get meningitis," Colleen said, almost hopefully. "Remember Jackie last month? It's a diagnostic procedure. Somebody would do the same to us."

"You sound like the SABC," Fiona said.

"I do not," Colleen argued, familiar with Fiona's fairly new habit of accusing her, and everyone else—African housekeeping staff, even right-wing Nationalist Party girls from Tygerberg hospital—of political apathy.

"It must be Malcolm and all that ganja," Fiona said.

Colleen ignored her and went back to her charting. Since the state of emergency, Fiona had become preoccupied with racial issues, as if she'd never considered them before. Colleen and Fiona had driven over to Pollsmoor prison in Malcolm's bakkie, and sat in the parking lot, wondering where Nelson Mandela was inside, and exactly what he might be doing. Colleen felt like a groupie.

Colleen believed that her survival of Zimbabwean independence reassured Fiona. So did her plans to return there. Her father was eager to have her back. When he'd sent her to South Africa—arguing that Zimbabwe was in flux, UCT more stable, Groote Schuur a better training hospital—he had seemed surprised at her lack of protest. She had secretly thought she would come down and do something subversive, something brave, like her high school history teacher, who'd been deported for smuggling nonsyllabus textbooks into Rhodesia. Colleen had vaguely considered militant acts as if they were career choices. But once here, imagining such heroics was only a kind of mental duty, a tribute to the conscience.

When Colleen returned from her last holiday in Bulawayo, Fiona insisted on details—how the statues were gone and the street names changed. "I want to go there," Fiona said, wistfully. "Live there."

"They won't let you, with that South African passport," Colleen teased her.

"What if they don't let you back?" she asked. "What if they don't give you a job?"

"I don't know," she said, acting like she didn't care.

Fiona loved to speculate and predict. She was wiry and small with a pointed chin. She walked around the hospital, bobbing her head this way and that, and objects—signs, plants, patients on gurneys — stood out, conspicuous under her regally nodding acknowledgment, her fast eyes.

She had started a group at her flat where they passed around copies of *The Second Sex* and sipped Drambuie from glass jars. She always mixed up feminism with being a lesbian, and Colleen would feel compelled to defend things like procreation.

Fiona had a series of lovers who were fat and menacing. One occasionally drank a bottle of Nyquil as a suicide attempt, and Fiona would talk about guilt. It was difficult to know what to say. "Janet does have nice breasts," Colleen might say, or "I love her throaty voice," but she disliked them, how they made her feel possessive.

Finally Fiona met Gail. They all had dinner in Sea Point and walked along the promenade. Fiona and Malcolm sat down on a bench, side by side. Gail and Colleen stood by the seawall. Waves sprayed up. "I really love her," Gail said, stretching one arm along a red iron railing. The tide was in. She raised her voice. "I taught her how to play squash yesterday." She laughed and Colleen nodded, realizing she was asking for approval, as if Colleen were Fiona's mother, or father. It seemed they should have cigars or cups of tea. Gail's eyelids were a faint dewy blue, and drops of water gathered on her face, which Colleen found herself staring at, moving from one to another. Colleen reached in her pocket for a tissue, but Gail had already swiped the droplets away with the back of her hand.

On the bench, Malcolm had that strained look of polite endurance he always succumbed to around Colleen's nurse friends. He felt that nursing, for her, was a phase, a response to an inner call to humble herself. He disapproved of what his father called "real jobs." He despised his father, who was half-Gujarat Indian, for crossing the color bar. Malcolm's only known relatives were the white ones, his mother's, Progressive Federal people, "parlor talk liberals," Malcolm called them. Malcolm's father never spoke of his Indian family in Natal, the people who raised him. His father had taken the double-barreled British name—Lang-Smith—of whoever had fathered him.

Fiona and Malcolm joined them at the rail. Seagulls flew up. "Fiona says she's telepathic," Malcolm said. She had found a way to keep his attention. She knew about his gifts of colored crystals, how he would weave rosemary into Colleen's hair ties for fidelity. They passed binoculars around, focusing and refocusing on Blouberg strand.

Fiona often talked about powers of the mind. She believed, for example, that Zoliswa did not have permanent brain damage, that Muriel would go into remission again. "One day they may both be walking the streets," she'd say. It made Colleen think of the second coming of Christ and evangelical chalk artists—the Americans who used to come to their school assembly once a year—who drew gold rays of light piercing lavender clouds. Hearing Fiona talk made her uneasy.

At night, Muriel and her mother emerged in terry cloth robes, with toothbrushes, and walked past them to the bathroom, gripping the IV pole. Their faces were two molds, as if they wore face packs. Muriel had lost most of her hair after the first chemo treatments. She had a few red strands at the back, which she kept in a finely threaded plait. Colleen imagined Muriel's mother slowly wrapping the hair around itself, careful not to pull. Otherwise Muriel's head was white except for a line of freckles where her side parting had been.

Muriel communicated to them through her mother. When the nurses hung IV bags, she stared at the floor. This exasperated Sister DeKock, but it was a relief to Colleen. She found she couldn't look at Muriel, or even at the blur of her. She felt absorbed by the force of her, which had to do with Muriel's knowledge of impending death. Her walk was heavy and weighted. She was tall, a deputy head girl at her high school. Colleen recalled the hypochondria of her teens, and her deep underlying secret belief that she had breast cancer or ovarian cancer, something reproductive and deadly. Despite this, or because of it, she did not know how to talk to her.

Zoliswa never protested or cried. She barely gagged when Colleen passed the nasal-gastric tube to her stomach. It stood out of her face like a horn. It seemed to pull her features inward, and separate them from their usual proximity to one another. What had been identifiable as this girl—her high cheekbones, black immobile eyes—appeared poised to spin, in a disorderly way, around a point. Her eyebrows were characteristic of certain prominent Africans: sharply curved, the proud brows of skepticism, the kind of woman she might have become. Above the gray tube, Zoliswa's brows twitched at random, irrelevant and purposeless. Colleen fed her, holding the tube the way she'd coil up the string of a kite, watching the fluid move between them. Sometimes Zoliswa would sneeze.

She was an easy patient, compared to the others, who tried to pull out their IVs and spat chicken broth. Her mother did most of the work. She changed nappies and pushed Zoliswa's flaccid arms into sleeves. Fiona knew some Xhosa from a handbook, and she and the mother worked on Zoliswa's range of motion exercises before ten P.M. tea, rotating the child's joints in mutual hopefulness. Zoliswa would slump in Fiona's lap. The mother had a fixed distant look, and when Colleen stood there taking her daughter's pulse, in those silences, the woman would turn her head away as if slapped, as if waiting for it to happen again.

There were three mothers who slept with their heads against cribs. Sometimes they might stumble off, their faces pressed and almost whitish, and follow Fiona to an empty bed in E2's spare private. Fiona taught them to make an admission bed, with fresh linen and crisp triangular corners, as if they hadn't been there each night.

Colleen came to get Zoliswa's mother the night of the long seizure. The intern on call was there, rumpled and sweaty and smelling of a woman, and he took the injections of phenobarbital, and then valium and more valium as fast as Colleen drew them up, pushing them into the IV site amid Zoliswa's tiny braids.

They watched her. She did not seem like a child or even a human or an animal, but a cataclysmic punishment of nature, raw nerves randomly stimulated, a series of shocks and unfelt returns to polarity. It seemed as if all of the world were in the room, the writhe of restless crowds. "She needs an airway," the intern said. Colleen ripped one out of cellophane and passed it to him. It jerked up and out of her mouth with each spasm, and the whites of her eyes showed, quivering white, as if she were holding her pupils up under her lids on purpose, the way Colleen used to scare her friend Penny at Hatfield.

Colleen thought suddenly of that childhood game. "I'm the coma girl," she would call to Penny, and follow her silently, pretending to sleepwalk, thinking of a *Sunday Herald* article they'd once read and clipped out, of a comatose girl who would not wake up. Later, she'd supposed that what she had wanted, or sought, vaguely, was someone to compare to her sister: if it were a contest Sarah would win, would surpass the girl in the paper. Sarah was better off than that, even after Rest Haven. She could talk when spoken to; she talked to herself, she read, she had ideas and beliefs, it didn't matter what. Colleen and Penny never discussed it side by side, the coma girl and Sarah—and Penny had been about as familiar with Sarah as she was. Colleen wondered now if, in fact, the game did not have to do with Sarah—not everything did, she knew that—or not much really seemed to. She remembered how the *Herald* printed subsequent headlines and more fuzzy pictures, of a girl whose eyes stared, and whose hands dangled over the sides of a wheelchair. Colleen and Penny would gaze at the pictures, grimace at each other, and practice making their eyes go cold. Sometimes, traveling in the hostel van, they'd hold their feet still until they were numb and stumble out of the van, arguing about the coma girl, speculating about how much she could feel. Colleen dreamed she was her, stretched out on a stone slab in a stone hallway, unable to move and trying to speak, at first wanting to plead or beg, but she no longer knew words, even in her thoughts. There were only variations of moans, deep inside the throat, barely audible as discordant humming.

"Let's give her some oxygen," the intern said. Colleen turned a knob and the wall unit began to hiss. They adjusted a mask over Zoliswa's face. Her milk teeth gnashed beneath it.

"Get her mother." The intern sat very still on the bed, his head tilted and confused.

Colleen ran down the hall into the brightness of E2 and opened the door to the mothers' room. The women slept intertwined on the one bed, arms about each other. The room was hot with breath, and a sweat that smelled of maize and fire, as if these things were part of their bodies, even in the city. Colleen saw the orange of Zoliswa's mother's dress. She lifted her head from someone's lower back.

"Zoliswa is having a seizure," Colleen whispered, and Zoliswa's mother stood, immediately alert. She rushed barefoot through the doors, muttering Xhosa to herself, "*ngozi*," something Colleen recognized from signs. It meant danger, a warning to burglars in posh suburbs like Constantia. It was posted on gates beneath pictures of snarling dogs.

The mother lifted the child and spoke to her in a low voice. She pressed Zoliswa against herself, and her arms trembled with her daughter's movement. Then they both became still, and Colleen blinked her eyes hard, wondering if she had become so familiar with the tremors that she didn't see them anymore. But the seizure was over.

"Did you know this woman brought her child to a clinic twice?" the intern asked later in the nurses' station. He flipped through the chart. "Here. The physician sent her home. Told her the kid had febrile convulsions." He spread some golden syrup on cold toast from the tea trolley.

"Does the doctor know?" Colleen asked. "Know what happened?"

"That he overlooked the beginning of a meningitis outbreak? That he made somebody a retard for life?" The intern looked at her irritably, but the anger was multifocused, impersonal, like his friendliness.

"Wouldn't care either," Fiona said.

"He might," Colleen speculated flatly. She wrapped her arms around herself. They were restless in the cold bright room, with injustice like a rainy season repeated, and no real way to react— bystanders, uncomfortably self-righteous, and despite their generations of over-documented history in Africa, oddly kinless and estranged.

"How long does she need the oxygen?" Colleen asked.

"Go ahead and remove the mask," the intern said.

Zoliswa sniffed and snorted as if she were laughing. Warm air blasted through the ambulance's jammed side window. Zoliswa's eyes were fixed on the roof, which was low, and marred, and rusting in odd patterns, but her eyes did not move from one patch to another. They glided through traffic like a float in a parade. Colleen imagined herself perched in navy blue satin amid a theme of flame lilies. Zoliswa would sit beside her. She could be a flower girl. She'd look good in yellow. They would both be alert.

A line of cars followed them. People hesitated to pass. They bumped across manholes, and Colleen placed another pillow beside Zoliswa's rolling head. The ambulance was dark inside and muted. It seemed to require curtains.

The driver turned at Rosebank. Colleen could see Malcolm's flat down Tafel Street, the fan in a window, its gray blur, on high. Malcolm liked white sound. The sun had already risen above the veranda. Colleen wanted to sleep, and roll face down into his imprint on the mattress. He would be awake, in the kitchen, smoking. Lately he slept during the afternoon, the same time as her. It had to do, he said, with her peds night rotation.

Malcolm had actually been staying up all night since base camp in September. After dropping out of UCT, he had spent his time avoiding conscription. It was a kind of hobby, requiring him to move from place to place, without a permanent address. When the SADF people found him—he'd been waiting for them, afraid to answer the door, eventually convincing himself that they wouldn't come—they recited the option of camp or jail. He lasted two months, the final week on the base's psych unit, and when he returned home, he'd been admitted to K4. Mental illness was a good permanent solution. Colleen wondered why he hadn't thought of it before.

"We were shooting black beanbag targets," he told her more than once—she thought, for awhile, that something had happened to his short-term memory—on K4, it was the first thing he said after days of speaking in monosyllables. But insane or not, Malcolm had changed. He made jokes about classical guitar and sold his guitar to his duet partner. He built marimbas with his parents' gardener. He stayed in the African townships, Guguletu or Langa, and washed in cold water. He claimed to sleep on bare floors. He lived on raw vegetables and fruit. Colleen only saw him for sex, or when he needed to use her phone. His Xhosa was becoming fluent.

The people in Langa taught Malcolm percussion techniques. He kept one drum at Colleen's boarding house. It was mahogany-colored with ancestral faces carved in the side. It had a goatskin membrane. He brought tapes over to play on the stereo. Some were copies of professional recordings, others were scratchy tapes of the Langa sessions, with background sounds of footsteps and doors closing. People would chant to rattles and shakers and the beating of clay pots. Malcolm's voice was higher and more self-conscious.

Colleen's favorites were the chants. They represented the struggle of life and death, Malcolm said. He preferred an exotic metal instrument. He played one tape over and over again. Part of it was familiar to her.

"I think this part is from the soundtrack to *Apocalypse Now*," she said, finally making the connection. They had been having sex to it and the bed was a mess, and she was letting the bed dry before putting clean sheets down. "I feel, in a way, like I'm screwing that guy in the movie, Kurtz, Marlon Brando," she said. She was in a good mood, joking around. "Remember when they killed that cow?"

The tape was a collection of various unnamed pieces. "It *is* a copy of a copy," Malcolm said. He sat down in the pile of wet sheets. He was naked and vulnerable-looking. "What if you're right?" He was quiet for a long time. "I can't believe myself," he said.

"It's sort of weird, that you didn't consciously know what you were listening to," Colleen said. But he was taking it hard. "You're not like Kurtz, Malcolm."

"Everything I do is wrong," Malcolm said.

"No," Colleen said, sitting next to him on the floor. "It's just a coincidence. You're drawn to the tape's ethnic rhythms. That's all." She wished she hadn't said anything. It seemed that, in some way, she was just trying to turn him into another person driving downtown to work, at rush hour, around the mountain, changing lanes. "Why not?" she'd occasionally wondered. She admired those people, going about their business. Sometimes she detested herself, how living here made her feel, how Malcolm and Fiona made her feel next to them, so reasonable and unimpulsive, and rational-seeming. "I like what you're doing," she said. "I like the marimbas."

"Maybe I'll go to Natal for a while," he said.

"To find your father's mother's family?" she asked. That he had Hindu relatives on the continent greatly interested her. Malcolm's obsession with austerity made her think of the Gujarat Jain traditions.

"I don't know," he said.

"Gandhi was a Gujarat," Colleen reminded him.

Malcolm didn't answer. He appeared to be listening now to the music. His own nonwhiteness, the fact of his father's "passing," his particular background, seemed as irrelevant to him as Colleen's ancestors were to her.

"We don't even know what we're doing," he said, switching off the tape player.

It was shortly after this that Malcolm returned to UCT and met Sawi, the matriarch of a rebirthing group. The group explored ways of transforming subconscious impressions into what the founder, Leonard Orr, called "awakening events." Sawi threw large parties, exerting intense cultlike pressure on the guests. "She's a fat pig," Colleen told Malcolm after meeting her for the first time. Sawi had stood at Malcolm's door with sunflowers in the crook of her arm. She visited all her group members,

she'd said. The sunflowers were freshly cut from her garden. She
had been smiling widely.

From the ambulance Colleen thought she saw her, Sawi, crossing
Main Road in a billowy Indonesian smock. Sawi was not her real
name. She changed it after she'd been reborn. On her parents' postbox, the night of the Samadi party, Colleen had seen the name Versluth.
It seemed odd, that Sawi might once have had a surname. Colleen
wondered how she signed checks. Everyone in Sawi's group had given
themselves new names. Malcolm had named himself Mpefo, but he
only used it in the group. He told Colleen that he had acquired a new
consciousness, a different kind of awareness. He had relived his first
breaths. He tried to teach her to hyperventilate, which was key to the
rebirthing experience. "You're too tense," he'd say, but it was like a
religion he was only half interested in.

Something thumped hard and the ambulance jolted backward.
Colleen's head clanked against a fire extinguisher. "*Vok!*" the driver
yelled. Zoliswa gasped, lurching beneath straps. "It's OK," Colleen said
automatically, as if she were administering another unpleasant treatment.

"*Jou voken ma sy moer!*" the driver shouted. He climbed down from
the ambulance and stood in the street. Cars honked. Colleen stuck her
head out the window. A Renault had reversed into the front of the
ambulance. Pieces of headlights and brake lights sparkled white and red.

"I was coming out of that space there," a man said. He wore a
double-breasted suit, which made him look haggard and dwarfed. "I
didn't see you." He glanced anxiously at the ambulance. "God, I'm
sorry." He rubbed his forehead as if he were going to cross himself.

"Is everyone OK back there, nursie?" the driver called.

"Ya," Colleen said.

"Ya, well, I will ring the police then," the driver said. He still half
crouched in a kind of fighting stance and swung his shoulders back
and forth. But his voice was light again.

"Pick-n-Pay should have a phone," suggested the man. "I can call."

"I am transferring a very ill child. This is an emergency," the driver
said grandly. "I will do it." He strode past dwindling bystanders into

the store. The other man got back in his car and hunched over the steering wheel.

Colleen sat back down inside the ambulance and watched a woman getting highlights inside a salon. The stylist pulled long strands through a type of bathing cap. He jerked her head to the side. She seemed exposed, Muriel-like, a bare skull. The next window was Truworth's with its faceless styrofoam mannequins. They wore tube tops and black-leather miniskirts. Colleen listened to Radio 5's Saturday morning countdown. Speakers throbbed in open doorways of shops, Simple Minds, "Don't You Forget about Me."

At the Samadhi party, Sawi had ejected this song from the boom box. Her boyfriend protested and they snapped at each other. She wanted to play inspirational testimonies and a lecture on affirmations. She seemed entirely focused and single-minded and Colleen had half admired her perseverance.

She'd agreed to go with Malcolm to the party because Sawi was making her jealous. Sawi would call the flat and ask for Mpefo. Once she sounded like she was crying. That time, Malcolm's voice was tender, and he gave her advice from their rebirthing handbook. Colleen decided she did not trust her.

The party was at Sawi's parents' house in Constantia. Her parents had emigrated to Perth, but since the State of Emergency, property values had plummeted, and the house had been empty for a while, overpriced, awaiting a sale. They planned to rent it out soon, Sawi said. They'd take it off the market and hope for prices to go back up. Without furniture, the rooms were loud and bright. Water had evaporated from the swimming pool. There was dried algae along the sides. Colleen noticed dead lizards clustered around the base of the diving board.

They sat in the crowded Samadhi tank, which was really a hot tub under the vined roof of a veranda. Malcolm touched her feet with his. "Relax," he said. He lit his pipe of Transkeian and passed it to her. A woman was lying on her side in a puddle next to the tub, trembling and murmuring and contorting herself. Her jeans were drenched. A man rubbed her back underneath her t-shirt. "Is she rebirthing?" Colleen asked. Malcolm nodded. It reminded Colleen of an orgasm. She wondered if that was how she looked during sex, and she tried not to listen to the woman, embarrassed for her.

The jets were off, and all of their legs bobbed. Yellow-gray, under the water, the legs seemed lifeless and separate. Sawi stood above the hot tub like a school games-mistress analyzing swim strokes. She poured more red wine into Colleen's glass. "A good year for Delheim," Sawi said, indicating the bottle. "Yes," Colleen said. "It's lovely." Sawi wore a floral bikini top and a white muslin skirt. The roll of fat, suntanned, between the top and skirt, was accentuated by a belt of loose beads. "You breathe wrong," she told Colleen, watching her chest and stomach under the water.

They got out and dried themselves with towels. It was dusk. There was smoke in the distance over the Cape Flats. Sawi's boyfriend flipped some switches for the garden and pool lights. Steam rose from the hot tub.

"And over there," Sawi said, gesturing toward the valley, "there is no hot water, no water to bathe in, no toilets."

Many of them nodded or bowed their heads, the way people do in prayer. There was the usual pause, the moment of silence, before conversations. The comment seemed like grace before a meal. Sawi gazed at the horizon. She glanced back at Malcolm.

The girl who had been rebirthing lit one of the pipes at a patio table. She inhaled a few times and put it down. She was wearing her boyfriend's jacket, a trench with deep pockets, and she walked around the swimming pool twice, her hands deep in the coat. Her teeth chattered. The third time around, she pulled out a gun. Colleen peered at it. At first she didn't trust her judgment. She thought it was a comb, the way the girl lifted it up to her hair. It looked like an SADF pistol, with a magazine in the handle, an officer's weapon. Colleen recognized it from home, from the commissioner's cache at Nyadzi junction.

"Laura, put the gun down," her boyfriend called from a group by the servant's quarters.

The girl stood there, turning in a circle, around and around, laughing.

She must be getting dizzy, Colleen thought. She could hear people's feet scraping on the concrete and the starting up of automatic sprinklers. The girl began to hiccup, giggling, coughing. She clutched her stomach with her free hand. She made Colleen want to laugh too; Colleen felt that strange irresistible urge to laugh hard, the way she used to get in church, or school assembly. That hilarity.

The girl was familiar with the gun. She pretended to aim and concentrate. She cocked it and swayed on her feet.

"Laura, you're mad," Sawi said in a bright way.

A bulb glared from the middle of the empty pool. The girl gazed into the bulb, tilting her chin, letting it shine on her neck. She presented her profile to the light. The boyfriend walked up to her in a straight line. His gait was fast and steady and mechanical. His chest glowed with sweat. He grabbed a glass of wine from the table and drank it. He regarded her. The gun was at the level of his chest. It seemed slippery in her fingers. She gripped and regripped it. When he struck it from her hand, Sawi screamed. The gun clattered to the bottom of the pool without discharging. The man jumped in and picked it up. The gun had settled by the drain and was covered with mud. He climbed out, wiping it on his pants. Colleen heard the gate click shut behind him, the slam of his car door behind the hedge. He drove off. There was the sound of his brakes around curves.

People started talking. The girl sat down on a cushionless chaise lounge. Colleen stared at her. She felt alone with her inside a kind of humming sound. Maybe her ears were still plugged with water. The girl's eyes stared back at her. They were like the eyes of Sarah's cat after she was put to sleep for rodent cancer.

"She's on Vesperex," someone explained.

Later in the evening, many people rebirthed. The fear had triggered a required panting reflex. The front lawn was dark with convulsing shadows, and others on knees, like Malcolm, assisting them. Colleen sat on the hill, trying to be conscious only of her breathing.

Colleen watched the slow movement of Zoliswa's ribcage as she slept. Her eyes were closed now and fluttering. Occasionally she trembled. The ambulance was getting warm. Colleen unbuckled the leather straps and fanned her with the cardboard transfer folder. On E1 Zoliswa often would lie sleeping for whole shifts, rarely opening her eyes for pressure care. Yet the huge doses of phenobarb did not control the seizures. Sometimes Colleen would hear her crib shudder on its wheels. Her thin body would jerk against the rails, where padding had dropped down below the mattress. Her hands would be fisted as though rattling a cage. The seizures were subsiding more quickly than before. Still there was always a faint tremor about her, a kind of palsy.

Zoliswa's mother had asked a doctor about bringing her home.

"It was quite a scene," Sister DeKock had told Colleen. "The interpreter made it worse. Of course Doctor Eliot explained that Zoliswa must learn how to be fed with a spoon. How was the mother going to deal with a feeding tube? She has other children, one younger than Zoliswa, did you know that? What about them?" She gazed at Colleen, biting for a moment on her lip. "He told her about Ionia. They have a rather good rehabilitation program there."

"They do?" Colleen asked.

"Oh, Colleen, I know about that field trip for students. They show you all the vegetables. The freakier, the better. That chap who runs the place is a sensationalist."

"I remember seeing the OT department," Colleen said. "But still."

They had visited Ionia during bathtime. Colleen had realized immediately that it was worse than Rest Haven, or Nkachini, or any place Sarah had been. Strong women heaved adult-sized bodies into tubs. There was a lot of screeching, and people with misshapen heads curled into fetal positions, trying to hide. Later whites and nonwhites ate lunch together at a long table. They drooled and scooped macaroni into their mouths with their hands. They did not seem to notice each other. They kissed all of the student nurses. Most were quick and strong. Afterwards the group was invited to sit around the lobby and talk about it. Several nurses sobbed, and the director put his large arms around them. "Sometimes it is best not to question God," he had said soberly.

"Anyway, the mother made a great fuss," Sister DeKock said. "She lugged the child to the front door of the hospital, wouldn't even sign an AMA. Then she came back. Didn't say a word. Put the girl in her crib and sat next to her. I thought it best to leave them alone, give them some privacy to say goodbye. Ach, it was sad."

"I agree with you. Her other kids must need her," Colleen said. They both spoke in a hushed way as if Zoliswa might hear.

"Ya, but to hear the woman cry was quite distressing." Sister DeKock's face became flushed. She turned away from Colleen. "It was a high-pitched sound that would make a dog go mad."

Before she left, the mother had taped a picture of Zoliswa to the bars of her crib. Zoliswa stood posed in the African way, unsmiling, actually pulling the sides of her mouth down as if someone had just said, "Stop smiling now." She wore an orange, knitted jersey. She was intent, and Colleen recognized her ruffled frown between the arched intelligent brows.

Colleen would place Zoliswa on her side, with a pillow behind her back. But it bothered her to watch Zoliswa facing the direction of the picture. Colleen imagined something darting back and forth across the space. She wanted to take it down, but Fiona became quite hostile about it.

"Her mother wanted to remind us that Zoliswa is a human being," Fiona said, in her didactic way.

The other Kei River patients had started to play quietly with toys. Many had gone home. Without the mothers, it became louder. The children dragged chairs around the large room, away from bedsides, and lined them up. "Please sit," Tembalani, their leader, would say to Colleen, and they'd all be on a train, going somewhere, all of them facing forward. Someone would be a bell, a whistle. They pursed their lips and made engine sounds.

A child might call out after bed, *fune songa* or *fune kama*, then another, and they would run in pairs to the echoey bathroom. Colleen and Fiona brought toast with peanut butter to their beds, and sat on edges with the rails down. Everyone pretended to forget about the lumbar punctures. Fiona said that since they spoiled the children maybe they had been forgiven.

Muriel began to emerge from the side ward on her own and walk in the hall. It had been rare in the last week to hear her vomit. Porters brought a TV and VCR into the room.

Fiona did not like Muriel. "She's a bitch," she muttered under her breath one night after retreating into the office. Colleen could hear Muriel's IV stand rolling along. It clinked over a doorway.

"What did she do?"

"Ignored me, looked right through me like I didn't exist. Like *my* life's the waste. Don't even say it, I know what you're thinking: how insensitive, after all, she's dying, all that *kak*. I'm so sick of both of them." She threw her head back in the direction of Zoliswa's crib. "These zombie girls."

"There's only so much anybody can take," Colleen said. "I mean, they make me feel like I'm talking to myself."

"You know then," Fiona said. "Because you are talking to yourself. They are not alive, they're gone. We are alive, we're the ones." She paced across the room and back. "I'm furious," Fiona said. "She must never look at me like that again." She sat down on the desk and dropped her chin hard onto her knuckles. Her mouth was a small line, a few centimeters. Colleen thought of Tembalani's drawings earlier in the shift. He had knelt at the ward table and drawn on several pages in a notebook.

"This is you, *nesi*." he said. He had climbed from his seat to show his sister. Colleen peered down at the drawings from over their heads. Her eyes were two dots. Her mouth was a simple mark. Each picture was the same. He had made a line coming off the circle in one, Colleen ran her finger across it. "It is this," he explained, tugging her ponytail. Colleen looked at the sparse round faces on the drawing paper. Except for the sharply open points of eyes, she could be asleep. "*Mnandi,*" Colleen complimented him.

Zoliswa slept. Colleen dabbed at sweat on her face. The sun made poking metallic sounds on the roof of the ambulance. The doors to Pick-n-Pay snapped open and the driver came out carrying a plastic bag. He passed a bottle of mineral water and some yogurt through the window to her. "Breakfast?" he asked. He offered a plastic spoon. He sat on the hood and nibbled from a bag of chips.

She gathered Zoliswa up and propped her on her lap, supporting her back. She felt like a ventriloquist. They faced the marching people outside. Colleen splashed water on the spoon and brought it to Zoliswa's mouth, hoping some would trickle past her gritted teeth. She swallowed. "Good girl," Colleen said hopefully. But Zoliswa clenched onto the spoon and it crackled into pieces. Colleen pried her jaw open to remove them. She rearranged her on the stretcher, sighed, and yawned.

Cars darted around them. It seemed as if they were still moving, as if they had drifted in a light boat. Colleen began to nod, dragging her head back up. She closed her eyes. She saw the bed, the Rosebank flat, Malcolm trying to teach her the fox-trot. "Count, Colleen, one, two, step aside." He pulled her to him, let go.

"You are entirely beyond hope." He laughed, falling back into a folding chair, breathless. They looked at each other, he was still smiling, but the music became fuzzy and abrupt, like long-distance phone calls, voices across cable under oceans.

They had become submerged in warm water, heavy with salt, maybe one of the bays beyond Cape Point, within shark nets. They rolled about in the silence, Malcolm, or someone like him, and the person that seemed to be her.

She plunged up alone. The sound was that of a conch shell. Three women stood on a rock. They wore orange and red blankets. They had necklaces of Zambian jade. On their skin were etchings of tribal scars that reminded her of fossils.

Colleen wanted to go back down under. She stopped treading. The air was cold on her shoulders. The women regarded her with quizzical eyebrows, silent. One by one their eyes rolled up to white, the way old home movies end—jumpy, white, and final. Colleen's tongue was thick, she could not speak. "Help," she heard herself call out inside the ambulance. She covered her mouth. Her skin was cold and damp. She peered around, swallowing hard. Zoliswa blinked on the stretcher and her pupils were great circles, entrances to caves. Colleen looked away from her, out the window at people's sunglasses, round, square, cat-eyed, at the brisk world reflected in them.

10: LAYING OUT THE PATIENT'S BODY

COLLEEN SAW AS SHE CAME BACK TO THE WARD THAT SISTER HAD been closing privacy curtains. Besides the light by the sluice room, there was only the lamp above the man's bed. Sister had left it on since midnight round. She'd told Colleen it could happen at any time, and afterwards they must draw every curtain around all the beds. It was the opposite of a fire drill. The windowpanes were dark and fogged with breath. Other men snored in various depths and rhythms, but the man's breathing had finally stopped. All night Colleen had been sure it was done. Then it had started up again—quiet, deep, faster, and becoming soft—then nothing, the alerting pause. Later it would begin: quiet, deep, rapid, soft. She knew his respirations like a chorus. She'd sat anonymous to him with her textbooks and penlight, and the man's suction machine whirred: his drainage had moved away from the high, taut mound of his stomach. It hovered in the tube and flowed forward and dripped back down. After a while, Colleen could not imagine herself out of the night. It seemed to have always been there. But Sister had relieved her.

"I'm glad you're back," Sister said now, and Colleen blinked in the dark ward. "Almost irresistible," Sister said, "my urge to do rescue breathing on him."

Colleen put down their to-go tray and began to help Sister draw the curtains. They'd wait for the doctor, Sister told her, and then they would wrap the man. "A good experience," Sister said. "It will be easier since you don't know him."

Colleen agreed. She pulled the curtains as quietly as she could along the metal rods. The curtains covered the foot of each bed and hung neatly down the length of the ward with a uniformity she had never before noticed. They absorbed the light in such a way that she thought it was already dawn.

"Let's eat then," Sister said. She removed her stethoscope and washed her hands. "What the bloody hell. We can't do anything else yet, can we?"

They leaned against the counter by the ward sink and finished their sandwiches. Sister ate hers with a plastic knife and fork. They stared down the corridor between the two rows of beds and the two lines of curtains all the way down to the sluice room. It was the beginning of the month, Colleen's new rotation. The ward looked the same as the other Nightingale wards on D-wing. Upstairs were the patients she had known on D2 last month. She'd been listening wistfully for any sounds above her, quizzing herself about those patients' names, or guessing at various footsteps. It had helped her stay awake. She never liked the week of changeover. Fourth-year students had told her about D1 nights—its steady overflow from intensive care when D1's own census dropped. The extra patients wore yellow "No Code" wristbands and had prominent stickers on their bedside clipboards—the glaring yellow, and a green one—which indicated their organs were too diseased for transplanting.

When the doctor arrived to pronounce the man dead, he and Sister opened the man's curtain and Sister pulled it back around them. The doctor asked if he could borrow a stethoscope. "Hello, Sir," he said, "Hello, Mr. Van Zyl." There was only weariness in his voice, but the name, out loud and unacknowledged in the long room, startled Colleen. Silence hung about like a form of obedience. The doctor and the sister expected nothing else. It made Colleen impatient with the man and the idea of such illness.

Sister asked Colleen to remove the man's tubes while she called his family in Outshoorn. Colleen went down to the lamplit curtain and looked inside. The man seemed the same as when she'd left for the cafeteria, except that his chest was not moving. His stomach too, which had been bloated and heaving under the hospital gown, did not move. The man's eyes had been rolling up all night; there had been no consciousness in them, at least not that Colleen had felt or seen. They were closed now, or partly open the way of a young kitten. There was not going to be very much to it, Colleen began to think. It was almost the same as anything else. And Colleen had never known the man before this night. Sister had told her he was a sheep farmer outside Outshoorn, in the Karoo. He'd come over from oncology because they'd filled up with chemo admissions. He was a large man, and he had been difficult to turn on her own.

Colleen decided to start with the IV tubing. The IV was still going, dextrose and saline at a hundred an hour. Colleen turned the knob down. She pulled the drip set from the pump. An infusion light blinked, and the pump began to beep before she could switch off the alarm. She heard the other men rustling under their sheets at the sound of it. She reached behind the bed and unplugged the pump at an outlet. The men rumpled around on their plastic mattresses. But the pump had gone to battery mode and it beeped again. She pushed STOP, and she pushed OFF, and finally there were no more lights on the machine. She nudged it away. The IV pole rolled up against a metal locker and bumped gently until the wheels settled. People seemed to be sleeping again.

With her scissors, she cut the man's "No Code" wristband. She picked at edges of clear adhesive across his hand. She turned his hand over. Someone had used too much tape. She could not find the beginning of it. The calluses on his palms gave her a surface to tear the tape away from. He was bruised around the veins, and cool to the touch, and she ripped and tore at the cellophane and peeled back moist tape underneath. It came away easily from the hairs on his hand. She realized that he did not feel pain. She would not need to be careful. There was nothing to hesitate about. The IV glided bloodlessly from the hand. She thought she should still tape a folded square of gauze down, and she pressed it against the small bones below his knuckles.

When Colleen tried to pull the catheter, she removed the binding along his thigh and tugged quite hard, but the catheter would not come out. She wondered if the urethra had closed off—did that happen when the body died? Or maybe all the tumors had pressed down on the tube, constricted the tube in there, she wasn't sure. It made her embarrassed, and she blushed with humiliation for the man as she pulled and pulled at the tube. She could not think the problem through. She would have to ask Sister. Blood had begun to ooze from the man's penis. She had caused that—injured him like that. Colleen sniffed back angry tears. She tugged harder—what was holding it in? She became wary of the perversity she thought might be restrained inside herself, how alert she appeared, the way her respect for the dead was not seeming to occur as an instinct. She should feel worse for him, more regret. The outrage of it, she tried to think. She covered him quickly and went to the office.

"What am I doing wrong?" she blurted.

The doctor looked up from the desk. Sister was xeroxing the death certificate, and the machine whirred and flashed several times.

"I can't pull the catheter," Colleen said.

"Just deflate the balloon with a ten-milliliter syringe," Sister replied. She reached for a syringe from the cart. "Here," she said.

"There's a tiny balloon on the bladder end of a Foley catheter," the doctor told Colleen.

"It's what keeps the catheter in situ," Sister told her.

"Thanks," Colleen said.

"You never know what the students have learned yet on these rotations," Sister said to the doctor. "It's touch and go."

Colleen returned to the man. He was the same as she had left him. This time she examined the catheter more carefully at his thigh. She did not want to have to return to the office. In the drainage bag, clots of blood floated around in the urine. Colleen noticed a port now, forking off from a rubber connection to the drainage tube, and her syringe fit into it, and she pulled back as far as she could on the syringe. She had all five milliliters. The tube began to give way. The catheter started to pass from the urethra on its own. Colleen drew it toward her, lukewarm and bleeding, until it was all out of him.

Colleen felt it was respectful to focus on the man's history as she tossed the catheter away in the waste can and covered his genitals back up with a sheet. She recalled the Little Karoo—it was all she knew about him—the brightness out there and heat, the flatland beyond Sir Lowry's Pass. Yes, there were plenty of sheep farms. The man would speak Afrikaans: his name, Van Zyl. Possibly he owned a Cape Dutch house in some disrepair, with various outbuildings. He would likely have farmhands to help with the sheep. He was an Afrikaner. He might call himself that with a certain pride and perhaps humor. Colleen thought of it the way she would make conversation with him if he'd been conscious. They would carefully avoid politics—she would. But she realized it was all speculation. Even what she imagined about him seemed dead and contrived on her part.

Colleen remembered a time she and her father and sister had driven through the Karoo on their way back to Rhodesia. It had been during a December school holiday, and Colleen had taken photos of ostriches and sheep in vast corrals as the car sped past them. Later the pictures had all turned out streaked with glare and motion. Concentrating, Colleen could also recall Outshoorn, its Christmas lights wired from one palm to another. They were switched off in the hot afternoon—multibeaded Christmas shapes glinting with sun. She'd not been able to tell red from green beyond her sunglasses. She'd only looked out at the lights because her sister had told her to. But perhaps the man, Van Zyl, knew these decorations? He would most likely have seen them. Might they have been bells or candles? She couldn't remember. He'd need to park there along that street when he came to town. Colleen recognized an impatience she'd felt earlier, standing there in the ward; its energy seemed to come from nowhere. She was certain that the man would have been indifferent about the lights. *Who wouldn't be?* she thought to herself, as if defending him, as if the lights should have mattered in some way to either of them.

Colleen had been avoiding the man's face. It was fairly easy to do since she'd left the nasal gastric tube for last. Even on a live face, the tube, like a kind of trunk, confused a person's features. Sister had switched off the suction pump at the time of death. This was partly the reason it seemed so quiet around the man. But after the nasal gastric tube, Colleen would be done. The layers of adhesive were crossed damply above his nostrils, and they came away as she touched them. She guided the tube straight up his throat. She heard the tube passing over the area of vocal chords maybe, a catch, or for a second, a bit of humming—possibly air, she told herself—air the tube had released as it moved behind the windpipe. There was her own voice too. She had breathed in, made some kind of sound. It could have been her—was it her or him or both of them?—something unified, and uttered. She was reminded of people praying, eyes closed, her own eyes closed. The ward felt cold and the ceilings were high. When the man gagged, Colleen jumped back—he was supposed to be dead, he was dead—and the tube went with her, all the way up, coiled and glistening. It slipped from the man's nose and dropped from her hand. His eyes stared. His mouth yawned. His face free of the tube had reclaimed itself. This was Van Zyl. The face was changing. It was moving. The vomit erupted with a force that turned the man toward her. He gazed straight at her. It would happen again. She leaped away from another blast. The curtain had become brown now from the spray. The man convulsed and the fluid shot outside the curtain. Whatever expressions Colleen had not known were mimed there on his face, a wincing, a protest, an anger, as if shouting. She thought she could see him in his life. He would take nothing from no one, and she liked that. He was a baby—fierce, defiant—a boy crying, his cheeks high up under blond-gray lashes that refused to blink. Colleen saw in his eyes the same flat blur of her Karoo pictures, the streaks of light which were caught in the movement of those photographs, her father's car moving so quickly down that road. *He's alive*, Colleen thought, *they made a mistake*, and she stepped outside the curtain waiting for Sister to come. At one point, she'd thought she must have cried out down the ward, or said "no" or "oh," she thought she had called "help." Her ears thumped. None of the other patients seemed to be awake. No lamps were snapping on. She wondered if she had overreacted, exaggerated the situation to herself. But she could smell the acid of the man's stomach. Vomit dripped steadily on the floor from the curtain. She heard herself call properly for Sister. Then she peered back inside. The man gaped, and fluid continued to come up gurgling from his mouth, but he was otherwise still. Even if he'd been alive that one second, if he'd been startled back alive by the vomiting, he was not alive now. Colleen slid carefully back toward him through the puddle on the floor. She reached for a tissue and wiped his nose.

"It's all right now," she whispered to him, the way she might console anyone else who had just been so sick, and she stood there, and then she grabbed his hand, and held it tight, and waited. It seemed certain that what she must do was stand and not move. She understood him better. She felt she had some understanding of him this time.

After a while, Colleen began to think about the mess around the man, and what she must get for him—she would have to do something with his mouth, stuff it, gag it, tie it up. She would find some towels in the sluice room; she also needed a linen hamper. Her shoes smacked around as she shifted position. How long had she been standing with him? On her watch, fifteen minutes had passed. She lifted the blind and looked down at the alley between the Florence Nightingale wings and the maternity wing. There were several laundry trucks removing bundles of linen. The drivers called out to each other in Xhosa. It was the time of early morning for the incinerator. She could smell the plastic of syringes melting, soiled bandages and cellophane, now blended into the mist coming down Table Mountain. She turned around to find Sister behind her, and Mr. Newton, the patient from the next bed. They were at Van Zyl's feet.

"Yes, Mr. Newton," Sister was saying, "that could be you if you don't get back to your oxygen."

"Let me help," Mr. Newton insisted.

"You're supposed to be at strict bed rest, aren't you now?" Sister said. "It almost serves you right to see such a thing."

Mr. Newton ignored Sister and clutched the bed board.

"But go on now," Sister insisted. With an armful of linens, she leaned over and blocked Mr. Newton's view. "Are you all right?" she asked him.

"He's only dead," Mr. Newton said, nodding at Colleen, and his nostrils pinched and flared, and she nodded with him in vague agreement. He backed out into the dark ward, his glasses flashing.

"Do you think we should change the time on the death certificate?" Colleen whispered as Sister came in close next to her, dropping a sheet down on the floor and moving it about with her heels.

"No, no. This happens sometimes when the NG gets removed. Look at the fingers there." Sister pointed out, reaching for his hand. "No, he's been dead a while, love. He's stiffening up. We should get on with it. His family's not coming in, thank God."

Colleen filled a basin, and Sister dipped cotton wool into the water, wringing, pressing down hard over the man's eyelids as she shut them. Sister tied a strip of gauze from his chin to the top of his head. The mouth was closed tight now. Colleen felt relieved that Sister had taken over. Beyond the curtain, Mr. Newton's own lamp had been turned on, and

Colleen heard him cranking his bed. She saw the silhouette of his open novel, his mound of pillows. The water in the basin was warm, almost too hot for a normal patient. Colleen soaped up their washcloths with a bar of Dial. She passed one across to Sister. They scrubbed at the filmy brown residue. Vomit had settled into the folds of the man's groin. Colleen rinsed the cloths in the basin, and they rinsed his skin down, and Sister ran the towel briskly over him. Colleen was glad for the hot water.

"Grab the draw sheet and let's pull him," Sister told Colleen. "We're turning you now, sir," Sister said. "Talk to him as if he's still alive," Sister instructed breathless, to Colleen.

"We're turning you now," Colleen repeated, reaching across his back as Sister hoisted him again toward her. She waited while Sister dabbed at various spots they'd missed. He was turned in her direction, and she held him close so he wouldn't be dropped, and steadied her feet.

They taped the required t-bandage under him and between his legs and worked at bending his arms into a fresh gown. They shoved him damply from side to side. Colleen tried to straighten the arm on her side, and it was tough and firm and resistive to her pressure. The muscles held on. They were no longer the man's. In its new phase, the arm seemed able to avoid inertia. She hadn't thought it would be this way—she'd never really thought of it at all—the shutting down of the body, this evolving separateness. The body would have formed once as an embryo, in that time which must have been before its mind, as intent on its purpose as it was now. There had always been a ready sequence. Colleen tried to tell herself that it was nothing to admire.

Sister said they might as well leave the arms, and said that, in any case, they could bandage the wrists together across the chest. The tape went round and round. Colleen had begun to feel tired. She noticed the absence of a certain pressure she felt she needed to stay awake. With a loudly squeaking marker, Sister wrote Van Zyl's name and birth date across an index card and tied the attached string to his foot. Colleen liked the familiar odor of the drying ink. She had become quite comfortable. The man's—Van Zyl's—body was there with her and Sister, and there were systematic workings in each of their bodies.

By now it was six o'clock. Colleen knew they were running late for temperatures. Sister flicked on all the overhead lights while Colleen shook thermometers down. Colleen did not think about the man as they passed basins. On her way to the sluice room with a bedpan, she walked by his bed, but she thought nothing of it. She'd emptied all the kidney dishes, slopping with toothpaste foam, into the hopper, and was setting up Mr. Newton's nebulizer when the orderly rattled in with a gurney. "Poor bugger," some of the men had been saying from behind their curtains, and four or five were now joking in a nervous way. Colleen could tell they were glad to be talking about it. They seemed relieved. Sister peeked in behind Colleen's curtain; Sister was flushed and alert—it was almost the end of the shift. They must wait to open the curtains until the orderly leaves the ward, Sister told Colleen and backed into the corridor. Colleen heard the body lowered onto the clashing gurney.

"Thank you, Sir, you're quite strong," Sister said to the orderly. Beneath the curtain, Colleen saw the wheels of the gurney wavering heavily and Sister's foot kicking at a brake. The nebulizer began to steam and hiss as Colleen handed it to Mr. Newton. There was no other sound but the rushing of oxygen. Saline popped against the nebulizer's plastic pipe. Mr. Newton sighed and then drew on the mouthpiece. His eyes bulged; he seemed fixed on the breathing.

Colleen came out and looked at the empty bed. She peeled the fitted sheet away from the mattress and stuffed it into a linen hamper. She sprayed the liner with Dettol and wound the bed down to flatten a crease where fluid had pooled. It would need to be carbolized. She tossed her cloth in the hamper and stood at the sink and washed her hands for a while. The gurney was still parked outside Sister's office. Day shift had arrived. They sat waiting to start report. Sister was releasing the body to the orderly. Sister used the gurney rail as a writing surface and signed her name on the release form. When the double doors swung closed, Colleen tied all the curtains back neatly for breakfast and morning rounds. The men sat upright, resting against their fluffed pillows. They seemed shy and quiet now that the curtains were open. Some of them slapped on aftershave, clean shaven and ready for the day.

11 : BASE CAMP

THE YEAR COLLEEN MARRIED NICK, MALCOLM EMIGRATED TO Australia with his rebirthing instructor. Nick and Malcolm had been guitar partners at UCT before Malcolm dropped out of the music program. Colleen and Nick had graduated, and found jobs, and planned to stay in Cape Town. Nick taught music at Wynberg. They lived in a nearby flat. Nick led the school band, and practiced at home with his own wind instruments so he could understand problems his students had with tonguing and reeds and embouchure. Sometimes he performed guitar duets in a small theater at Michaelis with a new partner. Colleen received her community health pin and drove around Mitchell's Plain for home visits. She liked being welcomed into the people's houses. In the afternoons, she helped at the TB clinic. She'd chosen the job because she had weekends off.

Colleen saw Malcolm the day before the plane left—a Saturday morning. She had gone across the street to the kiosk, and stood in line reading the paper. Malcolm was in front of her. He'd just been to the pawn shop to collect money on his instruments. He walked back with Colleen to the gate at her block of flats. They crossed Main Road. Next door to the flats was an old church with white walls and elaborate windows that occluded the morning sun. An organist practiced for the next day's service. It was chilly between the buildings. Colleen was eager to get back inside and take a shower. She and Nick had plans to climb the mountain later. Nick wanted to take the trail over to

Silvermine. Colleen held the plastic bag with the newspaper and two bottles of guava juice and Nick's pasty. It was a breezy, pleasant day.

About Nick, she heard Malcolm say, "He keeps you in line."

Colleen thought how placid Malcolm's indifference was; how it made her feel dull and numbly agreeable.

He also said, while they stood there and cars rushed by, "Look me up if you're ever in Victoria."

He gave her a kiss, a quick, moist pressure, dutiful—worse than reluctant—what seemed to have to be done. Colleen thought that if Nick had looked out through the balcony and seen this, he would have shrugged his shoulders; he was not easily threatened. He often said that he pitied Malcolm. She still wished she had groomed better before leaving the flat. It was always times like this that she met people she hadn't seen in a while. She rubbed at what she knew to be smeared mascara from the previous day. She gathered her hair up from inside the back collar of her T shirt. Malcolm himself smelled as if he'd also not bathed. She remembered this about him after the Defense Force, after his subsequent week on K4 (he'd been admitted only days after coming home and had only vague memories of the time there); he'd taken pride in his lack of hygiene, flaunted it.

The gate to the flats had locked behind her when she'd left for the kiosk, or someone else had gone through and closed it. She searched around in the grit at the bottom of her purse for the key. She removed her wallet and several tubes of lipstick.

"When did you use your key last?" Malcolm asked her, as he rechecked the latch himself.

"I don't know—I think yesterday," she said. The situation—being locked out of the courtyard—annoyed her more than it normally would have. She was always losing the key off the ring to her car keys. She found herself resisting having any conversation about such a dilemma now with Malcolm—he was leaving the country; she would never see him again. It all seemed above such matters. She shook out various rumpled envelopes. She would either have to yell for Nick, or the gardener, above the sound of traffic, the closed windows, or climb over the gate.

"Have a good trip," she said quickly to Malcolm as she pulled herself up the chain links. She dropped down to the other side, stum-

bling as she landed—she was wearing sandals with a wedged heel—
the links rattled, her feet crunched on the gravel.

When Malcolm left university the first time—this was before
SADF started sending him call-up papers—he'd spent a week in the
park in Gardens, drawing what his father called, dismissively, "the
bergie sketches." The homeless people in the park did not seem to
notice Malcolm. Most had purple faces from methylated spirits.
Malcolm managed to charcoal this as a faint gray stain along sunken
cheekbones. Before music, he had studied art. Colleen tacked one
sketch in her room at the boarding house, a *bergie*, now dead, with
eyes that moved like a 3-D Jesus bookmark.

"He looks like you," she'd told Malcolm.

"Do you really think so?" he asked her.

"In a way," she said. "His eyes? I can't explain it. I love him."

"He was Cape Malay," Malcolm said.

"That's probably it," Colleen said.

Sometimes race was a sensitive subject with Malcolm because of
his half-Indian father. Colleen was never sure who Malcolm really
wanted to identify with. Often he raged to Colleen about this issue
of passing—his parents refused to discuss it. The idea fascinated him,
crossing the color bar, like changing his own name on a birth certificate. The application had been filled out in the late 50s, decades
before, when Malcolm's father had moved from Mitchell's Plain to
Bothasig, and then on to Constantia. Malcolm had told her all this
proudly (not of his father, Colleen was meant to understand, but the
renounced heritage) and defiantly—despite the conditioned careful-
ness of his Western Province prep-school English, and in his soft
voice, his low voice, he had told Colleen to keep it a secret.

Colleen remembered how she and Malcolm had sought places to be
alone back then, anywhere, undoing buttons, kicking at trouser legs.
The last time she saw him before the draft—this always seemed clearer to her than any of the months following—they'd been at a film fes-
tival in Gardens. They were talking about going to Scratch, the multira-

cial club, to see some amateur bands. Nick might be playing. Malcolm
thought they should show their faces. They'd stopped on a bench in the
park, reaching into each other's clothes and then startling to someone's
footsteps on the pavement, a rustle of a brown paper bag, a staggering
figure disappearing, their own breaths returning. Later they'd found
their discarded Peruvian jerseys, and shook out their long hair. It was a
clear night with no moon. They left the park, sandals flapping against
their soles, going into dark doorways between shop windows to kiss.
Already, they heard live music coming from Scratch. Colleen noticed
mannequins behind Malcolm, past his dark, warm caves of eyes to their
chipped facelessness inside glass. Streetlights bore through the fabric of
the mannequins' clothes, men and women's domestic uniforms, faint
pink, pale green in the darkness, handwritten price tags hanging from
string. The glass reverberated with sound emerging up from the basement on Longmarket Street, the glass trembled deep and slight like their
bodies, the tags on the mannequins moved and fluttered.

Colleen and Malcolm used to go to Scratch before police started
closing it down every week. Someone kept reopening it. Fiona had
been there once when it was teargassed and had complained for several days about feeling "like a skinned knee." Malcolm liked to go because
he could easily purchase ganja. At Scratch, everyone danced to reggae
as if alone. This was the best thing about the place, Colleen thought—
how people went out and moved and swirled around, and gazed past
each other, slow-motion to the pauses of the bass. She'd get propelled
from one side of the floor to the other, and people would mill around,
brushing past. They all did the same sort of dancing or anti-dancing,
which diffused across minds and bodies—not that whites tried to copy
blacks; this just happened, like when Colleen read an amusing novel and
acquired strong wit for a week until the feeling dwindled, all used up.
So even the dancing was a form of exploitation, she told Malcolm once,
with a gloominess she had not really felt.

On this night, whites with punk cuts paced the foreground tugging long cords of microphones. They yelled out isolated names and
symbols of things that were bad about South Africa ("apparently very
much in the know," Malcolm joked to her), like "influx control" and
"Crossroads" and "Independent States."

"There he is," Malcolm said, laughing fondly.

Colleen recognized Nick from Malcolm's classical guitar duet at Baxter Hall. On this stage, Nick was shirtless and thin and sunburned, and paced back and forth with an electric guitar dangling from its strap. He reminded her of the larger cats she'd seen in game parks. He rounded his shoulders in a way that seemed both resistive and obliging. At Baxter, he'd been sitting on a folding chair next to Malcolm, their faces concentrated on their fret boards. Both of them had strong, graceful hands. They'd been playing a required piece called "Oriental" that they had been working on for months. But this night at Scratch, Colleen could see, even not knowing him, how nervous he was. When his turn came to call out a word, his voice was tense and forceful and carefully steady. Whites in the crowd nodded, began tentatively to chant. People halfheartedly tried to dance. Africans milled upstairs to hallways. Everyone stood with red, glossy eyes.

"Absolute crap," Malcolm said, pushing back to Colleen through a narrowing crowd with their Cokes. "I must tell him tomorrow. He shouldn't waste his time like this."

"They seem to mean well," Colleen said.

Malcolm looked at her irritably and back at the stage.

"They clash!" a girl snapped at her. "Apartheid is so self-perpetuating. Look at them."

Colleen and Malcolm stood alongside a spray-painted wall. Pieces of moss advanced through small cracks. It was an old building. Colleen thought of a time in Cape Town when the hole was dug, when heaving bodies dug this hole, placed bricks inside it. She ran her finger along knobby plaster, pieces of brick from hot fires of old kilns. Beyond the drumming, a hardness seemed to thud inside her like a shovel hitting ground rock. She felt embarrassed for the loud, white, crestfallen boys, their attempt at cohesion, and the stoical Xhosas behind them.

"*Phumla ngoku*," "Take a break," people called to the performers. Nick immediately knelt and began to unplug his guitar from the amp. "Bob Marley," someone suggested. Speakers crackled, a needle was dropped on overused vinyl, and "Redemption Song" began. People crept back on the dance floor, bobbing in slow and singular motions.

When the SAP came down the steps, "Rebel Music" kept going until it skipped, then stuck. The disc jockey had disappeared. The police lifted the needle and rubbed it scraping back and forth across the record. As Malcolm pulled her toward the door, she saw the stereo blinking green gauges of amplitude, as if someone might want to know.

The next week, Malcolm received call-up papers rerouted to his latest address, and after that Colleen didn't hear from him. His phone had been disconnected, and he refused to answer the door of his flat. Colleen took the train back to her boarding house, humiliated. He had gone somewhere to dodge the draft again and hadn't trusted her this time. She started to imagine him dead from types of suicide, his body inert and rotting in a private, chosen place. How desperate had he been? She could not make a decision about what to do. It was Nick who phoned to let her know that Malcolm had barricaded himself in a friend's flat in Tamboerskoof, but when the SADF arrived, he'd followed them willingly.

While Malcolm was at base camp, Nick asked Colleen to meet him at the Pig and Whistle. He wanted to discuss options for Malcolm. They drank a pitcher of beer. Nick's hair had grown out, and he brushed it impatiently away from his eyes. On a small pocket notebook, he copied down a list of contact numbers he thought they both should call. They talked about the End Conscription Campaign, which had just been founded. Nick said he wanted to get Malcolm out of this. Colleen was feeling angry with Malcolm and said that if he'd stayed in university, none of this would have happened. "I can't really see him leaving basics to go on a hunger strike in jail," she said.

"You despise him now," Nick said, out of loyalty to Malcolm. He seemed surprised and intrigued.

Malcolm was given a two-day leave. Colleen waited for him at Observatory Station, and they walked the few blocks to her boarding house. He'd been in basics for over a month. They didn't talk. He clung to her hand. He wore the brown uniform and combat boots. He put his beret on her head. They pushed the half-open front door into the long, dank hallway of the Cape Victorian.

"Your landlord needs to put a lock on this door," Malcolm observed. "You were lucky it was just a drunk you tripped over that night on your way to the loo."

Colleen opened her room. Early sunlight filtered yellow through the ivy outside her window. She set her keys on the mantle and percolated coffee on a hot plate.

"You've never worried about that door before," she said. "I guess they're teaching you about the total onslaught." She actually dreaded going to the toilet in the middle of the night, took baths during the day, while everyone was in the kitchen, and, if necessary, would clutch her Philips-head screwdriver in her robe pocket and tiptoe to the back *stoep*. She'd pause there, adjusting to courtyard darkness—Table Mountain straight ahead, the remote solitary light of the cable-car building, and dim roofs of sheds behind old shops of Lower Main Road—and step down, waiting at the corner of the next wall before she ran the last few steps. No one would be hiding except the landlord's tortoises and guinea fowl.

Malcolm lit a John Player. Colleen asked him about base camp. He said they shot at black targets, tightly stuffed hand-sewn black scarecrows winding up on pulleys from pits, human sized. The stuffing could not burst, even with barrages of bullets. He described the bed making, and the shoe polishing, and on-the-spot marches, left turns, right turns.

"If you wanted structure in your life you might have chosen a different major," Colleen said. "You like it, I think."

"You have no idea," Malcolm said.

Later, they went to his parents' house to swim. His mother had invited them for dinner. The sun pressed down gray through her sunglasses like a kind of eclipse. Colleen had been lying in an inner tube, studying for a Monday exam, holding her notebook high away from her, and she felt chilled, her buttocks cold under clammy spandex. She stood dripping on the concrete while Malcolm uncorked a Nederberg and passed her a glass, touching her nipple playfully, but a naturalness had gone, their freedom with each other had disappeared. They gulped their wine, viewed the great aqua pool, its lurid blue stillness, drowned insects by the ladder, floating.

He poured more wine into their glasses. Colleen was warm now, calmer, curled sideways on her towel near his lawn chair, wishing his parents weren't home, that they'd done more in her room that morning than talk about base camp, breathing in his drying chlorine and sweat, these elements, these minerals and molecules all from his skin and the air and her nostrils, the red Cape wine a part of her tongue and her mouth, her saliva and blood. She held her glass up before the sun. Red fragments of light danced on their bodies.

"You mentioned the total onslaught," Malcolm said. "It's all they ever talk about, Colleen. *Die swart gevaar*, black danger. How blacks will rise up and sweep us all into the sea. One chap, a lieutenant, gave this bizarre lecture." Malcolm was laughing; he had emptied the wine. "He told us that communists infiltrated our society with certain symbols, to create decadence among whites, to weaken us. 'We need to be morally strong,' he said."

Malcolm gazed down the hill at the road without interest. Servants cycled along ringing jittery bells. Ten speeds passed with helmeted cyclists on their way up and over Constantia Nek, and their long winding coast down to Hout Bay.

"I don't know what's wrong with me," Malcolm said. "I've become clumsy. I can't even clean my R2, can't even take a breech block out to clean it, or put it back in. Semi-automatics aren't really that complicated. I feel like an idiot."

"That's weird, considering your mechanical ability," Colleen said. "I mean, you fixed up that old Lancia. It's only because you don't want to use the gun. Who would?"

Malcolm swallowed hard and suddenly covered his face, and looked away, blinking rapidly at the sky.

"It's OK," she said. "It is. A good thing maybe." She reached through the lawn chair for his hand.

"Is it?" Malcolm said. "Sometimes I can get the magazine on." He rose from the lawn chair. "I'm going to the cellar to get more wine, perhaps that Roodeberg."

Malcolm did not call her for several weeks. His mother said he was learning riot control. "Next thing we know, he'll be over at

Crossroads shooting people," his mother told her grimly.

Colleen heard the gate open one day and looked up from her desk at the window. It was Malcolm, in a blue exit uniform, the collar unbuttoned, a half-empty bottle of Mainstay in his hand. He hesitated by her landlord's goldfish pond. He petted a cat. Colleen's landlord stopped and stared at him on his way to the postbox. "You look bloody awful, Malcolm," he said, and clicked open, clicked closed the gate.

Malcolm invited Colleen to Cape Point for tea. He asked her to drive. He said he had to sober up; he'd just gone through a robot on Lower Main Road. She pulled a jersey on. It might be cold there, she thought. The old Lancia smelled of cane, foam rubber, and crisp, peeling vinyl. Colleen unrolled the window. She rounded sharp curves, turned her face down long, red cliffs to the ocean. Malcolm slept, oblivious.

She parked in front of the tearoom, which was closed. A few people were posing for photos by the lighthouse. Baboons rummaged in one of the dumpsters. A west wind punched the small car. Malcolm wanted to go out on the rocks. They stumbled around. They found another path that led out onto the fynbos and walked in a vast circle. Her ears hurt. She and Malcolm rushed back—the car was warm from the sun and protected. They faced what they knew to be the merging current of the two oceans. She thought she saw a long ridge of whitecap dividing them, but such waves were everywhere in this wind. She tried, every time she visited Cape Point, to identify where or how the water came together, but she was always in doubt.

Because Malcolm had still been drinking the Mainstay, his voice wavered. He told her he would never have to return to the army, not even for weekend camps. An incident had occurred, and afterwards—when he'd spent a few nights without sleep—he'd been sent to the psychiatric unit on the base. Then he was discharged. The incident had happened during a night of guard duty when his gun accidentally fired. The new guards had been instructed to search everyone. It was required that they demand ID from even the most highly ranked officers. One officer had shoved Malcolm aside. There was a scuffle—Malcolm said he had persisted; he must search; he'd thought it was a trick, some test of his thoroughness. The machine gun fell and fired across the ground, spinning away. No one had been hurt. The alarm went off, and then the emergency spotlights. Other soldiers surrounded them. Malcolm had been punished along with his whole platoon.

"That was it," Malcolm said. "Everyone wanted to fuck me over after that. These blokes in my platoon from Pretoria, all scrubbing me down hard with a steel brush in the shower. Don't look at me like that. They beat me up, I admit it, I couldn't stop them. Not once did I block a single blow. They weren't even big guys. It happened for a couple of days. Everyone knew about it."

Colleen could not speak. Then she said, tentative, "They didn't try to . . ."

"They did not," he said.

"They called me a *goffel*." He shook his head. "I must begin to stay out of the sun. Do you think I look Cape colored?"

"No," Colleen said. "But . . ."

"Do I?" he asked her again. He grabbed her arm hard, and let go, pushing it away, into her lap under the steering wheel. Crossing his own arms, he settled back in his seat. "Say it another time! '*No!*'"

She obeyed him with a kind of fear, or caution. She said his name to him—Malcolm. She heard herself saying the name, as if imploring him in some way—he must repossess himself—it seemed she could demand it of him if she made an effort. But there was something inside her that seemed to resist such effort. It was more than the sudden revulsion of the moment, tempered hastily by pity, and her rage against the army itself, the ready object of blame. She had a dreamlike sense of watching him, as if he were a patient dying some fast death beyond her control—but his turn, not hers, not her turn. That same awful relief, a respite. As if his was not her ordeal. They stared at each other. Perhaps Malcolm understood this, and in all the months they stayed together after K4, when Colleen took pride in her commitment, and Malcolm grew stronger again, and other women wanted him—valued him as she had not—she knew the meaning of his disappointment in her.

Colleen suggested they start back to town. She touched his arm, and peered in the backseat hoping they had confiscated his R2. She pushed hard the gear into reverse.

12: THE CRY ROOM

IT WAS THE LAST TIME SOMEONE EXPRESSED DISAPPROVAL ABOUT Gavin. Colleen clenched hot chips in a handful. She looked up at a woman in lint-free crushed velvet. She was all black and red, like something Colleen colored before kindergarten, thick and waxy, something she had taken the sharp end of her mother's scissors to scratch designs across. Colleen examined the woman's square bob, its perfect symmetry. The hair swung over the first forming of jowls like a curtain.

"How old is your baby?" the woman asked.

"Four months," Colleen lied, four instead of five, an attempt at prevention. Gavin gnawed his teething ring and spun it wet across the high-chair tray. Nick lifted his head from the road atlas and rubbed his face. He had not shaved.

"Oh." The woman smiled, polite. Colleen waited. "But he's so small, don't you think, for four months?"

Colleen nodded. Gavin, in fact, was skeletal. His neck was a long stem and his bobbing chin pointed.

"My babies were all in the top percentile," the woman said. Gavin whimpered. "Poor little guy," the woman said. She stood with her tray of hot sandwiches.

"He has a heart defect," Colleen explained, but the woman was talking brightly to her children at a table behind Colleen. Two boys removed wrappers from their food.

Colleen could not swallow. Nick drank his coffee. The red of the

woman's blazer wobbled around on his pupils. "You weren't exagger-
ating about this sort of thing," he said. He gave Gavin his rattle from
the floor. "The hospital's right off N1," he said. "Come look."
Colleen sat next to him and they held the road atlas upright, a kind
of partition, like a cereal box at breakfast, bright with mazes.

At the hospital, Gavin was lively and smiled between heaving sighs of
breaths. A nurse placed him in a metal crib. His blue-gray fingers gripped
the bars and rattled them. He rolled over and looked out at a crying baby
across the room. Gavin gummed the bar and stared. His brown eyes took
up his whole face, a wide-eyed gazing, attentive and sometimes dreamy.

The nurse asked Colleen to remove his playsuit. She syringed chloral hydrate into Gavin's mouth. He sputtered and kicked. "Don't breastfeed him now, Mrs. Evans," she said. "He could vomit." Gavin became
a pressing weight in Colleen's lap. He snored, rapid, high sounds.

Nick paced and the other baby cried and Gavin kept snoring.
"You might as well go find the hotel," Colleen suggested. She was
aware of her tongue moving against her teeth—thick, half-numb, and
newly autonomic, with its matter-of-fact prepared statements.

"All right," Nick said, in a similar bland way, putting on his
jacket. He stared inside Gavin's crib for awhile. "I'm just glad he
doesn't know."

"Me too," Colleen said, her part in what seemed to her like a
litany. At first, Colleen used to say it, "*It's good he doesn't know what's
going to happen,*" insisting to Nick that she was not being pompous,
not borrowing clichés to define her child's crisis. A month ago Nick
still ranted about ethics. "I would like to persuade him when he can
understand the odds." "This should be his decision, not ours." But
now, this last week, *He doesn't know, I'm glad*, was Nick's line to any
caller, even the insurance people. He'd repeat it like a continually
sudden realization. The change had to do with the new camcorder.
Nick's guitar partner had brought it over after their Saturday per-
formance, and they'd all tested it out after dinner, passing it back and
forth. They bounced the picture off ceilings, zoomed in on plates of
chicken bones, and then Nick, almost incidentally, focused on Gavin,

struggling to breathe, propped up in a baby seat. Nick stood still, filming, perversely. "Stop it," Colleen had said. But he kept taping, directly, no more wide angles, and Colleen and the friend had been quiet and uncomfortable.

Colleen waited for the pre-op echocardiogram, relieved that Nick would not be there, staring in that transfixed way at the screen. A large dark man with a prayer cap peered around the door. "Mrs. Evans? Is this Gavin?" He shook Colleen's hand, told her he was the doctor on call for the night. "The baby's had echoes before, right? You know how it goes. Shaw likes to have a good picture before surgery."

The basement hall was very still. Colleen heard the rumble of a generator, the sudden clatter of a vending machine. The doctor waited by a door. Gavin's head swayed over Colleen's shoulder. Her blouse was wet with drool.

Gavin lay sprawled on a vinyl table in his diaper. The doctor rotated a sensor across Gavin's chest. Colleen held his limp fist. The room was dark and warm. The screen shimmered, multicolored, with arrows over throbbing shadows. The doctor pressed the keyboard and made white crosses, centering them over certain places, a map, contours.

"This is your son's heart," he said. Colleen saw the jumping mass. "Here's the ventricular septal defect, the hole, the blood moving back and forth between the ventricles. It shouldn't be doing that."

He hunched before the screen with his forearm paused over Gavin. He held the sensor tight. "This is a good sized VSD," he acknowledged. Colleen almost felt proud. "No wonder he has heart failure. The surgeon will just put a patch over that. Sort him out right away." The screen changed after a while to cross sections, television-screen static. The room was warm and dark green, some kind of womb. "Here's the mitral-valve defect. Wow, he's really overcompensating."

Gavin suddenly began to thrash about. He woke up from the chloral hydrate. The doctor asked Colleen to hold him down. She leaned across the table. The baby's eyes flew open and glared emptily; they seemed covered, veiled, Saran-wrapped. "Kids don't act themselves with the chloral hydrate," the doctor commented. "Just a few more pictures and we're done."

Gavin dozed again, his skin green-blue from the monitor, which switched from light to shadow as his heart, or pieces of it, convulsed hurriedly, running a race. The room sounded like rain falling fast. "How will they stop his heart?" Colleen asked.

The doctor typed a final entry and reached for the light. Colleen sheltered the baby's face from the glare. "With Pavulon," he replied. "It slows the heart right down." He suggested they look at the heart-lung machines over in OR. "You're the kind who'd like to see them," he said. Colleen wondered what kind of person, not her, but maybe a person with a preference, a choice, alternatives. She walked beside the man, clutching her son in a bath blanket.

"What do you do?" the doctor was asking her.

She told him she was a community health nurse. She did not feel like one.

"Oh yes, you'll understand this then. There's the machine." He pointed through a long window. "It's a pump. It simulates the pumping action of the left ventricle. An oxygenator functions for the lungs."

"How do you get the blood out?" Colleen wondered.

"With cannulas," he replied, as if this was something to be assumed. "It gets filtered, oxygenated, brought back to either the aorta or the femoral artery. The heart and lungs are bypassed. A surgeon's free to work."

Colleen liked the man. She imagined him adhering to the rules of Leviticus, buying kosher meat. "It's called extracorporeal circulation," he said. "Outside the body."

Colleen hardly noticed Gavin's roommate, the other baby, during the night. Its cries were muffled by the reverberating generator, the heat blowing soft out of radiators. The other baby's apnea monitor beeped. Nurses tiptoed in, pressed a reset button, tiptoed out. Colleen watched them through a plexiglass partition. They disappeared down the hall. Colleen had been awake, her face sticking to the vinyl chair-bed. She thought about getting up, taking her shower before the other mothers. She needed to get her makeup on, she could not feel ugly. She remembered intensive care in Gavin's first week of life, the rocking chair by the baby cart, rocking back and forth, breastfeeding him with all his tubes scratching her skin. She remembered seeing herself in the mirror in a public bathroom. She had been fat, she'd looked pregnant in a deflated, vacant way, wearing that white, stained maternity tracksuit, waddling around with pads sliding up her pants, her despair, her lack of control. She could not feel like that again.

Gavin sat up in his crib. He pushed his face between the bars. He smiled and tugged at Colleen's sleeve. He curled next to her to breastfeed, pausing often to catch his breath, intent, fervent, sometimes looking up at her to grin. Colleen touched his two white bottom teeth in a game they played. The teeth were square and pale in the darkness, reflecting the bright hallway.

The nurse walked past and stopped. She reminded Colleen about the feedings, one more at 8:00 and then nothing before the surgery at 3:00. She frowned, sympathetic. "You're both going to have a long day. He's going to be furious with you. Mom right there and no milk." Colleen agreed. She realized that she could not see beyond the exact minute.

Nick arrived. It was 10:00. He took Gavin and walked with him. His footsteps had a deliberate lilting sound, a kind of quiet dance. Colleen applied mascara in front of a blurry towel dispenser. The other baby cried. Maybe the daylight was too strong, over by the window. The crib looked cold and exposed, gray, part of the outdoors.

Nick and Gavin gazed down into the crib. "What's wrong with her?" Nick asked.

"I don't know. I didn't ask," Colleen said. "Is it a girl?"

"Here's her name, Ramona."

"She cried all night. Whimpered. Cried and cried and cried," Colleen said. "But I hardly even heard her. Just another white sound."

Nick shifted Gavin, and smiled, a grimace. His dimples became great fissures. "Benjamin Spock comes to mind," he said with cheerful disdain. "Leaving a baby to cry."

Colleen felt irritable. "I'm not the world's mother," she snapped.

Nick did not answer. His eyes were bloodshot, she could hardly tell brown from white. The silence felt like accusation.

Colleen stepped over and peered into the crib. The baby was lying on her back at the bottom of a row of bars. She must have just rolled over. Her face was creased into pink criss-crosses from a loose blanket. Her hair could be called blonde. It curled about her head in sweaty tufts.

"I don't know what you're being so self-righteous about," Colleen said, glancing back at Nick. "You got to sleep in a bed." She craved the normalcy of a bad mood, perhaps even an argument, and his paced responses, instead of this evasive polite hospital Nick, a hospital husband.

The baby, Ramona, regarded Colleen with eyes of a doll—blue, glazed play jewelry. They opened and closed, and her hands too, clenched and then fanned out. She was even younger than Gavin, all tiny bones covered with veins and skin. Her mouth pulled down, uttering little same high sounds. Colleen put her hand into the crib, open palmed, the way she might win over an untamed animal. The baby gripped her finger. She was still and alert before the next cry.

Colleen thought about last night, pacing in the room. She had worn the wrinkled yellow scrubs they gave her with the bed linen. She hovered by the outer window, viewing other windows in an opposite ward, going up, up in rows to a heavy, yellow-black city night sky, electronic lights of suspended televisions and monitors quivering in variance. A nurse had snapped a bedlamp on behind her, by Ramona's crib. The baby began to suckle formula. The nurse spoke gently to the baby, rocking her, stroking her thin hand. "Don't pick this baby up, OK?" the nurse said. "That's our job. The crying's hard to listen to, I know, and we're so short-staffed, we can't be in here all the time. But—it's a liability thing." Colleen had nodded.

The day nurse was feeding Ramona. She sat in a rocker and talked to Nick, told him she was working on a postgraduate degree in nursing from UNISA. "Ramona is a cocaine baby," the nurse told Nick.

"She is irritable. She can't thrive. I really shouldn't be saying anything." Colleen hid behind her novel, half-listened to the nurse sending out jargon to Nick like a scent. He flicked the mobile above Ramona's crib. Colored cardboard fish glided through the air on bobbing string. Their eyes stared, around and around. Gavin reached out from Nick's shoulder and batted at them.

Gavin started to get hungry. He wanted to eat. He could be distracted no longer. He tugged at Colleen's blouse. He threw back his head and wailed, stopping to heave quick breaths. Silence was filled immediately by the other baby's whimpers. Colleen and Nick took turns. Colleen walked a tiled line in the hall, showed Gavin the dimensionless pictures of clowns and animals, placated him in a high, self-conscious voice. Gavin screamed. Colleen saw the UNISA nurse flowing down the hall in culottes, probably a size eight like Colleen, but Colleen felt a thickness of anxiety about her own shape like an aura. Her head was heavy and huge, a great expanse of murk. She trod the hall, rubbed Gavin's tear-oiled face, his bluish fingers.

Another nurse gave Gavin a shot. He glared at Colleen in a fierce way, his lower lip pouting. Colleen wondered if this was his last aware moment, ever. She closed her eyes, saw roads ending, bridges collapsed, rivers stopped at cracked dams.

Colleen was the only one allowed in the holding room with Gavin. He slept across her chest with his mouth open. A teenage boy lolled next to them in a wheelchair. He could not sit upright. His body jerked and quivered. The room itself seemed to tremble.

The anesthesiologist was young with black eyebrows and brown eyes that did not look away. Colleen ached to trust her, remained focused on the doctor's steady gaze. She passed Gavin to her. The doctor's voice was earnest. "I'll take good care of him," she said. Colleen watched Gavin carried through a doorway to a glaring white hall.

Colleen found Nick in the parking ramp, practicing his next duet in the front passenger seat. The car door echoed as she slammed it shut. She stared ahead at spackled concrete, water stains, the hood of their car, filmy with ocean salt. Nick's guitar hummed as he set it aside. They held on to each other. Their jackets rustled. Nick touched her vertebrae inside the jacket. He pressed one, then another, and on down. The bones seemed like part of some old ritual or superstition, and Colleen began to relax.

Nick went back to his guitar. It was the incomplete sound of an accompaniment. Colleen ran her fingers through his coarse brown hair. She tried not to listen. The sounds required melody. He needed his partner. The sounds were atonal and lonely. She sensed vast spaces and gaps, she imagined the aloneness of dying. She was far away from her son and her husband. They were each alone.

Hours passed. Two women expertly played Jenga in the waiting room. Colleen heard each block being pulled from the wavering tower, expected it to fall, sat upright to watch. Her breasts leaked when it finally clattered to the table. She crossed her arms over the faint damp circles. Nick said the spots could be anything, Sprite maybe.

A nurse showed her the breast pump, a square black machine. The room was crammed with IV poles and wheelchairs. Colleen sat in one and attached a tube to the machine. She turned it on, listened to its drone, put the suction cup, clamping, hissing, to her breast. Milk started slowly, a drop, then one or two sprays, four, five. Milk converged into a stream. The bottle began to fill. Her breast was pulled, wrung, released, pulled again.

Colleen blinked, drowsy, and watched the white substance of her blood shooting through the funnel. She heard this pump, and imagined the other, with red blood spouting along clear plastic—that pump, those cylinders, an oxygenator bubbling a foamy column of blood, her son's blood, and the packed cells of her O-negative, in rubbery Red Cross bags in a refrigerator waiting. Gavin's heart stopped still, a long job to be done, and a thing pumping his life outside of him, his head extended backward under the brown-eyed woman, and the sharp domes of white light, and the evergreen canvases all over in tents, all dark red and bright red and green. But he was only a baby. She was glad she'd only known him five months, not counting all the kicking and hiccuping before he was born, and their shared fight to get him out, and she thought, he was no more than a newfound friend. It wouldn't matter so much, it wouldn't be as if she knew him for years.

She capped and labeled her two four-ounce bottles and placed them in a freezer next to stashes of other people's milk. Some bottles were frosted white slush-gray.

Gavin had come back. His body was suspended tightly, tied across the bed like drying meat, a pelt, the skin a swollen ice.

"Why is he so cold?" Nick asked. He shuffled next to the bed, and picked, bewildered, at the square of sheepskin under the baby.

The ICU nurse explained: the body was kept cold during the bypass to slow it down, to decrease its requirements while on the heart-lung machine. "He'll thaw out now." She smiled.

Gavin's eyes were slits in a strange mushroomlike face. He flinched and the alarms went off. Nick turned his head away. Colleen touched rubber and plastic tubes. Pieces of fluid started and stopped inside them. Red blood slid in, dropping down from a labeled bag, hers maybe, the bag she gave two weeks ago, lying back in a recliner. She'd pressed hard a ball inside her fist, expelling viscid sluggish matter, watching it leave her, wishing it all would go away, waiting for embalming, to be cleared through and filled by something more sustaining, to be preserved, pickled. Nick and Gavin had been at the Red Cross refreshment table. They played with a puppet, a marionette. With Nick's hands, the marionette danced and jumped. Gavin had giggled outright.

The ventilator forced air into Gavin's open mouth. The pipe hissed fake wind—on, off, on, off. Colleen sat, mesmerized, nodding to the false movement of her son's slashed, wired, taped chest.

Five days later Colleen tried to recall Gavin's mouth and nose without tubes. His lip was taped sideways in a kind of sneer. She held Gavin's hand and talked foolishly to him, read stories, held picture books before his drugged eyes. She felt invisible, the possum in

Possum Magic. Gavin did not see her. He startled at objects gripped by her void body. She stared at illustrations in the books, at talking animals in bright-colored overalls.

Colleen would sit or stand, mostly looking at Gavin on the bed, talking to him, observed by the vigilant ICU nurse on her rolling stool. Or coming up from the ramp, sudden winter light, or back down into the ramp, dampness, burial vault, she rushed through to the door with her car keys jingling and entered the mauve and pink warmth of the children's hospital, the gingerbread house in the foyer, murals, plants, long carpeted halls under skylights, her son's hot, sealed room, the breathing of the ventilator.

Or she and Nick were in the hotel, where Nick practiced Ravel, *Pavane for a Dead Princess*, and *L'Encouragement*, his parts of a duet scheduled for early August. He would not cancel. He would progress through all his chords. Colleen listened to the repetition, his mistakes, curses, the ceaseless cry of the guitar.

On a Saturday night, they returned to the hotel late. It was after midnight. A band played in the bar. People had overflowed into the lobby wearing dresses and sport coats. Colleen and Nick plodded to their room. Colleen pushed herself down deep in the tub. She heard Nick through the hot water, playing a kind of blues. He stretched the strings and held them. Notes were bending and whining. She watched him as she dried herself. The copper tube on his little finger pressed down. His hair was in his face. The sounds became higher, stupid, they clashed with each other. Nick drummed his guitar. It made a long wail. It resounded off the headboard. Nick had tossed it. He was crouching on the floor, sobbing, odd coughs, a type of choking. Colleen stood there. It did not go away. She turned the radiator knob to high. The fan roared and muffled the sounds like a blanket. She knelt and picked up his clenched fist, unbending his fingers one by one, rubbing her thumb over the calluses.

Nick muttered all night in his sleep. Colleen sometimes dozed. She dreamed of her mother. They were at church in Umtali. The minister's evening sermon echoed over the microphone. The sun had just gone down. It shone faint yellow through thick, blurred windows. Colleen's mother took Sarah to the cry room at the back of the church. Colleen saw them through the glass wall. Her sister cried, but Colleen could not hear her. The minister prayed. Then Colleen heard the long wails of an RDF siren, an alert (an earthquake, her father whispered), followed by quicker, faster sirens of distant ambulances. "Amen." The minister stopped his prayer. People milled down the aisles. But Colleen's mother stayed in the cry room. "Come on." Colleen beckoned to her. "Mommy." Her mother was huddled in a corner of the glass cry room. Sarah was gone. Flames licked around Colleen's mother's body, she wept and gnashed her teeth. *She has gone to hell, she must be saved*. Colleen felt a pressure, a heavy vaporous weight pushing her body down flat, she could hardly lift her head. An old dream, nearly forgotten.

Gavin woke up. He fidgeted with the ventilator tube and the nurse re-tied his wrist. He finally began to breathe on his own. They returned to the room with Ramona. Nick argued with the nursing supervisor, demanding to be moved. "Our only privates are the isolation rooms," she told him.

Nick went home, back to work. Colleen and Ramona and Gavin breathed and fed and dozed under the glare of the fluorescent hall light. It was the first night back in the room. Gavin had started to breastfeed again, grasping her fingers, looking up at her, earnest. She touched his scabs and bruises, the peeling tape across his chest, the scaly redness. His hands and feet were warm and pink, unmottled, entirely without blueness. Colleen squinted to make sure. Ramona had not moved from her place at the outer wall. She whined and gasped. The apnea monitor beeped aimlessly. Nurses reset it. She seemed smaller, flailing around in her hospital-issue, one-piece undershirt.

Colleen would lie awake in the chair-bed. She tried to sleep, heard nurses laughing, she could smell their buttered popcorn. Her mother tells her stories in the dark, a Donald Duck night light, time to go to sleep. Colleen dreams about a bear sneaking down the hall, her heartbeat the padded paws on the parquet floor of her bedroom. She opened her eyes, frozen. Gavin's back was striped with the crib's shadows. He did not move. Colleen jerked up onto her elbow and blinked through the bars. She waited for his breath. "Help," she yelled.

The nurse panted from running. She put her head to Gavin's face and prodded him with her stethoscope. She touched Colleen's shoulder. "We'll have to get used to him breathing normally," she said.

Colleen watched the slow undulation of his chest. "I thought he was . . ."

"That's OK, Colleen," she said. "He was on the vent for so much longer than usual." The nurse looked at her. "You haven't been sleeping, have you?"

Colleen shook her head.

"The worst is over," the nurse said.

Colleen tried to sleep. "It's over," her mind told itself.

Nights and days passed inside the room. Gavin slept deeply. He never seemed to hear Ramona. Colleen rocked her in the rocking chair when no one was around, usually at change of shift. She was limp and heavy, Colleen's waterlogged lullaby doll. She pulls her dripping from the dirty dishwater of the kitchen sink, soaking pans resettle, maybe Sarah put her in there, she's always playing with Colleen's toys. Colleen rocked Ramona, back and forth with the crying that never stopped. She looked straight down into the blue stone glitter eyes.

The surgeon was impressed with Gavin's scar. He noticed that breastfed babies heal faster. "Otherwise this would still be a nasty looking gash." He traced the red line. "He'll grow now." He smiled at Colleen. Her face was a slab. She tried to move her mouth.

"The crisis is over, Mrs. Evans. Get some sleep." He backed out of the room. "Sleep while he sleeps," he added.

This word, sleep, flourished in Colleen's mind. It would get said separate from her own thinking. The word became itself a voice, a person's voice, it forbade its own meaning and function. Colleen stayed awake. She did not read, she could not concentrate, and blankly watched children's shows on TV, chef shows after that, listened to the vigorous voices, to didactic purpose. One compartment of herself remained moving for the babies. Gavin began to smile again. Puppets were strewn all over the room. Colleen was a good dog; she made friendly animal sounds. She could deftly control the marionette.

It was night again. Ramona was crying, crying. Colleen's body ached, her head buzzed, her eyes opened and closed to outer and inner sound, the train clattering into a nearby station, the whine of the brakes, the stupid same word—sleep. She wore her yellow cotton scrubs. She was lying on the chair-bed clutching its arms. She must have closed her eyes. Behind her lids was the imprint of the bars of both cribs, shadowy lines inverted to white rods. A haze. Ramona clenched her fists up to her mouth. She thrashed from side to side, moaned, howled, caught her breath. Colleen's pillow prickles under her ears, the feathers crinkling, scratching, a nest. Colleen stands over Ramona, drops the pillow down, no noise, pushes against the feathers with her hand, pushes the soft feathers. Colleen sleeps. She wakes up, cozy, warm, fuzzy, sees Gavin next to her behind the bars. The room is silent. Colleen goes to the window, faint white-gray of morning over Ramona's crib—mute girl, dolly. Colleen screams.

Nurses charge the room. "Call a code," one yells. Gavin cries. His eyes dart back and forth. Colleen holds him. She stares at Ramona in the bright light. They squeeze a black bag over a mask on her face. The room fills with people. A nurse pulls a curtain across the center of the room. "Stand back," a woman shouts. People push the curtain backwards. Gavin's table scrapes across the floor and his crib rolls. Colleen stands between the furniture with her live baby.

The room was empty, cluttered with used syringes and tourniquets. Ramona was lying underneath a sheet. Colleen balanced Gavin on her hip and lifted the sheet from Ramona's face. Pulled it up, lifted it off, over and over. Looked at the dead baby. Over and over. Gavin reached for the sheet. He thought it was a game. Colleen pulled his hand away. She remembered the dream. "Was it a dream?" she asked. She remembered the soft pillow. "I did it. I killed her." She placed Gavin in his crib.

The nurses wrapped and taped Ramona inside white plastic. Colleen stood there. "How did she die?" Colleen asked.

"Respiratory arrest," one replied, tying a tag around the feet. She looked at the male nurse. "We need to get biomed to have a look at that apnea monitor," she said.

An orderly rumbled in and out with a squealing gurney. He took Ramona away.

Gavin's nurse cleaned the empty crib. Colleen curled into the chair-bed, wrapped in a sheet, touching the pillow, picking white feathers from a hole. They floated to the floor. "You killed her," she told herself. "You stood there and smothered her with this pillow." All was clear.

"I did it," Colleen told the nurse. She blurted out her secret. The nurse dragged a chair next to Colleen and sat and looked at her. "You were asleep," she said, firm. "Dreams are strange. You may have sensed something was wrong."

Colleen shook her head.

"You're losing it," the nurse said after a silence.

Someone permitted Colleen to push Gavin in a stroller around the halls. She was haunted, nothing mattered, not this healing baby perched forward, looking ahead, side to side, kicking his feet. There had been a sacrifice; she had the knowledge of it. She was dangerous. Over and over came the thought. Dreams and reality layered on top of each other, and behind each other, mixtures and reminders of wrongdoing and banality and the covert. She trotted behind the stroller, on down the corridor.

13 : KAMGA

BEFORE THEY REACHED THE N2, GAVIN HAD TAKEN TWENTY-FOUR pictures of goats. The goats were everywhere, following the road, crisscrossing it, picking their way through mud in groups—males, females, babies. Some disappeared into the bush.

"I don't know if they'll have film in Kamga," Colleen said. Gavin's other roll, developed after the game reserve last weekend, was mainly blurred elephants inside cloud shadows, many with his thumb, but he had one clear shot: a locust climbing several blades of grass. The camera was Gavin's first one, part of a spy kit he'd ordered with his cereal-box coupons. Colleen slowed the car for him again.

"I still have film in here," he said. "Because it isn't rewinding." He took a tinted plastic spyglass out of his vest pocket and covered the lens with it. The back of his neck was upright and intent and vulnerable looking. He aimed the camera in various directions. The lens buzzed in and out, the goats passed slowly by, but he did not click again.

They'd driven a half hour from Morgan Bay, sliding around on the clay road, yet if Colleen listened carefully through Gavin's open window, she could still hear the waves. It had just stopped raining. She told Gavin it was too misty to see Mpetu Kop, the Boer War battle-ground where, according to their Eastern Cape travel book, Boers and Xhosa had fought each other with bayonets in 1901. There had been no survivors on either side, no one to carry the bodies down from the low rocky hill—the kopje—and it became known as *Mpetu*

Kop, a Xhosa-Afrikaans blend meaning "Maggot Head." Although the name itself fascinated her, she'd recently wondered about the battle with her husband; both had been confused. "Don't they mean British or Zulu?" Colleen had asked. "Were the Xhosa in the Boer War?" "They're thinking of battles during the Voortrekker times," Nick had said in his gurulike way. "Bloody idiots. Who put that book together?" Colleen and Nick themselves were vague about their South African history. "Lies," Nick usually called it, with a certain practiced disdain. He claimed to have read "the only true record," *Time Longer than Rope.* Back in Rhodesia, Colleen's regional history textbooks had always reminded her of soap operas. Their blithely ignored contradictions used to make her blush with a personal shame, and throughout high school and college she'd preferred Europe. She recalled latching onto Europe with an almost blind loyalty, like some adopted children seek a biological mother.

Ahead of her, Colleen could not tell clumps of mist from the goats, and her feet kept moving to the clutch and brake. She relaxed once she turned onto the highway. She knew she shouldn't. She had been warned by her father-in-law about the roaming livestock, new drivers on the road without licenses, the pedestrians, the speeders, the perils of the N2. Colleen was convinced that Nick's parents' retirement, which coincided with the end of colonialism, had made them at least mildly paranoid. But everyone felt that way now, including herself. "One has to be," Nick's mother pointed out. "It's a form of survival." So it made sense to Colleen, their recent listing of the Morgan Bay cottage. The tenants had emigrated months ago. The cottage could not be left empty.

It was Nick who balked at his parents' real estate decisions, especially this one. Colleen wasn't sure if it was greed or nostalgia. Nick would not say. "It's difficult for you to understand," he had said. "Zimbabwe's not the same thing." After his parents' burglary in April, they'd sold the house where he'd grown up and moved into a gated community across from Pollsmoor prison. Nick had teased them about their view of Table Mountain through the chain-link fences. The mountain loomed up, blue-gray, fortresslike behind the new Cape Dutch condominiums. Nick joked about his father playing golf in full view of the prison tower across the road. "Who's the prisoner?" he asked.

"They have post-traumatic stress," Colleen had said, repeating back Nick's own jargon. "It was a very bad experience. Maybe even worse when you're older." The burglar had been in the house with Nick's parents. A knife had been held to their throats. The man was unstable and the knife had trembled. Colleen felt compelled to emphasize this fact.

"Their stress is nothing," Nick had said, passing her a newspaper with the latest statistics on AIDS.

Yet when Nick's parents received an offer on their cottage with contingencies, Nick agreed to help with repairs. He wanted to see the bay one last time and show Gavin the tidal pools there, all the unusual sea anemones. Gavin was on school holiday; Nick had already been off since the school band concert in late November. Colleen traded vacation hours with another nurse. They'd all flown to Port Elizabeth and spent a weekend at Addo, and ended up driving, the five of them in the rental, the last stretch after dark. Colleen had been in the back seat, pretending to sleep through the hairpin bends of the Ciskei. She tried to block out her husband's frustration, her mother-in-law's odd new road terror. Even after the burglary, it was not Gwyneth's style. That night, Colleen had only half-recognized her, the way she might know her inside a dream, with faces and names intermingling and no set place.

Now, a week later, Colleen realized the narrow width of the two lanes. Paved shoulders had disappeared. She was reminded of the strip roads near her father's farm. She noticed that the usual cautionary road signs were nowhere to be seen this far east: reflective orange billboards and their electronic numbers, tallies of traffic deaths per hundred kilometers. Those signs, like digital clocks outside banks, changed in some other instant when Colleen wasn't watching. Whose job was it? she'd wonder. Who sat behind a computer and entered such data? That someone was keeping track reassured her. Colleen would try to squint beyond the billboards, especially when the sun glared, appalled at the bewildering surge of relief she'd get, as if the numbers weren't deaths but lives saved, or some other statistic, cricket scores maybe, advertising polls.

It would be much easier, Colleen thought, if they could just buy groceries down at the BP station. The convenience store was now a rest area complex, built onto the old Transkei border post. "It has everything," her mother-in-law had told her, even fresh fish from the Kei Bridge. But Colleen had offered to make copies of the original land survey. She was supposed to fax it to Johannesburg if she could. The assignment gave her a vague sense of purpose. It was the most useful she'd felt all week, freed up from the sorting of Nick's old souvenirs, conch shells, and rocks, her always having to ask, "What should I do with this? And this?" The cottage's buyers—a white couple who annually hiked the Strandloper Trail—wanted proof that there was always an easement for the rondavels next door. "Bloody Transvaalers," the estate agent had said. "They've already done their own survey. And you won't find copy machines in Kamga," he told them. "Faxes, anything of that sort. The place was barely a dorp before. And now?" He'd lit a cigarette. "You know then, hey."

The tires droned over a cattle grid, and Colleen looked around for livestock. It was not a likely place for grazing—near the Kei River, she thought, too much rock. She did not see the cow sitting on the no-pass line until she was right upon her. Colleen veered sideways. She braked, but forgot to gear down, and the car stalled on the shoulder. Without blinking, the cow turned her head toward them.

"I thought she was mud," Colleen said to Gavin. She glanced up at the seeping embankment. "How did she just come up on me like that?"

"She is a mud color," Gavin acknowledged.

The cow sat between the two lanes as if she'd been there for a long time. Across the road other cows rested on the ground, like rocks between boulders.

"She's going to get killed, Mom. Why is she doing that?"

"I don't know," Colleen said.

"Maybe she's already been hit. Maybe she has a broken leg."

"No—look at her." There was something obstinate about the cow that Colleen felt ashamed to admire. They called to her. Colleen whistled. Gavin practiced his whistle: the cow turned her head away. Gavin opened the door.

"I'm going to get a stick," he said.

"Get back in here," Colleen said, and she fumbled with the automatic locks of the rental car.

When they first heard the lorry, it was distant, then close, then distant, perhaps because of the way the road cut through hills, or the way rocks might muffle sound and then amplify it, and then contain it again. Colleen started the car. They would need to get out of the way. The cow had not moved.

"Go, get up, get up," Gavin began to scream to the cow. He was in the front seat with her, out of his seat belt, leaning across her toward the open window. She drove along the shoulder in first gear. She was afraid to get back onto the road, the truck was coming too fast. She could hear the rattle of the engine, the speed. It was coming downhill from the direction of Umtata. She wondered: Could the cow be deaf? Could cows be deaf? She remembered Gavin's eighth birthday last year—Gavin on his new full-sized bike with hand brakes, riding down a sudden long hill in Cape Town. He'd panicked. He'd forgotten how to use the hand brakes. She and Nick had probably not cycled enough with him on level ground. Colleen had been too far behind him. She'd been distracted by a persistent group of beggars, wavering on her bike, searching for Rand coins in her jacket pocket. Gavin wailed for a full city block. He spun the pedals backward. Colleen followed him. "Your hand brakes," she yelled, but the wind was strong on the hill, and her voice seemed to whirl inside the gusts. She watched Gavin fly through an intersection. When he finally stopped the bike with his feet, he stood astride it, ferocious, wailing. She thought of this wail as he shouted now past her ear, her helplessness, her uneasy sense of spectating.

The cow raised her head and shoulders. It seemed she might be lifting herself, but she settled back down again. The truck had not yet rounded the curve. The cow was behind them in the rearview mirror, far away, miragelike, part of the road. Colleen felt certain that the cow would not move, could not move. Colleen felt a pulling down or heaviness in her own body as if at this moment, were she to try, she herself could not walk—bumping carefully along the roadside, immobilized against her seat. She willed the cow to move, but there was no power in any of her intentions. It seemed that the cow's will was greater than her will, or that the cow had no will at all. Languidly sprawled across the road, about to die, this cow had a kind of will which was stronger and more determined in its inertia. Colleen felt influenced by it, and threatened.

Colleen hardly heard Gavin's screaming. She pushed him back into his seat and belted him in and started to turn the car around. She had to do something else. Her mind felt released, clear—she would go back and warn the truck, drive back that way and wave to the driver. Why hadn't she thought of it before? Then she saw it rounding the long curve, but it was not a truck, it was a bus, a red Shushine Ltd.—dark inside with people standing, people pressed into seats. A driver twisted the wheel. The destination sign said Bisho. Gavin was quiet. Colleen turned away. She felt her fist at her mouth. The time was longer now and she waited. The bus screeched. Colleen looked back again. The bus swerved, it was not on all its tires. It was overloaded, shifting balance—people slid on top of each other in one direction—yet it seemed light too, able to bounce, capable of flipping. Luggage wavered on the roof carrier, garbage bags, a mattress, flying rope. A suitcase spun out clacking across the road. The cow stared. The bus righted itself, and then it passed them. In a cloud of black smoke, the cow stood and stumbled into the acacia bushes.

The bus was unloading in Kamga. Colleen parked a few spaces behind it. The bus idled loudly. It would be leaving soon for Bisho. Several passengers, Africans, stepped down. They peered at the rooftop carrier through rain and oil fumes. One woman smoked a cigarette. 'She is relieved to be alive,' Colleen thought. The woman ignored the street vendors trying to sell kiwis in egg cartons.

Gavin held the suitcase in front of him, his arms stretched widely around it. The case was scratched from sliding across the road. Rain tapped on the hard plastic, an old Samsonite, popular when Colleen was a child in the early 70s, she had begged her father for one, seen them advertised at movie cinemas before the shows. This case was missing a handle, which may have fallen off during the impact. Gavin pressed it close to keep it together. The original duct tape was now curled with moisture. He struggled with the weight of it.

Back on the highway, Colleen had run to the suitcase and thrown all the contents back inside—clothes, small bags of food, samp beans, mealie meal. The sugar bag had broken across the grass and she left it there, near the resettled cow. Only the photographs Colleen had taken time with. Someone had bound them with a thick rubber band, and they'd landed in the sugar and the wet grass. She'd smeared the photos across the grass and wiped them against her jeans.

The bus driver climbed the ladder to the rooftop carrier. He began to drop labeled garbage bags onto the curbside. Colleen had been to Kamga once before, after she and Nick were married. There had been a drought, and at that time she owned a pair of brown-tinted sunglasses which made the street appear drier, more yellow, more parched. Now, in the rain, she fidgeted with the burglar alarm device attached to the Avis keychain. She was used to Nick working it. For their own car in Cape Town, she locked her steering wheel with a Club. Finally the alarm made two concise shrieks, louder than the rumbling of the bus. It was set. Colleen gazed furtively inside the storefront window, beyond the door held open with a stick. She didn't want anyone to know that she feared having her car stolen, that she even considered it a possibility.

The store was dim. Its only light came from the display window, and the veranda roof blocked much of that. An African was sweeping. He stacked benches against the wall, his back turned to her. He wore a tweed sport coat. The floor was scuffed from hard-heeled shoes. Parquet tiles had been damaged by torn out store shelves. The checkout counter had become a desk covered with cords and rotary phones, and a long row of province directories. The man rolled the swivel chairs back from the desk and swept underneath. Colleen finally read the sign—Tembisa Funeral Brokers—stenciled in white across the far window. She was used to the crematoriums in Cape Town, brick and churchlike and set apart.

At the bus stop someone had already claimed the suitcase: the woman who'd been standing with the cigarette. She and Gavin stood under the veranda of Spar Groceries. The woman was tall, thin, but

not the emaciated thin of AIDS, and looked older than she probably was, maybe because of her gray hair, which was almost white
against her face. Reading glasses dangled from a ribbon around her
neck. She seemed familiar. Colleen had glanced at the wet photos of
a man, a young boy, as she'd passed them to Gavin in the car. Possibly
this woman was the person's mother. Colleen wasn't sure.

"These are all the same guy," Gavin had said in the car, drying the
pictures in front of the defrost fan. He'd scraped granules of sugar
from one with his dirty thumbnail. He was restless since the near-
accident, aimlessly tapping the automatic window button. He fanned
the pictures out in his hand like playing cards. "Look," he'd said, and
he waved each photo in her face while she squinted at the road with
a new, almost phobic caution. "Here he's on a soccer team. The one
with the glasses. The goalie." She'd seen the pictures for seconds, but
had seen them twice—a boy in school uniform, professional baby
photos, a young man in front of the Morgan Bay Hotel, wearing
some kind of orange maintenance jumpsuit, thin and diminished in
it, with his glasses sliding down his nose. Gavin placed the pictures
across the dashboard near the vents, and they reflected back in the
window. After a while, Gavin had put the rubber band back around
the pictures and sat holding them.

The woman from the bus propped her suitcase against her leg. She
and Gavin were talking about sugar, Colleen recognized the word,
and cow, *komo*. Colleen smiled at the woman and she nodded.

"*Inkonyana*," the woman said. Colleen was confused.

"It looked to her like a calf," Gavin explained. He seemed very little between them.

The woman said some other things, mainly to Gavin. Once she
shook her head. The woman pressed a two-Rand coin into Gavin's
hand.

"Oh, no, that's . . ."

"Why not?" the woman asked Colleen in clear English, glaring.

"*Nkos*," the woman said firmly.

"You're welcome," Colleen said.

The woman held the case under one arm and walked away. The bus had gone, and so had the street vendors. Rain blew in two directions. People sat together on the sidewalk, legs outstretched, under storefront verandas along both sides of the street. Colleen and Gavin were conspicuously white. Gavin picked up a piece of tread from the curb and stepped back out of the rain, and put it in his pocket with the two-Rand piece. Colleen took her mother-in-law's list from her backpack.

"We can buy bread here in the Spar," she said, although the doors had been closed and the checkout lane was empty. She peered back at the dim aisles.

"Your Xhosa is bad, Mom," Gavin said.

"I didn't get to learn it in junior school," Colleen said. "Anyway, what did she mean by *umhloli* and all that?"

"I think she was saying 'miracle.'"

"Miracle to get the case back."

"She didn't think there was anything she could do. *Ukudana.* Try to say it."

Colleen remembered her family's trip to Johannesburg when she was in high school. Sarah had lost a suitcase filled with assorted things she'd packed without anyone's supervision—rarely used toys, unsorted junk mail—and Colleen and Sarah's baby pictures, their mother as a girl, their grandparents in their youth. Afterwards, Colleen tried to recall the suitcase, where it was in its place on the cartop carrier, but she could never see it. Everyone argued about when they'd heard it dislodge. There had been so much shuffling about on the car's roof. Colleen's father said they should have stopped when they heard a piece of the tarp flapping. The windows had been open, loud, blasting hot air, and they drove back fifty or sixty kilometers, scanning the ditches.

As they came upon each place, Colleen imagined it there—by the scenic lookout where they'd briefly stopped to use the lime-pit toilet, in the dry riverbed under a low bridge, among bones of dead springbok. At roadside markets, her father talked to villagers. "There's nothing we can do about it," her sister said grimly, repeatedly, in the front seat, watching their father gesticulate under long, thatched roofs.

He gave up. They turned back toward the city. They'd traveled hundreds of kilometers that day, and the suitcase could be anywhere. There was nothing they could do. "Do you have to keep saying that?" Colleen finally said to her sister in an irritable way.

"*Ukudana*," Colleen said to Gavin. "It doesn't require a clicking sound."

"Clicking is easy," Gavin said.

There was lightning now and thunder. People leaned against the wrought-iron pillars and watched the rain. Gavin tried to put his face under a drainpipe splashing from the roof gutter. "Don't drink that!" Colleen yelled from the ATM outside Spar.

"The ATM will not work," one of the Africans said. He spoke loud above the rattle on the corrugated iron roofs. "This whole side of the street has power down."

"I wonder where I can make copies," Colleen said, feeling in her backpack for Nick's parents' land-survey document.

"The post office is down," the man said. "You can try Guns and Ammo."

"Across the street?" Colleen asked. "I think they're closed. I saw someone try to open that door a few minutes ago."

"It is a buzzing door. For you they will buzz in."

When Colleen had visited Kamga before, it was called Paternoster. Guns and Ammo was then a cheap hotel. She and Nick had eaten lunch there. They'd argued about the mothballs at the hotel, which must have been used to store tablecloths and serviettes in the offseason. She was pregnant and the smell made her retch. To her own self, she'd sounded petulant. She admitted that she was probably being unreasonable. Maybe they should just go back to the cottage now, or go somewhere else to eat, further up the Wild Coast? He'd pushed back his chair and left her sitting in the sun with her plate of river fish and curried beetroot—she suddenly was hungry—while he went into the men's bar. She'd heard him in there, clinking glasses with a gregarious man who'd been sitting at the corner table, and she ran back to the bathroom and vomited.

Guns and Ammo was nothing like the old hotel. The floor did creak in the same way, and now it sagged. The joists needed to be raised. But all she recognized was the location of the bathroom. On the bathroom door was an out-of-order sign with red letters underneath: DO NOT USE. The white woman, the first one Colleen had seen since her mother-in-law that morning, showed them the copy machine. Colleen photocopied the land survey and let Gavin copy his hand, and while she was paying for the copies Gavin walked along the gun racks. He touched the stocks of a few rifles displayed lengthwise behind padlocked cables. The white man—the husband, Colleen decided, or brother—wore a mint-green safari suit, and stood with his hands behind him ready to serve someone.

"Just wait at the door. We'll buzz you out," the woman said. Colleen could not understand the door. She pushed it when it buzzed, but it re-locked itself, and then Gavin was whispering urgently to her.

"Do you have another toilet besides that one?" Colleen asked.

The woman laughed, a kind laugh. Colleen warmed to her.

"No, my girl, but this one is not really out of order, see."

Gavin was in the bathroom and out in a matter of seconds, and the out-of-order sign closed behind him, and Colleen heard the toilet flushing.

"We only have that sign up for some people," the woman said. She nodded knowingly at Colleen. "Now this time give the door a good push when it buzzes, see."

Colleen pushed, she shoved the door hard with her shoulder, and stood again with Gavin on the sidewalk, bewildered. "I'm not sure I heard her right," Colleen said.

On the lit side of the street, they passed more shops converted into funeral brokers. Some were carpeted, some were painted purple and aqua, some had track lighting. Doors were open. Fans oscillated and trembled. Gavin took her hand, but let it go when someone walked by, and then reached for it again. Across from Tembisa funeral brokers, Gavin ran to the car ahead of Colleen. The curbside was ankle deep with rainwater surging around a drain, which Gavin waded toward, peering into it, absently reaching for the car door. Colleen had not heard the car's full alarm before. Car alarms went off in Cape Town all the time, distant sirens, but hers, this one, reminded her of the screeching of certain birds.

Colleen fumbled in her jeans pocket for the keys. She aimed at the red light next to the ignition. She aimed, and aimed again. She shook the device. It did not seem to work. She unlocked the door and aimed again. The sound went around and around. Colleen got behind the steering wheel and twirled the device like a wand. It seemed the car had become the town's center. Her ears rang. These sound waves came from here. Everyone had this knowledge now, her white fear, her lack of trust. She was unsure what to do.

She pulled the car manual out of the glove box. She would not try for a moment. Gavin was pacing back and forth on the sidewalk with his hands over his ears. He gave her a quick, guilty look. Inside Tembisa funeral brokers, the lights were back on. Colleen took a breath. Gavin saw her too: the woman from the bus, the Samsonite beside her, one ear to the phone receiver, her finger in the other ear. She looked out past Colleen over her reading glasses. Colleen swung the alarm device back at the red light again, and the noise was done.

Rain dripped. The smell of undiluted Dettol wafted out from the Tembisa doorway as if it could not before make its way through sound. The floor had been mopped, and benches were set up in rows, as if for church, and the suited man sat behind the desk.

"Sorry," Colleen said. She did not even have to call out. It was so quiet now. There was the murmur of the woman into the phone, and the roll of her swivel chair. The woman held up her hand to them in a type of wave.

Colleen drove out of town.

"I think she was just using the phone in that place," Gavin said hopefully. "I didn't see a pay phone anywhere." He put his head back outside the window.

At the intersection of R63 and N2, a truck rattled slowly past, and Colleen waited for the procession of cars behind it. There was a strange flash that might have been lightning—the sky seemed gray enough for another storm—but the camera was rewinding. Gavin had taken a picture through the back window of a green sign that said KAMGA 2 KM.

This word sorry circled around in Colleen's head, the sound of it after the din—sorry—for what? For the intrusion of the alarm? Someone was dead—the woman's son?

She caught herself saying it again out loud, as if rehearsing something, although it was over.

Colleen bought bread and samosas at the BP. In the miscellaneous section she found the wood glue Nick wanted. After a while they were back on the dirt road to Morgan Bay. The mist had cleared since morning, and they could see Mpetu Kop now, its rocks covered with lightning marks and bird droppings. Several cows were following one another along a path. Their bells clinked in a blunt, rusted way. Colleen got out of the car and stood looking at the battleground. She felt it was required of her, with the mist gone, and the kopje's actual form right there to be seen. She watched as the cows made their way around to the other side. The grass all over was trampled and grazed. Gavin ate his samosa inside the car and said the hill did look like something to be claimed and used as a boundary, but neither of them could imagine a battle there. Colleen felt nothing except the plainness of the hill itself. There was, she acknowledged, the land and the climate all the days and centuries before the battle, and the decades after, and the time to come. She remembered what her mother first told her as a child about God: "the alpha and omega, the beginning and the end," how back then her mind skipped like a heartbeat with its odd, clear idea of infinity, moved backward and forward as if she were not limited by her own life or herself, nor were others limited. Colleen startled at a snapping in the bush and rushed to the car. Gavin was laughing—"It's just more cows"—and the cows, like the others, moved out of the acacias toward the kopje. She heard the whistle of a distant herder, and distinctly, the scraping open somewhere of a low gate across gravel. Colleen could not help but notice that the cows climbed their hill with the resignation of soldiers.

14: THE VISIT

IT WAS STILL SUMMER IN HARARE, AND AFTER BURYING HER FATHER, Colleen returned to Cape Town with a tan on her forearms and irregular white lines across her wrists. She'd worn Sarah's bangles there: Sarah had offered Colleen a set, carved, wooden, the kind Colleen wore at fifteen, confiscated by prefects. Colleen fidgeted with them constantly, twirled the bangles, twisted them. After those six days, she could still feel the bangles, dropping from one bone to another as the arms moved.

They gave some of their father's clothes to AIDS relief, and left the rest for the squatters, although Colleen did keep his favorite jersey. He used to wear it in Cape Town during his annual visits. Colleen also kept a pair of shoes, one pair of trousers, a familiar plaid shirt, and his cap. She put these clothes into her suitcase as if they were her own. She had tossed them in on their hangers.

When Colleen unpacked, sitting on the floor with Gavin, she pushed aside the clothes, rummaging around in the case for gifts. She found the Great Zimbabwe bird replicas. The two birds had slightly different beaks. One closely resembled the real Shona artifact. They had been purchased from an especially languid roadside vendor. They had not bartered. The vendor had been sleeping on a straw mat alongside the other carvings: soapstone lizards, giraffes, wildebeests, all well oiled with Canola. Colleen told Nick and Gavin about her. She realized that, besides her sister and stepmother, the woman was one of the only people she'd noticed.

Colleen carelessly draped her father's clothes over the sofa. He liked to nap on this sofa. He would cover his face with his tweed wool cap, which always made him look like he should be standing, posed, next to a vintage car. He might suddenly remove it, if he sensed Gavin watching him, and roar, and chase him in a game they called "Scary Man."

The clothes stayed there for a while—possibly a week, two weeks, until Nick asked Colleen what she planned to do with them. He suggested the attic, or their closet, if she wanted to see them every day. She imagined the clothes, whisked past, hangers sliding along, every time she selected an outfit for work, part of that cold, early morning resignation or frenzy.

But she felt stubborn. She felt irrational and selfish. The shirt stayed on the sofa on its hanger, with its sleeves contorted, the pants underneath, the cap on top. Gavin would sit on the floor, or on the sofa next to the clothes, watching the VCR. He would absently play with the shirt's cuffs. He began to wear the cap, backwards, forwards. It settled itself over his eyes. He'd adjust the narrow visor. He would put it back, somewhere in the vicinity of the shirt's collar. The cat slept beside the arrangement. It did not startle her, or turn her head. Colleen had dreams about her father, waking up from his nap, in the sleep-wake state of newborn babies, not recognizing her, not aware enough for bewilderment.

Colleen believed her father would have lived longer if he'd kept the coffee farm at Nyadzi. The land was not yet being repossessed there. Fifteen years ago, her father had bought a ground nut farm outside Harare so that Sarah could live at home. Sarah kept getting admitted to Rest Haven after she finished school. The new farm was only twenty kilometers away from Rest Haven's outpatient center. Nyadzi sold quickly—after the war, the eastern highlands had become productive again. Colleen was in Cape Town during the sale and the move. Nothing about it had ever seemed real to her. She only vaguely knew the Darwendale area—a long stretch of bush and small kopjes, across town from her old boarding school—except for a large dam, which the Fairbridges used to take them to on picnics. Sarah had been brought to this new farm, and she arranged the furniture the way it had always been at Nyadzi. The rooms were the same except for the dining room. Sarah measured proximities of chairs to one another with a tape measure. When Colleen visited, she would tell Sarah that this farm in Darwendale felt like home.

On the night Colleen left for Zimbabwe, their father had been in coronary step-down at Harare Hospital. He had blamed the heart attack—his second one—on the squatters, who'd been making beer and selling it at the highway in his cement buckets. "My name is on those buckets," he had said. "They have turned the place into a shebeen." Colleen did not think for a minute that he was dying. He was only seventy. She understood his condition, how it could go either way, but despite her nature, she'd never really considered the worst. She viewed his illness as an opportunity to take leave from work and spend some time with him. She was curious to meet his new wife, Carine. Carine had not come with him to see them last spring. Colleen also hoped that maybe she could convince Sarah it was time to leave the country. Her father had said, "I doubt it." Sarah had been talking to herself again, yelling sometimes at the voices. "Under the circumstances, this is actually good," he had said. "The squatters are frightened of her. People are never sure she isn't a witch."

Colleen found out he was dead at the airport in Johannesburg. She'd made her connecting flight, but the plane's landing gear had not come up, and they'd circled and landed again. She stood at a phone booth outside the duty free shop. Someone called out flight numbers over the intercom. She plugged her outer ear. She could remember the city code for Harare but not the country code. She and her father usually wrote letters. She waited for an operator. She gave her the calling card number. Her English was precise. Colleen waited for someone to answer the phone. It rang and rang, the double rings of Zimbabwean telephones. This was good. Perhaps it meant that he'd stayed in the hospital. Sarah finally answered. She mumbled, then ranted into the receiver. "*Get out of here*," she said through gritted teeth. "*Go on now*, 'voetsek'."

Colleen winced, then reminded herself, dubiously, that Sarah was probably not talking to her. It was hard to tell, not being able to look at her eyes. Colleen didn't take Sarah's insults personally, at least not when she addressed the wall, or an open doorway. Sarah finished scolding. She paused to blow out cigarette smoke. Colleen could hear her. It was a good line.

"How's Dad?" Colleen asked, unnecessarily loud, competing with any other questions, or accusations, she might be listening to. Colleen hadn't seen her sister in two years. She always forgot any previous attempts at seeming casual about the hallucinations. Colleen tried to talk to her like she would before the breakdown—this was difficult to remember—keeping the protectiveness out of her voice.

"He's not really dead." Sarah exhaled again.

"No, it's just a heart attack," Colleen said. "Right?" She fumbled with the phone. "What do you mean?" Colleen asked, but she kept on talking. She told Sarah about her conversation with their father that afternoon. He had wanted to leave the hospital. He'd feared a blood transfusion. "You had a small heart attack," Colleen had said. "Why would you need a transfusion?" She'd carefully asked him if the doctors had mentioned an angiogram, or a bypass—if so, then he would need blood. He was scheduled for an angiogram. He admitted he'd been approached about the possibility of surgery. "But I'm not going under the knife!" he'd declared. "Not around here in any case." Colleen repeated the whole dialogue to Sarah. It prevented her from answering.

Sarah made strange statements. She sometimes created new words. The words were the opposite of euphemisms, enunciated with a haughty deliberateness. She would speak, then pause and listen. It reminded Colleen of their childhood, when she and Sarah would stand on the crumbling wall and yell swear words across the valley, waiting for echoes. But Sarah's sentences could be oblique. She might talk around a thing. "He's not really dead," probably meant, "He's seriously ill." Colleen was out of practice, trying to decipher Sarah's codes.

"*No*," Sarah snapped. "*No it's not.*" She was snarling at her voices. Colleen felt responsible; she had distracted her. Then Sarah said, "They sent him to the morgue."

"But you said . . ."

"He was still warm. His hands."

"He did die?"

"He did not." Sarah seemed exasperated. She was talking aside to someone, possibly a voice. "I tell her 'morgue' and she thinks he's dead."

"Dead people go to morgues," Colleen hissed into the phone.

Sarah was laughing. "Tell her. Explain to her. Shut up. Not you. You."

Colleen slammed the receiver down and stared at it. There were people waiting for the phone, a couple. They seemed to be speaking in Flemish. Colleen stood aside. She stood there next to them. She could not seem to think. She wandered into a main terminal, with its high ceiling, time zone clocks, a skylight. Babies were crying.

"It's a delusion," Colleen said to herself. She went back to the phone. She wanted to shout at Sarah. She was furious. She couldn't board again and fly the next few hours like this. Sarah had gone too far, playing her ambiguity game. 'She knows, she's not that insane, she knows what she's doing, she does.' Colleen called again. Sarah answered right away.

"What are we going to do?" she asked Colleen.

"I don't know," Colleen said, immediately floundering.

When the plane bumped along the runway, gathering speed, shuddering over the ruts, Colleen did not have to fight panic. She watched her seatbelted body, her hands, lurching, as if her movements were no longer voluntary.

Sarah was not at the airport. Colleen took the shuttle bus downtown. It was nearly midnight in Harare. The bus was lit with flitting iridescent tubes, the same light as the arrival lounge. Besides the driver, it was empty, and the air conditioner rattled. If Colleen pressed her face to the window, she could see outside, the bike path along Queensway, jacaranda branches against an occasional streetlight.

She and her father had often cycled the airport path. They would buy orange Fantas at the BP kiosk, and drink them standing against the open bar, handing the bottles back to the kiosk clerk. The bottles would clink into a metal tray. Her father would try out new Shona, slang greetings he'd heard on the farms. The clerk would be guarded and polite. They might hear an approaching jet in the distance, usually the SAA DC–9 from Johannesburg, and get back on their bikes, peddling hard past the runways, changing gears. If they hurried, they would be standing on the deck when it touched down. He would shout things to her, gesture at the plane and point, but she couldn't hear him. He loved to watch planes.

The familiarity, the tall hedges, the shopping centers, all seemed infused with a presence of her living father. They were not tainted yet with the everyday passing knowledge of absence. The lit places emerged from hedgerows like stuck slides in carousel projectors, or they rushed by like movies, both static and continuous. They reassured and tormented. The city was the same as yesterday. The city had gone on without him. Colleen turned away from the window and blinked.

It had happened. It was just that no one knew. "My dad just died," she'd wanted to say to the customs official. People looked clearer, as if she saw them through tears, but she was not crying. 'They don't know' she kept thinking. Their not knowing seemed to mean something, that this death did not happen, or it could have, or she, Colleen, was dead, or she was unconscious, a child, or an adult, thirteen, seven, forty. She was wearing hard-heeled flats yet she could not hear her feet. Everything was separate and had taken off on its own. Her senses were outside. They were outside like the things they sensed. There was nothing that was her. There was no world without her father. She was sure she was finally becoming like Sarah, but she had no fear about it.

At the airport, Colleen had cashed a traveler's check and asked questions about the exchange rate. She heard herself talking. She thanked people. She might be in a typical dream, the way she jumbled up South Africa and Zimbabwe and places on BBC *World News*, and the shore became some jagged peninsula in the North Sea, with baobab trees, and the landmarks contradicted each other until she was nowhere.

The shuttle bus passed the industrial park. It circled a roundabout, rushed beneath the railroad viaduct, more lights, neon lights, billboards, small businesses. There were cut-price coffin stores advertising bargains in bright colors. One sign said, "You bury your dead, not your future."

The bus dropped her outside the Holiday Inn. It waited, rumbling, for ten minutes. Colleen pushed through the revolving door and came back out again, deciding to flag a taxi. The street was quiet. Traffic lights buzzed at the intersection. Down Jameson, she saw three men at a light pole with a long net, capturing locusts. Colleen was not sure what to do. She had actually not given the fine details of transport any thought. In the back of her head, she'd assumed her father would be there, a combined image of him, all the times he had picked her up, at school, train stations, airports, in shirtsleeves, his elbow outside the car window, or on a platform with the dog on a leash.

Colleen stood there in the oval. An occasional tire hissed through a puddle. It was rainy season. Jacaranda blossoms were tramped into the concrete. To pass time, she made a comprehensive list of the cars they'd driven, as if listing was now required: the Renault, the Combie, the Minis after the war, the series of Peugeots. She thought about the different ways their horns beeped.

Sarah had detested bikes, even the ten speeds, but she liked to drive, especially the Mini. On the farm in Darwendale, their father had decided that a car would keep Sarah out of Rest Haven. From the start, she coordinated the clutch and gears without stalling. Colleen recalled one visit with them, riding hunched in the back, her father in the passenger seat with a newspaper. He joked that Sarah's driving lessons were a great relief to him after teaching Colleen. He reminded Colleen of various mishaps, years ago, on mountain roads. Sarah steered with a detached precision—idling, stoical—through military roadblocks. She never required maps. She refused to talk, or argue, or joke around. Not while she was driving. Once, even before the Mini's white and red *L* learner plates were removed, Sarah disappeared for an entire day; later it turned out she'd been waiting in line at a petrol station.

★ ★ ★

They left the city, the power lines. They took the Chinhoyi Road. "This time of night, it is the better road to Darwendale," the taxi driver said. The closer to the farm, the more impossible it all seemed. Maybe Sarah had feared the worst. She believed wholeheartedly in her stories. She could never be called a liar. Colleen asked herself why she hadn't called the hospital, or her father's wife on her cell phone. "My father is sick," Colleen told the man.

"Everyone is sick now," he said. "It is very bad."

"Those pole barns outside Highfield . . ."

"Yes," he said. "Those are new morgues." He turned on the radio, *mbira* music. "A gibbous moon tonight," the man said. Clouds hung low and gray-white over the plateau. They did not seem to move. They passed each one. They passed rocky kopjes. Colleen's ears sometimes popped. The grass, the bush, even during the rains, was a translucent green-yellow that, at night, reflected back the moon like snow.

Inside her father's gate, the headlights flashed on what must have been the squatter camp, the corrugated metal sheets. She had been told it was right up by the road. There were shimmering black garbage bags duct-taped across plywood, and pathways, doorways, and tents. They drove past cooking fires, embers now, and smoke—possibly a breeze had been stirred up by the movement of the car. Everyone seemed to be asleep. The driver did not comment. Did he see this kind of thing every day? Had he heard of the looting? Nothing phased him, Colleen supposed. He believed in his driving, the safety of his car. Possibly he carried a gun. But Colleen wasn't afraid either. She breathed in the wood smoke. She thought, "This must be the squatter camp that has been so much trouble."

Sarah sat at the dining-room table drinking cane and coke. Their father's jacket hung over the back of a chair. His keys were next to the Mainstay bottle. His desk lamp glowed in the adjoining office. Both Sarah's eyelids, especially the left, were swollen as if with insect bites. She peered at Colleen from under puffed lids. Colleen kissed her cheek and leaned against the table. She thought she should wait for Sarah to speak.

"Does Dad have any Castle?" Colleen asked after awhile. She went to the fridge and opened up a beer. "Is Sustena still saving bottle caps?" she asked.

Sarah held out her hand for the cap. "*This* one I want her to have. From a beer opened tonight." The maid's son constructed *mbira* instruments for ancestral religious worship. He built them individually for select musicians, who played for spirit mediums in ceremonies. Colleen recalled what little she knew about the *mbira dzavadzimu*, part of Shona culture for over a thousand years. It required snail shells and, recently, bottle caps to provide its underlying buzzing sound. Colleen sat down, wishing for this cyclical music, wondering if all the dead really could become alive and speak inside sounds. She looked at Sarah, almost envying her voices, her neurochemical anomaly, how most Africans revered her. Surrounded by the evidence of her father's last days, she drank the beer. She wondered vaguely where her father's new wife was.

"We're making coffins now," Sarah told Colleen suddenly. Colleen knew that Sarah worked, possibly ten hours a week, at a skills center. It had started out as a craft market for the blind, but had eventually included the mentally ill and the mildly retarded. She'd insisted early on that she could not work in the morning, when the voices were active, or—if she took the Haldol—when she was sleeping it off.

"No more magazine racks, and things like that." Colleen felt slightly wistful. The skills center was well known for its geometrically designed carpets.

"We use some of the same hinges and nails." Sarah had their father's watch on the table now, his wallet, a comb, things they had probably given her at the hospital. She pushed his driver's license down the table to Colleen. She slid the comb along. Her hands smelled of acetone, and her nails, clipped short, had sediments of nail varnish, hot pink, electric blue, in the nail beds like newly stripped woodwork.

"They must be beautiful," Colleen said about the coffins, imagining carvings, sides of church pews.

"No."

The comb was a typical black pocket comb with bits of dandruff.

Colleen plucked it. She dropped a tiny scale to the floor, as if she'd just removed a crumb from her son's face.

Sarah talked about the various coffins. They were a new design, intended for easy transport to remote areas. The demand was high. "Collapsible coffins. That size." She indicated Colleen's suitcase on the threshold. She described the whole process, sewing the canvas shroud with machine stitches, pulling it right side out, hammering it to a wooden frame. It then folded into a bag. People could carry their coffins home on buses, or in the trunks of cars.

"Like our old cots when we camped in the Chimanimanis."

"Everyone is buying collapsibles now," Sarah said.

"Maybe we should get one for Dad," Colleen said. It was a stupid thing to say, contrived. Colleen knew he had made pre-arrangements after his first heart attack. He had told her, and probably Sarah as well.

"Colleen," Sarah said. "He already bought a metal coffin."

Sarah never said Colleen's name, anyone's name. Everything was a pronoun. It had been this way for a long time. Colleen was suddenly tearful. When Sarah stopped using names, no longer said "Colleen," it seemed as if Colleen, herself and her name, had undergone some sort of division. Later, attached to her married surname, the name had acquired the feel of a pseudonym. Colleen remembered the way her son, as a baby, first said "Ma," looking up at her, and later, "May," his word for milk. He would tug at her shirt. "May," he would say. That Colleen was called something, a mother, even a food source, that she was this name, at first amazed her.

They finally began to talk about the hospital. "Was Carine there when he died?" Colleen asked. She knew Carine would have facts, the chronological details she half craved—this, this, this. He is this. At what hour and what minute. Whoever this Carine was, she would know. She would tell. Yes, Carine had been there, Sarah said, and she was still in town at the other house. They had all been moving into it before Colleen's father collapsed. Did Colleen know about repossession, the government land reform act? The farm workers had all been let go. Sustena was in town now too, with a job at Lobel's bakery. After reciting this information, in the monotone of a child learning to read, Sarah turned her head sideways as if listening for a cue. So their father had not mentioned this move into Carine's house, which Carine had been using after they were married as a counseling center—why ever not? Why hadn't he said, "We've been moving, we're forced off the land, it's happened"? It wasn't as if it was a secret. Colleen had heard about it on the news practically every morning for the last two months. But this was her father, avoiding, forgetting to state the obvious. Or had losing the farm been such a defeat? "Inevitable," he had said once, about land reform. But when it personally happened to him, he had not been able to tell her. He would have said something eventually, when he had grown used to it— "Here's our new number, the address." Colleen realized that by living so far away, she had made it easy for him to be oblique. She had chosen it, justified it.

Sarah started mumbling to herself, pulling at her long, thick plait. She'd not once looked Colleen in the eyes, even in the mirror above the sideboard. 'Should I bring her back to Cape Town?' Colleen thought with a type of dread. Here they both were, sitting alone at a half-abandoned farm twenty kilometers outside of town. "She's your responsibility," her father used to tell her, back at Nyadzi, when she'd convinced Sarah to walk out to the highway with her, to the small African grocery stores, which, after martial law, were closed and boarded up. Short wave radios used to blare on concrete steps, unfamiliar stations, not the sleepy, cajoling RBC. Sometimes Colleen would buy cigarettes, and light them, one after another, striking wooden matches on a rock, letting Sarah smoke the stompies.

In recent years, Colleen would ruminate about one of her netball games. Sarah had been in form one. Colleen was in Sixth Form, her second year of *A* levels, with the Sixth Form lounge, and separate, womanly uniforms with darts. Sarah was standing alone, watching them play through the chain link fence. Colleen hardly saw her at school, maybe when they lined up by forms for assembly, and filed into the assembly hall, settling themselves, crosslegged on the cool tile. At the game, Sarah rattled the fence, and waved, but the ball was moving fast; they all ran, skidded, kicked. Sometimes, even now, Colleen would wake up at night, startled, dreaming of this game, in a sweat. It seemed worse at night, the acuteness of it, the badness, the irreparable damage. Colleen would sit awake against the headboard, her heart beating fast, watching the darkness of her husband's back, his slow breathing, like a kind of rationality. How could she have waved back? She had been concentrating, it was a game. "No one gives a damn about their family at that age," Nick sometimes pointed out.

Sarah sat across from Colleen, but she did not seem to see her. She squinted her eyes and tilted her head. Colleen might not even be there. Colleen wondered what the voices were telling her—perhaps it would be useful—what were they to do? At forty, Colleen felt for the first time a certainty that they were no longer children. She saw the ten speeds parked inside their father's study—brought in from the carport, probably before the looting of the outbuildings—and she went over to them with the vague idea of pushing one around a little and listening to the steady click of the tires. They were padlocked. Seeing Sarah in the overhead light, her own self in the mirror, her smeared mascara, it was their own age coming on, their aloneness, there was no escaping it now. Sarah had gained weight from the Haldol, and even the pills they called atypicals—all the different things they'd tried. Colleen could not see her cheekbones. They were both tired. Colleen wondered if there were any beds still in the house.

"A morgue is a refrigerator," Sarah said. She stood up abruptly and began to pace in front of the buffet table. It was almost morning. Doves rustled in the trees. Sarah's teeth had begun to chatter. "He's not dead." She was starting up again. Colleen wanted to go along with it, wanted it to stop.

"Is Dad the only one who knows the numbers on this padlock?" Colleen turned the padlock to various combinations. What numbers had he chosen? A certain date, an age, an equation? She thought of her husband, a musician, who chose "5454" for many of his computer codes, the odd inane things one knew about people, or didn't know. Colleen could not stop thinking about this knowledge of her father's. It was a small thing he would remember automatically, a habit—he might walk over and turn the lock, or say, "It's two and six and five"—this would never be disclosed. But her mind kept going around, trying to solve the problem.

"You'll have to break the lock with a hammer," Sarah said.

When Colleen met Carine at her house in Eastlea the next afternoon, Carine reprimanded Sarah for going out to the farm. She had called the police, reported Sarah as a missing person, but had doubted whether they would do anything. "It was stupid for us to stay overnight there," Colleen admitted. She was already losing sight of their father. Everything began to change, turn over. It was like starting out at a different school, or the wrong job. Carine was a new person inside a house Colleen had never seen before. Colleen felt tall and clumsy. Sarah loomed heavily, shuffled her feet. They both seemed to have to answer to her. Colleen and Sarah had slept late; there was already the sound of roosters at the squatter camp when they'd gone to bed. They had woken up to hear women using the garden hose for their water jugs. Then they had driven back in Sarah's car. Sarah drove. They'd passed the women, walking down the driveway, carrying the containers on their heads. One had turned to them and steadied the water jug with her hand. They had driven past the camp like it was any roadside village. Colleen would never go back to the farm again. She knew it too, but she thought nothing of it.

After Colleen was settled in (she would be sleeping in Sarah's new room, on her own twin bed that still had peeling STP stickers on the headboard), they went to Eskimo Hut for ice cream. This was what Sarah said she wanted to do. "I like to reward her for verbalizing what she wants," Carine explained to Colleen as they stood in line. The sun glared. Colleen wished she had sunglasses. She avoided looking at beggars rattling tins in the parking lot. Below the parking lot was a ravine where someone had once told her they'd seen a crocodile. They sat on outdoor stools next to a tiled counter and licked their cones. Colleen was reminded of a shirt she had worn in her childhood: it had a picture on it with three girls sipping milkshakes, and on the back of the shirt, their backs, their different colored ponytails, dress ribbons tied into bows. Colleen could not remember who had given her the shirt. Who bought her clothes when she was that little? Her mother may have still been around, or her father? She had never thought to ask him about it. She had the strangely detached feeling that she and Carine and Sarah were those girls, the front and the back, some kind of pattern on a textile, and thought dully about how Carine could be the mother. Colleen had always thought of the dark-haired girl as the mother. Carine had that carefully colored chin-length hair. Colleen and Sarah could be the blonde ones, although Sarah looked older than any of them, and her hair had bleached early into a yellow gray from the sun. Colleen's mind was dull and trite.

Carine told her briefly about the cardiac arrest. She described the resuscitation efforts. They had managed to revive Colleen's father—he had answered the doctor and said something—Carine said she was too far away to hear and "in far too much of a state" afterwards to find out. Colleen thought that he had probably replied to the calling of his name. Then he went under again, and they kept shocking him. Carine said that after a while she had begged them to stop. "I couldn't watch it anymore. They had been going at it for over ten minutes. I said, 'Give him some dignity.'"

Colleen felt a rush of irritation with her. Who was this woman, telling them to stop? What if they had kept on going and brought him back? In any case, who was she? The way she made such a drama of it, taking that attention away from their father. The nurses had set Carine down and given her some warm Milo. Colleen could hardly stand hearing it.

Colleen noticed in the first hour of knowing Carine a determination to convey something to her. Much of the conversation was with Sarah, as if both of them, Carine and Colleen, were competing for her, trying too hard. Despite the previous night, Colleen was out of touch with Sarah, and she watched Carine with her—Colleen knew she was expected to—listening to all the names of people and places they both knew and she did not. Did Colleen know this person or that person? They would be coming to the funeral. All of them were people Colleen had never heard of; there had been such turnover. Then Sarah laughed at something Carine said. Colleen hadn't been listening. She tried to recall when she had ever heard Sarah laugh. Both of them were laughing. Colleen felt confused. She needed to pay more attention. For someone so graceful, Carine's voice was coarse, almost croaking. The voice seemed to come up from some other body, and seemed almost mannish, yet she was not at all self-conscious about it. Colleen decided she was not going to like Carine. She noticed it for sure in the laughing. It was all to get Sarah to laugh, and there was her sense of accomplishment as her eyes flickered past. Colleen wondered how Sarah couldn't tell she was being so manipulated. Carine must have seen her face—she turned to Colleen. "Have you heard of that Joni Mitchell song? Those lyrics, 'laughing and crying you know it's the same release?'"

"'People's Parties'?" Colleen said.

"I think that's it." Carine was collecting up all the paper napkins and some empty cups left behind by another customer. Sarah continued to gaze at Carine with what looked to Colleen like a blind faith. Colleen wondered if maybe she just wasn't used to her fixed stares anymore. Sarah might have been somewhere else, daydreaming; Colleen almost wished she was hallucinating. But, still, she wondered what would happen to Sarah if this woman lost interest. Why was she interested? What had their father thought of this? It surprised Colleen more than his death. Maybe it had even caused it, she thought irritably. It was so sickening, who could endure it?

"Jet lag," Carine was saying. "You need a nap, it's been too much."

"No, I'm OK, thank you. The flights were only a few hours."

"You're with family," Carine said.

The undertaker had wired her father's mouth, or glued it, or sewn it with thread. His expression reminded Colleen of her son's, how he held his mouth to play his recorder. This mouth made her flounder. The look on his face was something that had never been alive. This face had become what it had never been before. She thought of her old toy, a stuffed dog, Toby. Gavin had the dog now, on a shelf in his room, memorializing Colleen's childhood in a way that distanced her from it further, even seeing the dog every day, rearranged differently among his souvenirs every time he moved them. The dog had a small line of a mouth, several blanket stitches sewn on, decades ago, by Colleen's mother, after weeks of no mouth—the original had fallen off in the washer—a piece of red felt that had given him a look of eagerness or enthusiasm. The second mouth took awhile to adjust to, Toby's new catlike seriousness. Colleen would hold him out in front of her and look at him. She began to realize he was not animate.

They stood next to the coffin and shook people's hands. Colleen liked Carine temporarily. Carine was exhausted from the introductions. She seemed gaunt, with the shadows under her eyes. Colleen thought she could understand what her father had seen in her. The three of them now seemed, at times, to be a team. Sarah sat in a winged chair. Colleen could only see her profile. Sarah nodded to people, shook their hand when they offered. She was "holding up well," people said—Colleen agreed. Carine would reach out suddenly to pick a piece of lint off Sarah's blouse. Her forearm would dart out, taut and deliberate. It made Colleen impatient, but Sarah did not seem to mind. As Colleen stood there, listening to her father's friends talk about him, she kept wanting to turn around and include him, knowing he was behind her, behind her back, half expecting him to be standing there, tall and thin and a little stooped, coming forward to shake their hands.

They left the coffin in the plot, after the undertaker cranked it down. The workers driving the front-end loader were busy at another grave. Colleen felt worried, leaving his coffin exposed like that. They were a small herd, slamming car doors. Across from the cemetery there was a drive-in theater, with rows of soundboxes, and the screen, and the bush. The cemetery kept going, all the way down Marlborough Road; it had been extended out into the bush for another kilometer. It was loud with front-end loaders. Colleen thought of construction sites, demolitions. She remembered a time she and her father and Sarah had watched an implosion when they tore down a department store by city hall, how baffled they had been, silenced, wandering around looking for a tearoom without that landmark.

In the morning their father's lawyer, an African named Mutiswanda, read them the will. Nothing surprised Colleen about the money: there was none, or very little, except a second fund for Sarah's maintenance, which their father had set up somehow in South Africa. The farm was to be divided up by the government into five segments, Mutiswanda explained. Already there were thirty applicants for the land. He said the application process took time, at least a year, but he assured Carine that she would be compensated for the farm equipment. "And the land?" Carine asked.

"That's a different story," Mutiswanda said. He was moving to another page, tapping the second document neatly on the desk. "Why do you even ask me the question?" he asked her, glaring briefly over his glasses.

Mutiswanda read over the second page. He told them that Carine was to be appointed Sarah's guardian and would be responsible for any "decisions regarding Sarah's care."

"You have a young child in Cape Town," Mutiswanda said to Colleen. "Your father did not want to, shall we say, overwhelm you. You understand. There would have been problems because of her illness. He and I talked about it."

Although Colleen was relieved, she could not avoid Carine's odd triumph in the room, soft, controlled. The money in South Africa was barely enough for one person to live on. She could hardly be excited about that. Colleen wanted to say "Good," or "Rather you than me." But she felt defeated. Colleen knew that this woman believed her to be second choice, no matter how concerned her father had been for her own well-being.

"You know you may oppose the decision," Mutiswanda said.

Over tea in Carine's flagstone courtyard (Sarah was napping, her medication had been adjusted), Carine told Colleen about her divorce, her daughter's illness—the girl had died of a rare form of leukemia when she was ten. There had been years of misdiagnosis, one doctor after another. "They thought I had Munchausen syndrome by proxy," Carine said. "They accused me of harming Pamela for the attention." She grimly poured Colleen's tea and passed her the cup. 'That's great,' Colleen thought, trying not to look immediately suspicious. Had her father known about this? He could be so clueless. And Carine had waited to tell her until after seeing Mutiswanda. Colleen wondered why she'd said anything at all. But there had been a lawsuit, Carine assured her, after a pause that she seemed to enjoy. There had been a settlement; the doctors were proven wrong. Carine did not need to work—she spent the time completing a doctorate through UNISA. "I wanted to be a therapist all my life," she told her. "I wanted to help people." Colleen's father had met her during one of Sarah's hospitalizations at Rest Haven. Carine said she did not counsel at Rest Haven for very long; she had felt restricted by the acute setting. "How about you?" she said. "Tell me about yourself. Your father never said much. Not that I mean he didn't care about you. You know how he is." She laughed. "He transplanted those rose-bushes just last week, brought them out from the farm and put them in himself. I should've had Duncan do it."

The gardener was skimming Carine's pool for insects, talking to someone in the road on the other side of the hedge. Carine went back into the house for a tin of biscuits. She was wearing black tricotine pants and a Lizwear top, sleeveless. Her slingback shoes were more stylish than anything Colleen had seen recently in Cape Town—they were probably from Johannesburg. "I love that outfit," Colleen said when she returned, bustling around the table. There was a tension in the way she walked that seemed fluid and graceful, yet so rigid Colleen found it alarming. It seemed Carine had to be careful in some way, as if walking on ice or new cement—something very fragile—everything was fragile around her. Colleen realized that she walked as if she wanted it that way, all things fragile around her. She knew it to be that way. She was used to stepping, light-footed, across all delicateness with a quiet knowledge that where she was going and what she was doing was right, absolutely right, without question.

Colleen could see she had never been thoroughly challenged. Like Sarah, Colleen felt an urge to be compliant.

"Do you remember your mother, Colleen?"

"No, not really," Colleen said. The gardener began to use a Weedwacker up by the rock garden. He stopped and started again.

"How do you feel about that? Your mother? How does that make you feel?"

Carine folded her hands under her chin. Colleen assumed this was a pose she used in therapy. Her elbows had settled into the white metal latticework of the table.

"I don't know," Colleen said. She wondered how her father had dealt with Carine—whether she had irritated or overpowered him. Especially in these later years with Sarah around again, influenced by Sarah's thinking, he'd often seemed to circle a subject. Maybe finally, toward the end of his life, he'd needed someone like Carine, practicing at being therapeutic. Colleen tried to picture him responding to such questions, finding words.

"I'm going to take a nap," Colleen said. She had forgotten about these sleepy afternoons in Zimbabwe. The doves were cooing. All she wanted to do was sleep.

Colleen had three days left. Sarah returned to her job at the skills center. Carine saw her two clients in her office off the living room. She had introduced them to Colleen. They liked her South African accent and asked her what it was like in Cape Town. They wanted to emigrate. One was a pale-faced woman with a streaked bob who seemed to relish the fact that she had borderline personality disorder, and the other was a young man, a victim of a brutal robbery involving a crowbar. He seemed to have post-traumatic stress. Colleen could hear the sessions through the transom windows. They were doing a variation of Gestalt therapy, "my variation," Carine told Colleen, laughing. "You have to be flexible." They came over every day. The woman called Carine frequently on her cell phone. Colleen thought that Carine indulged them, but at least it was a type of income. It also seemed possible they might not be paying her, or not paying enough. She did not seem to do the sessions for the money. It reminded Colleen of a club, or a support group.

Colleen tried to get out of the house during the sessions. She had begun to envy all the camaraderie. She didn't have any of her own friends here anymore. Everyone from Hatfield had emigrated. Tambudzai worked as a teacher in Chipinge, but they had not written now in several years. No one had ever been sure about Heresekwe; Tambudzai used to speculate that he'd never returned from the war, like the thousands of others. And all this time people believed him to be alive, maybe prosperous, some kind of diplomat. Colleen had searched the Internet a few times and found no results, which, she'd always assured herself, could mean anything. Once, Colleen's father told her he'd seen his picture on TV—he hadn't been sure of the name—something about the Ministry of Education in the eastern province, and Colleen liked that, she liked to believe that. She understood that she might never know. She felt no sense of him here. She idly paged through phonebooks. She would walk to the kiosk and buy all the chocolates from her childhood: Lunchbar, Crunchie, Cadbury. She sunbathed on the veranda. Proteas were blooming. She sorted her father's clothes into cardboard boxes, and she and Sarah dropped the clothes at a donation center in Hatfield.

At night, they would go to a restaurant Sarah liked downtown called Buffalo Bill's. Then they would watch TV. Sarah smoked. Colleen and Carine drank several cups of tea. They took turns boiling water and setting up the tea tray. They watched the British miniseries *Rebecca*. Carine had never read the book, but Colleen and Sarah had both read Daphne du Maurier novels in their teens. It was difficult to get books in Rhodesia back then. Colleen knew all of her characters as if they were her set books at university. She rooted for *Rebecca*'s main character, who was only known as "I," "me," "you." In one scene of the book, Maxim had called her by name, repeatedly, but they never found out what it was. Colleen could never imagine what her name could be. Back then, they told Carine—in their school days—they had loved that character. Even Sarah said she had.

Colleen was disappointed to leave only because she could not watch the last night in the miniseries. "We'll let you know what happens," Carine reassured her, although Colleen knew what would happen—Maxim would confess that he'd killed his first wife, Rebecca.

She ached for the story. It was the only thing that seemed real, or worth contemplating, the only thing she cared to talk about.

On that last night, Sarah and Carine went to bed after *Rebecca*. Colleen watched the news on ZBC, the national anthem—footage of Victoria Falls, and the flag, the flashing emblems, Mugabe smiling. She switched it off and then back on. Programming had ended for the night. The static was loud, and she turned it down and stared at it for a moment. She'd read somewhere that it was the remains of the big bang, some kind of wave or sonic energy left over from the beginning of time. She thought of God and eternity, and her father out there with all the people who had just died.

Colleen finally fell asleep and dreamed she was in England, inside a hospital lobby on a snowy night. Her father pushed through a revolving door. It swished around and around. He stood long enough to tramp in snow, and stomp his feet, and then he was back out again, pacing, wringing his hands. He did not have gloves. Back in, his hands were cold, as if frozen. He pulled his hands away. Could she go outside with him, please? He tramped up and down. "Come on, let's go." They walked down a clay road. It was warmer and the wind stopped. A man was selling yellow bricks at a kiosk. We need to buy some, her father was telling her. He was rational and matter-of-fact.